The Duke Says I Do

Scoundrels of Mayfair Book 4

ANNA CAMPBELL

ALSO BY ANNA CAMPBELL

Claiming the Courtesan

Untouched

Tempt the Devil

Captive of Sin

My Reckless Surrender

Midnight's Wild Passion

The Sons of Sin Series:

Seven Nights in a Rogue's Bed

Days of Rakes and Roses

A Rake's Midnight Kiss

What a Duke Dares

A Scoundrel by Moonlight

Three Proposals and a Scandal

The Dashing Widows Series:

The Seduction of Lord Stone

Tempting Mr. Townsend

Winning Lord West

Pursuing Lord Pascal

Charming Sir Charles

Catching Captain Nash

Lord Garson's Bride

The Lairds Most Likely Series:

The Laird's Willful Lass

The Laird's Christmas Kiss

The Highlander's Lost Lady

The Highlander's Defiant Captive

The Highlander's Christmas Quest

The Highlander's English Bride

The Highlander's Forbidden Mistress

The Highlander's Christmas Countess

The Highlander's Rescued Maiden

The Highlander's Christmas Lassie

A Scandal in Mayfair Series:

One Wicked Wish

Two Secret Sins

Three Times Tempted

Four Christmas Kisses

Scoundrels of Mayfair Series:

The Worst Lord in London

The Trouble with Earls

The Last Duke She'd Marry

The Duke Says I Do

Christmas Stories:

Miss Barton's Mysterious Husband: A Mayfair
Christmas Romance

The Winter Wife

Her Christmas Earl

A Pirate for Christmas

Mistletoe and the Major

A Match Made in Mistletoe

The Christmas Stranger

His Christmas Cinderella (in the anthology *A Grosvenor Square Christmas*)

Other Books:

These Haunted Hearts

Stranded with the Scottish Earl

To my dear friend Rachel Bailey whose dedication to helping her fellow creatures inspired the character of Portia in this book.

This is actually my 50th historical romance to hit the shelves which is a big moment in a writer's life. I'd like to take this opportunity to thank all my wonderful readers. You've made my journey as a published author over the last 18 years a fabulous adventure and I'm so grateful for your support.

CHAPTER ONE

Wapping, East End of London, April 1818

*D*amn. *Damn. Damn.*

Alaric Dempster, the fourth Duke of Granville, paused under the overhanging eaves while with utter dismay, he watched the scene unfold before him.

The woman was in trouble. With foolhardy gallantry, she faced down the hulking brute with an even more disreputable-looking mongrel on a rope at his side. It was clear, as the lout crowded her toward a side alley, that all the courage in the world wasn't going to save her.

Alaric Dempster was praised as the perfect gentleman. He always did the right thing. From boyhood, proper behavior had been instilled in him. Proper behavior meant coming to the rescue of damsels in distress. He knew that. But by every saint in heaven, he wished that fate had presented him with a different damsel.

Portia Frain wasn't giving up easily. She did her best to hold her ground. He gave her credit for that, if not for good sense. As he knew to his cost, Frain women weren't overburdened with good sense.

He didn't like her. She didn't like him. She never had, even though he was accounted the most eligible bachelor in Britain. When his engagement to Portia's sister Juliet ended in humiliation and scandal, he'd sworn that he'd never again have anything to do with that ramshackle family. He had no proof, but he'd lay good money that Portia was at least partially behind last summer's disaster.

"Give me the dog and I'll leave you alone," Portia said with the dismissive self-confidence that always made Granville want to push her into a bush.

The commanding tone set the ruffian chuckling. Granville couldn't blame the bastard for his contempt. Portia was tall for a woman, but in comparison to the bruiser, she looked minuscule.

"Now, why the dickens would I do that, pretty lady?"

To his regret, Granville couldn't argue with that description either. Juliet Frain was a diamond of the first water. Portia, with her wheat-gold hair and sparkling blue eyes, might even surpass her older sister. It was a pity that she was such a firebrand. She'd frightened off most of the men who might want to court her.

She stood as straight as a soldier. Her valor only emphasized her fragility. By God, her opponent could crush her with one blow from those beefy hands. "I'll pay you. I have money."

Despite his growing fears for her safety, Granville couldn't help rolling his eyes. Now she really was in hot water.

The villain accosting her saw that, too. Another knowing chuckle. "That's good to hear. I'll have that. I'll have you. And I'll keep my dog. A fine day's work, I'd say."

Even at the distance, Granville saw that she paled. Those ruler-straight shoulders tightened. She might be a fool, but she wasn't so much of a fool that she missed the threat.

This had gone far enough. Noblesse oblige and all that. Sometimes the oblige part was onerous. This was one of those occasions.

Granville mightn't like Portia Frain, but he couldn't stand uninvolved while she was assaulted.

He stepped forward and put on his best ducal drawl. "I say, old fellow, let the lady go on her way. There's a good chap."

Two pairs of eyes leveled on him in astonishment. "G-Granville," Portia stammered. "Where on earth did you come from?"

"Just passing." Jolly lucky that he had been. These alleys near the docks were a maze where murder could be – and often was – committed, the body dumped in the Thames, and no culprit ever found.

A chill rippled down Granville's spine. Despite everything that rankled about Portia and her family, the idea of her beauty and spirit lost to a muddy grave made every cell in his body protest. She was a pain in the arse, but he didn't want her dead.

"Right, with Sir Lanca-bloody-lot turning up, you can go on your way, flower," the thug said, shortening the dog's leash.

Thank the Lord, the man was willing to retreat, now that Portia had someone to defend her. Where the devil was her maid? Her coachman? Well-bred maidens didn't wander around alone. Even in Mayfair. And right now, she was a long way from Mayfair. Wapping wasn't the usual beat for aristocratic females. How in Hades had she managed to stray so far?

Granville took her arm. She was bristling.

Outrage rather than fear, he guessed.

"Yes, come away, Lady Portia. This is no place for you."

"I'm not leaving without the dog."

"There are plenty of other dogs," Granville said in the soothing tone that he used on his slow-witted cousin George.

"I want this one."

Granville eyed the mongrel cowering behind the bruiser. An unpromising specimen of indeterminate breed with black and white patches. "I'll buy you a dog. I'll buy you two, in fact."

He'd buy her a whole bloody kennel, if he could just get her to safety and go back to ignoring everyone named Frain.

"This one's being taken to a fight that he won't survive."

Her crispness surprised Granville. Not quite as much as the heat radiating from where he touched Lady Portia. Perhaps he was coming down with something. The East End was mired in filth and disease.

He had gloves on. She wore a woolen pelisse, and he assumed a long-sleeved dress beneath that. The day was cold. Yet even through all the layers, the contact had an extraordinary effect. His blood rushed, and his heart crashed against his ribs. The reaction was unprecedented. On previous occasions when he'd danced with her, he'd suffered nothing stronger than a vague annoyance. "It's still none of your business."

"That's right, flower." The man's smugness was meant to goad, but Granville had no trouble keeping his temper. "Go along, and we'll all pretend this never happened."

"It is my business," Portia retorted. "Dogfighting is an abomination."

"Harmless fun," the bruiser said.

"Not harmless for the dogs. How much do you want for him?"

"I'm not interested in a few extra shillings. He's a good fighting dog."

"I'll give you five pounds," Portia said.

The man eyed her with sudden interest. Granville couldn't blame him. To most people, five pounds was a fortune.

Granville was desperate to get out of there. Not least because he wanted to stop touching Portia. He should let her go, but his hand didn't heed his mind's command. His mind dismissed this woman as a troublesome baggage. His hand enjoyed holding onto her more than it should. "If you'll give over the dog this minute, I'll give you ten."

Greed lit the man's eyes. "Let's see the color of your money."

Granville made himself step back from Portia, astounded at the effort it took. "Pass the dog to the lady and let her go. Then we can deal."

"How do I know you'll stick to it?"

Granville was unused to anyone questioning his integrity. He was renowned as a man of unshakable principle. To the point where wilder elements of the ton considered him a dull fellow indccd.

"You have my word," he said coldly.

"Your word is fine and good, but it won't buy me the froth on a tankard of beer. Pay the money now and I'll hand Jupiter over."

Despite the building tension, Granville couldn't help casting another glance at the dog. Anything less like the king of the gods was hard to imagine. "You've heard my offer. Take it or leave it."

The man made an unconvincing effort to look thoughtful before placing two fingers in his mouth and blowing a shrill whistle. The noise had the dog tugging at the leash and howling.

Portia lurched forward. "It's all right, sweetheart. Nothing's wrong."

Knowing it was a mistake to touch her again but unable to avoid it, Granville caught her arm. He wasn't letting her get within the villain's reach.

This time, the surge of heat didn't startle him, although it remained a puzzle. He was a man of sober habits – too sober, he sometimes admitted – and he didn't in general find unsuitable women alluring. But the urge to touch Lady Portia Frain and keep touching her was unmistakable. It was dashed inconvenient, but she wielded a power over him as unexpected as it was irresistible.

More reason than ever to eschew her company. But first he had to get her out of this mess. A mess totally of her own making, blast her.

The dog kept howling. Perhaps that was why Portia trembled under Granville's hold. He glanced at the unappealing animal. "Quiet," he snapped in the voice that always gained instant obedience.

This occasion proved no exception. The cur stopped making a din and sat, gaze fixed on Granville. The stubby tail moved in a tentative wag.

Unfortunately, that was the only good news. Now the dog was silent, Granville heard the sound of running feet.

"Wotcha, Jim?" a coarse voice shouted from a side alley. "Trouble?"

Hell, now they had two ruffians to deal with. Granville's grip on Portia's arm tightened, as he backed toward the wall behind them. Danger had always loomed, but the arrival of Jim's ally tipped the balance.

"Not for me, Alf. But these two downy birds are where they shouldn't be and sticking their long noses into stuff that don't concern 'em. I'm going to do some plucking. Thought you might like to share the pickings, my lad."

Granville wasn't surprised to see that Alf was even bigger than Jim. That was how the day progressed. It had been on a downward spiral since he'd first glimpsed Lady Portia on her ridiculous rescue mission.

Alf stepped up beside Jim. "Good of you, chum."

"I advise against violence," Granville snapped. To his annoyance, the voice of authority had less effect on Jim and Alf than on Jupiter.

"Do you indeed, my dandy?" Jim sneered. "Hand over your blunt, and we might let you and the lady go. Might, mind you."

Granville was wise enough to worry. He wasn't exactly afraid. The Dempsters had been lauded for their courage since Philippe d'Ans-Terre fought with William the Conqueror. However large Jim and Alf might be, he could handle them. If he was alone. But the rub of the matter was keeping Portia from harm.

Nonetheless, he believed that they could get out of this. Sacrificing a few pounds to these bastards might pique his pride, but hardly mattered. He could tell that any request for Portia to abandon the dog would prove fruitless. The Frains, he knew to his cost, were as stubborn as mules. If they weren't, he'd have been Portia Frain's brother-in-law this past year. A thought that filled him with horror.

"Think," Granville said. "London is full of dogs. I give you ten quid. We take the dog and go on our way. You get a nice pile of blunt to buy a dozen mongrels, if that's how you choose to spend it. No trouble for anyone."

"I've got a taste for trouble," Jim said slyly. "Ready, Alf?"

Stifling a sigh, Granville stepped in front of Portia and in one smooth movement, pulled the sword from inside his fashionable walking cane. "Don't be too hasty."

Surprise and something that looked like excitement sparked in Jim's eyes. "I hope you know how to use that, my bullyboy. It's still two against one."

"Whether he does or not, I know how to use this." Portia's voice was calm. "So don't do anything stupid."

Granville chanced a quick glance away from Jim to see that Portia stood a few inches back from him. One gloved hand held a pretty mother-of-pearl pistol aimed square at Jim. Her exquisite highbred face was determined, and her hand was steady.

"Give us the dog and let us go." Her voice was almost as imperious as Granville at his most ducal.

"I've got a knife," Jim said, although Granville saw that the appearance of weapons had rattled him. He brushed his thick leather coat back to reveal a large blade tucked into his belt.

"Is it worth risking injury?" Granville asked.

"Especially when you can still have your ten quid," Portia said.

Despite himself, Granville couldn't help but admire her nerve. She might be a fool, but she was a deuced brave one.

Jupiter whined and strained at the leash. "Stop your fucking wriggling," Jim snarled at the dog, aiming a kick at his black and white flank.

Portia gasped in protest. Jupiter yelped and broke free. Instead of taking off down the alley, he headed straight for Granville and skulked behind him.

Jim surged forward, only stopping when Portia raised the pistol. "Take your money and go."

"Grab the blunt, Jim," Alf said. "This ain't worth a bullet in your hide. Nor mine."

For a moment, Granville wondered if Jim, like Portia, would allow obstinacy to outweigh pragmatism. Then the thick shoulders lowered, and he spat at Granville's feet with a disgust that didn't disguise his surrender.

"Move left so we've got somewhere to run," Granville muttered to Portia.

Keeping the gun trained on Jim, Portia sidled around until the alley was behind her. For once, saints be praised, she didn't argue.

"Give me my money," Jim growled.

Granville withdrew his pocketbook from his coat and pulled out two five-pound notes. He dropped them to the cobbles and placed one glossy boot on them to stop them blowing away. Jim's attention fixed on the money. Alf's posture indicated that he'd lost any interest in a fight, thank God. As Jim bent, Jupiter gave a soft growl.

"Shut your trap, you useless cur," Jim snarled.

Granville jumped back and sheathed his sword. He grabbed Portia's hand. "Let's go!"

Jim lurched to catch the money before the wind carried it away. Portia pocketed her pistol and dived down to collect the frayed rope attached to Jupiter's collar. But the dog soon broke free to run at her heels.

Granville suffered a fleeting worry that Lady Portia mightn't be up to his speed, until she broke into a fast run. He caught a glimpse of surprisingly stout half boots, as she gathered up her skirts and dashed along the alley beside him. Even through his urgent need to escape, he noticed Lady Portia's lovely long legs and finely turned ankles.

If he wasn't running so hard, he'd groan. He'd always had a weakness for a nice pair of legs.

If anyone had asked him a week ago what he thought of Portia Frain, he'd have responded with a derisive snort and said something about chits with more hair than wit. But she'd been cool through the crisis and she kept up with him now without complaint.

As he and Portia skittered around corners and down dark passageways, his ears strained for the sounds of pursuit. But either Jim and Alf had decided that a tenner was a good return on the day's adventures, or he and Portia had lost them.

The problem was that Granville had managed to lose himself, too. He knew his way around the part of the docks where his shipping company kept its offices. But the twists and turns that they followed now left him bamboozled.

Jupiter released an excited bark and raced ahead. "Pipe down, you brainless beast," Granville panted. The last thing he wanted was for Jupiter's excitement to lead Jim and Alf their way.

"He's not a brainless beast," Portia said. "He's a good boy."

Granville very much doubted that, but this was no time to argue the point.

Eventually he stopped to catch his breath, leaning back against the filthy bricks in a litter-strewn courtyard. He needed to spend more time with his fencing master and less sitting around paper-strewn offices with his political cronies.

God alone knew what was smeared across the wall behind him. God alone knew what his coat would look like after all this rough treatment. Hobbs, his starchy valet, would have a fit when Granville finally made it home.

If he made it home between homicidal cockneys and featherbrained do-gooders.

Beside him, the hen-witted do-gooder's flushed cheeks and disheveled hair made her look ridiculously beautiful. Somewhere in their mad dash, she'd lost her very becoming bonnet. If Jim or Alf stumbled upon it, that would make a nice bonus on top of what Granville had paid for Jupiter.

As she caught her breath, her full bosom rose and fell in the most intriguing fashion. Granville fought the urge to kiss her. He must be losing his mind. Kiss a Frain? He'd rather have his teeth knocked out with a fence post.

Except…

"You can let go of my hand now," Portia said in an expressionless voice.

CHAPTER TWO

*T*he Duke of Granville had too much assurance to blush, so the heat that stung his cheeks must be something else instead. Although he couldn't recall taking Lady Portia's hand as they fled, he must have. "I beg your pardon."

He didn't blush, and he didn't regret it one bit when he released her gloved hand. And his hand didn't feel cold and empty, once he no longer curled his fingers around hers.

Jupiter sat on the muddy cobbles in front of him, regarding him with an air of expectation that made him uncomfortable. He met the dog's bright brown eyes and told himself that the animal could have no idea of Granville's discomfort with today's events.

By God, he wished he'd stayed in bed in his mansion in Lorimer Square today.

He didn't want to be stuck heaven knew where in the most dangerous part of London.

He didn't want to share the company of an addle-headed Frain woman. All his dealings with that family ended in disaster.

Most of all, he didn't want to find Lady Portia

attractive.

As he should by now have realised, fate or the universe or the Deity paid no heed to what His Grace of Granville wanted.

Self-pity was unforgivable, coming from a man with every worldly advantage. But he couldn't help feeling ill-used. He'd felt ill-used for years.

As if following his train of thought, Jupiter's whine sounded sympathetic. Which just went to prove that Granville really was losing his mind.

"Do you always carry a gun with you?" Thank the Lord, he didn't sound like he was about to collapse.

Lady Portia had come through the chase in better state than him, damn it. At least she managed to stand on her own two feet. Eyes the rich color of lapis lazuli surveyed him with cool dislike, familiar from his days courting her sister. "I do when I'm heading into the East End to rescue a dog. Do you think I'm a fool?"

Tact forbade an answer, although he suspected that Portia was well aware that he had no time for her. He hoped to hell that she hadn't picked up today's awkward reaction to her presence. "What the devil are you doing in Wapping on your own?"

The disdain that always nettled him arched her eyebrows. Except today he was too busy finding that haughty face beguiling to pay much attention. What in blazes was wrong with him? Had he hit his head somewhere and he didn't remember it?

"I don't believe you have any right to question my movements, Your Grace." The cool tone should dowse the heat in his blood like a shower of freezing rain. Instead, it made him want to kiss her more than ever. To wipe the barely concealed derision from those full lips until only passion remained.

"Perhaps so. But why not satisfy my curiosity?"

She sighed and brushed a wing of lustrous gold

hair back from her forehead. "I've been tracking Jim Jones for about a week. He runs a dogfighting ring in Seven Dials."

Granville stuck his swordstick under his arm and picked up Jupiter's leash. With his other hand, he caught Portia's arm and marched her down one of the alleys. This built-up area might all look the same, but he had an inkling that he wasn't far from his offices. "The more reason to shun his company, I'd say. He's clearly dangerous."

"Dangerous to dogs, anyway," she retorted. Jupiter tugged at the leash Granville held. Their prickly conversation upset him. When Portia glanced down, her expression softened in a way that did nothing to quash Granville's sexual interest. "It's all right, Jupiter. You're safe now. Nobody is ever going to hurt you again."

The soothing murmur made every hair stand up on Granville's body. Just so would she croon her pleasure to a lover.

Who was never going to be him.

No amount of unwelcome attraction could make him stick his head into that particular noose again. One engagement to a Frain woman was more than enough, thank you.

Nor did it escape his notice that the mongrel dog received kinder treatment than one of England's premier noblemen.

He wished to heaven that he didn't notice how beautiful she was. He'd always recognized that she was a diamond, but he'd felt no urge to cut himself on those sharp facets. Now it seemed that he wanted her, no matter how she sliced at him.

"And I wasn't alone," she said. "Rankin, my coachman, was with me."

"Not when I met you."

"We lost sight of Jones when we got to Wapping,

so we split up."

"That was a damned silly thing to do," Granville snapped.

When her eyes flashed annoyance, his grip on her arm firmed. Where did this sudden yen for obstreperous women come from? Her sister had always been so proper – at least until she turned out not to be proper at all.

She pulled free and stopped to glare at him. "I had my gun."

Granville stopped, too. They'd entered a more respectable part of town, a residential square of small, well-kept terrace houses. "Which has one bullet in it. Once you'd fired it, you were at the mercy of those ruffians. Do you think Alf would just let you go if you'd shot Jim?" The memory of his stone-cold terror when he'd seen her face down those brutes made his gut contract.

She had the grace to look a little sheepish. "I hadn't counted on Jones having an accomplice."

With another whine, Jupiter broke free. Granville waited for him to take off into the tangle of alleyways. Almost wished that he would. Even if Lady Portia was sure to set out in pursuit. But the dog merely shifted to lie at his feet.

"He likes you."

Granville told himself that he was being oversensitive to hear disbelief in Lady Portia's remark. "He recognizes the voice of authority."

"No, he's decided you're his master."

Dismay flooded Granville as he stared down at Jupiter. Who stared back with unmistakable devotion. "I'm not. I can't be."

Most men of his status kept kennels. Most men of his status had a normal upbringing where games and larks and friends and japes were part of the deal. Granville's grandparents had spent their lives training him to be the perfect duke. Pets weren't included in the arrangement. Pets were distracting and dirty and made a lad think of playing outdoors, instead of memorizing screeds of political history.

"You have to take him."

In general, Granville would crush the pretensions of any pest who dared to tell him that he should do something. That went double for troublesome individuals burdened with the Frain name.

But today set its own rules. For some reason, the cutting set-down that put Lady Portia in her place wouldn't emerge.

"I...can't." Even in his own ears, that sounded weak. He strove to strengthen his tone. "You rescued him. He belongs to you."

She shook her head and stepped back, physically distancing herself from responsibility. "He loves you."

Granville only just restrained a derisive snort. Love? That, like pets, wasn't part of his life either. Never had been. And he hadn't suffered from the lack.

Love, in his experience, made people do stupid things like break respectable engagements and rush off to marry scoundrels like the Duke of Evesham. Love promised an end to clear thinking. If the Duke of Granville valued anything, it was clear thinking.

"Well, I don't love him," he said shortly. It was high time he took control of a situation that threatened to break out of control. "He's going home with you."

Portia looked shifty. He wished to heaven that the expression didn't make him want to kiss her. It didn't seem to matter what she did today, he wanted to kiss her.

"Papa has threatened to get rid of all my animals if I bring back even so much as a canary."

Granville steeled himself, as a pair of limpid blue eyes changed from shifty to pleading. "Then you'll have to make other arrangements."

"Are you afraid he won't get along with your other dogs?"

His lips tightened. "I don't have any dogs."

Portia looked astonished. He couldn't blame her. The English aristocrat and his faithful hound were as much a symbol of the national character as John Bull and his shallow-crowned hat.

Along with astonishment, there was a hint of sympathy. After his failed attempt to wed Juliet, he'd become accustomed to people's pity. Pity that despite his wealth and prestige, he'd been judged second-best. Even worse, second-best a second time. In his youth, an engagement had ended because the bride had run away with the same sod who ended up marrying Juliet.

He'd loathed the sympathy then. He loathed it even more now. It made his skin crawl. Especially when it came from a blasted Frain.

He waited for Portia to say something crass, but while he might deride her as a nitwitted flibbertigibbet, she was smart enough not to remark on his loneliness.

Instead, that pretty jaw adopted a surprisingly daunting line and she focused a direct glare on him. "Then you've got room for Jupiter."

"I don't have the first idea how to go on with a pet."

The determined expression didn't ease. "You can learn."

His lips tightened. This inconvenient attraction almost made him forget how annoying she was. Lucky for him, she kept reminding him.

He put on the voice that had discouraged encroachments since he was at Eton. "My dear young woman, I have a country to run. The fate of one ill-bred canine hardly counts in comparison."

As he should have realized, the ducal tone didn't discourage Lady Portia. Her shoulders squared, and she stepped closer. Without budging from Granville's booted feet, Jupiter turned his head to watch her. "Of course it does. If a great country can't ensure safety for women and children and animals, it's not a great country at all."

Granville gaped at her. "That smacks of treason."

She shrugged. "It's the truth. Are you going to abandon Jupiter to his fate? I've followed your political career. I can't imagine the man who spoke so movingly about little children working in coal mines could be so heartless."

"Don't you dare try to shame me into doing what you want." His tone made Jupiter whine again. "It won't work."

"No, I can see that." He hid a flinch as disappointment flooded those beautiful eyes. "Even taking him for one night is too much to ask. Just to give me time to try and find him a home."

Granville should feel relieved. At last, she talked sense. He'd disappointed so many people in his life, no matter how hard he tried to do the right thing. His grandparents. His fiancées. Others too numerous to list. It shouldn't matter that Lady Portia was just one more.

Somehow it did.

"So you'll take him then?" he asked hopefully.

She shook her head. "I can't. Papa is stubborn, as you know. We'll have to let Jupiter go."

The dog's gaze fixed on Granville. Even the bloody hound thought he behaved like a cad, dash it. "Jim or Alf might find him."

Portia avoided his eyes but not before he caught a shimmer of what might be tears.

Great, Granville. Bravo. Three cheers for you. You've made the girl cry. They should give you a medal.

"He might be lucky."

Granville knew that Jupiter had no idea what the conversation was about. So that couldn't be reproach in the intelligent dark eyes. "You must have someone else you can ask to help."

"Everyone else I can ask has already taken in their share of mistreated animals. It's a huge problem in London."

Granville tried not to hear the break in her voice. He shouldn't care. She didn't like him. She'd never liked him.

Despite everything, he did care. He felt like the lowest worm on the ladder of creation. All because he'd upset a woman he'd once have been glad to avoid for the rest of his days.

"Perhaps my butler won't mind looking after Jupiter overnight," he said reluctantly. Partly because Sheriff would mind. And Granville had been brought up to consider his staff's feelings. The idea of introducing an untrained mongrel into the perfect clockwork of Dempster House was so unappealing, it verged on the impossible.

Portia looked doubtful, too. "Jupiter has bonded with you."

Granville bit back an irritable growl. "Then he can unbond."

"It's not as simple as that. I suspect he's had a hard life. I don't want to upset him."

This time, what Granville bit back was a sarcastic response. Upset Jupiter? What about upset caused to that esteemed personage, the Duke of Granville, whose ordered life disintegrated before his eyes?

"He's a dog, not a spinster great-aunt with a nervous disposition," he said with commendable mildness. "If I see he's fed and out of the weather, what in Hades else does he need?"

"Love."

Damn, that word again. He'd happily expunge it from the language. When he became prime minister – as was widely touted to happen before he turned forty in eight years – perhaps he'd draft the legislation. "The only offer I'm even considering for the animal is one night at my house, madam."

"In your company?" The scale of his generosity left Portia less than overwhelmed, curse her. "He'll fret with strangers."

"I only met him an hour ago. I'm a stranger." He could hardly believe that they discussed this flea-bitten beast as if he possessed all the delicacy of a duchess.

"Not in his eyes. You're his knight in shining armor. You saved his life. You can't abandon him to uncaring hands and people he doesn't know."

She was wrong about that. He could. Quite easily. If not for those big blue eyes watching him as if he could never let her down.

"This is a dreadful idea. I've never looked after a dog." He hated the waver in his authoritative tone. Hated even more that Portia would without doubt hear it, too.

"It's simple. Give him a bath. Feed him. Take him for a walk."

Now that he would indeed transport this misbegotten wretch of a dog to the pristine halls of Dempster House, the prospect of bedlam ahead filled him with horror. "He mightn't be house-trained."

Portia glanced at Jupiter, who continued to listen as if he understood every word. "I'm sure he is."

"No, you're not. You *hope* he is. That's not at all the same."

"He's clearly spent time in a household. He's accustomed to the lead, and he knows how to sit quietly. If he'd never been in human company, he'd run off and we'd never catch him."

Which right now seemed a preferable outcome. Although Granville didn't dare to say that. "Perhaps my fatal charm is keeping him here."

His wry remark made those spectacular eyes widen in surprise, and he recalled that she dismissed him as a dry stick, devoid of humor. It shouldn't sting. After all, he'd decided that she was an ineffectual do-gooder. But among all today's trials, perhaps the most astonishing was that Lady Portia Frain had developed the ability to affect his emotions.

"He might prefer men. Animals can express a preference for one sex or the other."

Every hair on Granville's skin rose as if he'd been struck by lightning. "Sex" wasn't a word well-bred young ladies used. While she meant it in the most innocent way, the sound of that short syllable on those lush pink lips had him standing to attention.

His cheeks were hot – this time, he couldn't even pretend that he wasn't blushing. Battling for self-mastery, he bent over to collect Jupiter's lead.

"We'll have to consider that when we find him a home," Granville muttered to the filthy cobbles, as he fumbled for the tatty rope.

He was in such a state that he only realized the quality of the silence had changed when he straightened. She surveyed him with a hint of uncertainty. That surprised him. Uncertainty wasn't Lady Portia's natural state. "Thank you. I wasn't sure you'd take him."

He frowned. "What the devil is wrong with you? Isn't this what you've been angling for this whole time?"

She didn't flinch under his impatience. He started to think that Portia Frain wouldn't flinch facing a cavalry charge. "Yes. Yes, it is."

"You can't keep him."

"No."

"It's only for one night."

"Ye...es." That emerged less emphatically.

"And we can't let him fend for himself."

"No." Stouter tone.

"So what else can I do?"

A tentative smile softened that cursed tempting mouth. If anyone had told him this morning that he'd be in a lather to kiss Portia Frain, he'd question their sanity. Now all he could think about was how those full lips would taste beneath his. "Thank you. I'm sure you won't be sorry."

"I'm not," he said shortly.

"Sorry?"

"Sure."

She spread her hands. "I'm very grateful."

He ground his teeth. "That's nice to hear. You're also going to be very useful. You're coming back to Dempster House to settle him in. And you're going to call tomorrow to take him away with you. I know you want me to adopt him, but that's not going to happen."

"Don't be ridiculous." She looked appalled. "I can't come to Dempster House. My reputation will be in shreds."

Given that she wandered around the East End without a hint of a chaperone, her reputation was likely to be ruined anyway. "I'm not dealing with this animal alone. That's my condition for looking after him tonight. Take it or leave it."

She sighed and regarded Granville with familiar displeasure. She'd been turning up that pretty nose at him since he'd started courting her sister. "You leave me no choice."

"Very sensible. Now we just need to find my carriage and we'll head off." So far, he knew that he was going to upset his valet and his butler. Phipps would be offside, too, once a dog badly in need of a bath invaded the ducal coach's luxurious interior.

Portia eyed Granville with a lack of faith that stung. "Do you know the way?"

"If we angle toward the river, we should be fine." The river was always easy to find. It stank.

He hoped to blazes that the carriage wasn't far away. He'd told Phipps to walk the horses while he completed his business with the shipping agent. He presumed that his coachman had been looking for him ever since. Their paths should cross sooner rather than later.

He gestured for Portia to turn down a side street. "My lady?"

Only as they left the square did he realize that in his attempt to best her, he'd made a disastrous error of judgment. Even worse, he had nobody to blame but himself.

He was attracted to Portia Frain, mad as that conclusion might be. He needed to un-attract himself and soon, or he was doomed to nothing but frustration. A virgin of Portia's class only came to a man's bed after a wedding. However much he might fancy the chit, no amount of desire convinced him that she'd make a suitable duchess.

That was if the impossible happened and she agreed to have him. Jupiter would start conjugating Latin verbs before that happened.

Granville had to nip this madness in the bud, before it took over his life. The best strategy was avoiding the lady's company until balance was restored.

Yet here he was inviting her into his house and

enlisting her aid and extending a contact that could only prove calamitous. By all that was holy, he needed to have his head fixed.

CHAPTER THREE

Across the maroon leather interior of the coach, Portia watched the Duke of Granville stare out the window with a pensive expression. Like a perfect gentleman, he sat with his back to the horses. He *was* a perfect gentleman. He'd even taken Juliet's rejection with notable gallantry.

She wished to heaven that she knew why his refined manners irked her so much.

They still drove through the East End. They'd stumbled on the duke's carriage soon after she'd obtained his reluctant agreement to take Jupiter in. From there, they traveled to the rendezvous point that Portia had set with Rankin, her coachman, so he knew she was safe.

Portia had a lot of respect for a good coachman. She couldn't manage her rescues without Rankin, and he took charge of her menagerie if she was absent. The duke's coachman was clearly another paragon. Phipps hadn't raised an eyebrow when his passengers included a disheveled lady and a dog of doubtful breed.

The dog of doubtful breed now perched on the seat beside Granville. The duke had tried to put him on the floor, but Jupiter was having none of that.

Portia, after a lifetime of dealing with animals, had observed the silent battle between dog and nobleman. So far, she'd put her money on Jupiter emerging triumphant. Just as she'd lay good money on Jupiter now having a home. She should be ashamed of herself for that blatant manipulation of the duke's finer feelings, but the cause was good and he'd benefit from having a dog. He just didn't know it yet.

Granville hadn't spoken since they'd entered the carriage. Nor had he looked at her. That should suit her down to the ground. It wasn't as if she liked him. She was probably the only person who cheered when Juliet had jilted that plaster saint, the Duke of Granville.

Nor did Granville like her. Although she had to admit that he'd proven a useful accomplice through today's adventures. Or at least he had when he wasn't staring down that imperial nose at her, as if she was something nasty stuck to his shoe.

She tried to ignore him as successfully as he ignored her. But in such close confines, that was more difficult than it should be.

If only he wasn't a pleasure to behold. Even when she'd dismissed him as a self-important bore, she'd acknowledged his good looks. One of the reasons that people treated him with such deference – aside from the ancient title and impressive fortune – was that he looked like the Angel Gabriel in an old painting. Nature had gilded him with golden hair and golden skin. Chiseled features. A lean, athletic body. Commanding height.

Today's events left him more disordered than usual. His once-pristine green coat bore stains from brushing too close to clammy brick walls, and his gray kidskin gloves were grubby. Scuff marks dulled his usually gleaming boots.

He'd removed his stylish beaver hat. His thick blond waves of hair were untidy. One lock even had the temerity to tumble across that noble brow.

Portia had observed the Duke of Granville across a plethora of ballrooms. He always dressed *comme il faut*, not a hair out of place. He'd probably shoot his valet, if the man failed to do up every button and straighten every hem.

Granville was famous for setting feminine hearts aflutter. Debutantes had been known to swoon if His Grace requested a dance. When Juliet attracted his notice, society applauded her on a major coup.

Until now, the sight of the Duke of Granville had never roused a moment's discomfort in Portia. Which, given that he intended to marry her sister, was a good thing.

She didn't like self-satisfied men. She didn't like men who set themselves up as arbiter of all decisions. She didn't like men who treated the world like a toy created for their private pleasure.

Unfortunately, that description fitted most males in the beau monde. Her dislike for dominant men partly explained why she'd refused the numerous proposals that she'd received.

So it seemed absurd that studying Granville now, she should feel an unaccustomed shortness of breath and a warmth on her skin.

She tried to blame both on running away from Jim and Alf. But she'd been sitting in this coach for a good half hour and her heartbeat hadn't regained its normal rate.

Perfectly presented Granville left her cold. Granville the worse for wear appealed to a part of her that she didn't like to acknowledge. Today, for the first time, he looked almost human, not like a visitor from heavenly realms, unaffected by mucky emotion.

This man looked like flesh and blood. He looked touchable.

Curse her, she wanted to touch him. She very much feared that if she wasn't careful, she'd start staring at His Grace the way Jupiter did. All starry-eyed devotion. Ugh!

Wouldn't that make Granville laugh? Even worse, it might make him feel sorry for her.

Jupiter smelled like a dog who had been on the streets too long. Despite the open windows, the reek of unwashed canine was overpowering. How was it possible that across the several feet separating her from His Grace, Portia was aware of another scent? Something clean and fresh and spicy.

She'd often danced with Granville – they'd both put a good face on their animosity for Juliet's sake. Never before had she noticed anything particular about his scent. Yet right now, if there were ten men in a room and she closed her eyes, she could pick Granville out within seconds.

It was jolly irritating.

Without warning, he turned his head and met her eyes.

Awareness jolted her, made her sit up straight. Good heavens. She needed to be careful. She prayed that he didn't detect her unwilling interest.

"May I close the blinds? We'll soon be back into the part of Town where we may be recognized."

"Yes," she said, then continued in a tart voice that didn't sound like her. "It would be a disaster if anybody saw us together."

A proposal grounded in scandal would be the end of enough, even if in the family tradition. Both her sisters had been caught in improper circumstances with the men they later married.

But Juliet and Viola had been in love with the gentlemen in question. Portia might suffer temporary insanity in finding the Duke of Granville appealing. That didn't mean signing up to a lifetime with the pompous idiot.

Her tone made his elegant golden eyebrows arch. "If you agree to take Jupiter, I'll arrange for your discreet return home, with nobody the wiser about our encounter."

She rolled her eyes. "We've been through this. If you think that dog intends to leave you this side of doomsday, you're cracked in the head."

To her surprise, he laughed. "You know, nobody else talks to me like you do. In fact, even you didn't talk to me like this until today."

She hadn't spoken to him since those fraught days last year at Afton Court, the family estate, where Juliet had rejected him. "I don't feel like I've got anything to lose with you anymore. I'm sorry if you don't like it."

Which was a lie. She wasn't sorry at all.

A frown, more puzzlement than annoyance, creased his brow. Portia wanted to grind her teeth in frustration. Could he look any more picturesque? The Archangel Gabriel sorrowing over humanity's foibles. The awful truth was that his beauty made her stupid stomach tie itself up in knots of longing.

"I wouldn't say I don't like it," he said thoughtfully. "Compared to all the fawning toadies, it's refreshing to know where I stand with you."

What a relief. That sounded like she'd managed to hide her sudden and inconvenient penchant for him. "I appreciated your help today," she said on a less belligerent note.

He laughed again, a grunt of self-mocking amusement that she would have assumed was outside his repertoire. On the strength of earlier encounters, she'd judged him to be totally humorless, too wrapped up in his own grandeur to laugh at anything. She couldn't remember them sharing so much as a wry smile. Then, as he pointed out, she'd been punctiliously polite to him in return. Not at all her outspoken self.

"I'm sure it hurt to say that." Like her, he must recall their chilly interactions.

He, too, was franker than he'd been in their previous acquaintance. Perhaps they might have found common ground, if they'd ever moved beyond banalities. "I'll survive," she said with a hint of grimness.

"Pleased to hear it." He pulled down the blinds. "I've got enough problems with this hound of humble parentage. I don't need an expiring noblewoman on my plate as well."

Darkness surrounded them. Warm, intimate darkness. She bit back a dismayed protest. Her heart lodged in her throat and threatened to stop her breath.

Not seeing the duke should make her less aware of his proximity. It didn't work like that. He hadn't shifted closer or hinted that she was anything except a nuisance. But with the blinds down, the space shrank. If she stretched out her legs, they'd tangle with his.

Portia wanted to ask him to raise the blinds. Except that was dangerous. Now that they approached the fashionable part of town, they were back in traffic. If just one person saw her sharing a closed carriage with Granville, her goose was cooked.

"My God, that dog stinks," Granville said.

His disgusted exclamation should destroy the suggestive atmosphere. Portia swallowed to moisten an unaccountably dry mouth and struggled to sound matter-of-fact. "He can't help it."

"Perhaps not."

Now that her eyes adjusted to the dimness, she watched Jupiter lie down and set his head on Granville's lap. She waited for the duke to shove the animal away, but to her surprise, he rested one gloved hand on his neck.

For pity's sake, she didn't want to like Alaric Dempster. She much preferred to think of him as a one-dimensional stuffed shirt with no care for anyone but himself. If it turned out that he had a kind heart, she was doomed.

At least with the blinds down, Jupiter's stench overpowered Granville's evocative scent. Imagination alone must make the duke's intriguing essence linger in her nostrils.

Portia struggled to concentrate on practicalities. She was good at that. She wasn't a girl who melted at the sight of a comely male. Or at least she hadn't been before. "We'll give him a bath when we get to Dempster House."

"You know, I've never taken care of a dog," His Grace said in a musing tone. The twilight inside the carriage made her far too aware of the beauty of that baritone voice. He was renowned for his speeches in parliament. Portia understood why. How on earth could anyone vote against him? "There hasn't been a dog on Dempster property for at least three generations. My grandparents brought me up and didn't want anything to distract me from my training to take over the title."

His words held a hint of sadness. An unbidden image of a lonely little boy forced to concentrate on his studies and denied any chance of a puppy made her heart ache.

Stop it, Portia. You have no idea what his childhood was like. He was probably ecstatic to be a swot. Just because you love animals, it doesn't mean everyone else does.

"He really will be better with someone else," the duke said.

"He doesn't think so."

He sighed. "You're pushing me to keep him."

She was. Jupiter saw none of the flaws in the Duke of Granville that she did. At least until today, when she'd lost her mind. "I'll see if someone can take him tomorrow, if you still don't want him."

That was a weasel answer, she knew. Since her father's ultimatum about no more animals, she'd farmed her rescues off to anyone she could think of. Viola and Toby had taken a whole kennel's worth. She doubted that she'd find a place for Jupiter.

The duke clearly had doubts about her honesty, too. His silence held a skeptical edge.

When he lifted the blind a few inches, a beam of light illuminated those remarkable features. Against her will, her gaze soaked up every detail. The deep-set green eyes, the straight blade of a nose, a mouth that conveyed iron self-control. She'd already seen all this, but today, for the first time, she noticed hints of humor.

His mouth fascinated her. She couldn't remember paying much attention to a man's lips before. The lower lip was surprisingly full. A sign of restrained passion? Plenty of noblemen had bad reputations with women. Granville didn't. But that didn't mean he'd never kissed anyone.

What would it be like to kiss him? The thought prompted a shiver. Not of revulsion. Odd, because when she'd tried to imagine Juliet and Granville kissing, she hadn't succeeded. They both seemed too stiff and proper to engage in anything as messy as a passionate embrace.

Portia had never been kissed. She'd never particularly wanted to be kissed. How bizarre that the first man to stir any curiosity about the activity should be someone she once found of no interest.

If she thought about it – and she thought about it far too much today – she suspected that Granville would be quite a good kisser. He was renowned for his competence. He'd been competent today, dealing with Jim and Alf. That competence had saved her bacon.

In fact, the only time that she'd seen him at a loss was with Jupiter. He'd even taken Juliet's rejection in his stride.

Not that she'd ever kiss the Duke of Granville. She might suffer an unwanted attraction. He didn't. Once she'd set him up as Jupiter's master – he mightn't know it yet, but he'd lost that particular battle – nothing would stop them reverting to their frigid distance.

How ridiculous that the knowledge made her burn with regret.

Because right now, sitting opposite His Grace, she admitted that she'd dearly like to kiss him. Even more shocking, she'd like him to sweep her into those powerful arms and touch her with those elegant long-fingered hands.

At twenty-five, she was late discovering the power of physical attraction. To think that Alaric Dempster was the man to awaken her dormant desires. It was almost inconceivable. Yet the merest sight of him had her hungering for more.

"We're turning into Piccadilly." He let the blind fall back. Outside, it sounded like half of London rattled and shouted and pursued their trade. Inside the carriage, Portia and Granville inhabited a different world.

The gloom's return assuaged Portia's fear that her expression might betray her unacceptable longing. The carnal direction of her thoughts troubled her. Her secret parts thrummed in a most unsettling fashion. Unsettling, if not exactly unpleasant. She shifted on the seat to ease the unaccustomed weight between her legs. It didn't help.

"Not far to Lorimer Square then." She hoped the duke missed the remark's breathiness.

The duke lived across the square from the house that Papa had rented the last two seasons. Portia had expected her father to give up the lease, now Viola and Juliet were married. But these days, he mostly stayed in Town. Perhaps after last summer's mayhem, he couldn't bear to return to Afton Court.

Portia didn't mind living in London. There were more animals in trouble here than in the country. At least the part of the country that she inhabited. Largely thanks to her efforts. She'd wondered whether her father might question where the constant stream of strays came from and curtail her activities but he never had. She supposed he imagined that people gave them to her, if he devoted even that much thought to her in between his dreams of theatrical fame.

Granville knocked on the ceiling, startling Jupiter from his snooze. He sat up and whined in protest.

"It's all right, boy." Portia was impressed at how he'd settled. Often rescued animals were so frightened that they were difficult to transport.

The duke scratched Jupiter's ears. He mightn't have any experience with dogs, but so far his instincts were good. She suspected that his air of quiet authority contributed to Jupiter's easy transition. Nervous animals appreciated a sure hand. So, it turned out, did she. The moment Granville emerged to defend her against Jim, she'd known that she was safe.

The panel above Granville's head slid open. In the gap against the sky, Portia caught a glimpse of the coachman's lined, benevolent face.

"Lady Portia has very kindly agreed to help with the dog, Phipps. But discretion is required."

"Aye, sir. I can manage that. If you'll wait in the carriage once we reach the stables, I'll send off those puddingheaded lads."

"Capital. The other thing is Jupiter needs a bath. We're probably better doing that in the stables, as well. Or perhaps the garden."

"I've got no authority over the gardeners, sir. Let's stick to the stables."

"Good thinking."

Portia had to credit Phipps for not betraying the slightest sign that these requests were unusual. Or that he minded the opulent carriage transporting a filthy mongrel from the London streets. Let alone a virgin of good family.

Although she knew nothing about the duke's private life. Perhaps he often lured women of pristine reputation to his house.

"Would you like me to look after the dog, Your Grace?"

Granville glanced at Portia. The open panel admitted enough light to read his expression. She saw him consider the idea, but to his credit, he didn't leap at the chance to pass Jupiter's care over to a servant.

This afternoon, she was astonished at how much she laid to Alaric Dempster's credit.

"I'll accept your help with pleasure, but I think it's time I learned how to bath a dog, don't you?"

Phipps's expressionless face hinted how bizarre he found this statement. "Very good, Your Grace."

"That will be all for now."

The panel slid into place, plunging them back into twilight. "He's right, you know," Portia said.

"About the gardeners?"

"About it being beneath your dignity to wash

Jupiter."

"He didn't say that."

"He didn't need to. And he offered you a chance to wriggle out of a nasty job."

Granville gave a dismissive huff. "As if you'd let me get away with palming Jupiter off on Phipps."

"I might have...expressed disappointment."

She couldn't see the duke roll his eyes. Somehow she knew that he did. This preternatural awareness was new, too. She'd never been interested in his reactions before. Now they loomed far too large in her consciousness.

"Might?"

"You don't have to listen to me." She wondered why, having worked so hard to obtain His Grace's cooperation, she offered him a way to avoid his obligations.

He didn't answer that. "Phipps was hired to drive the horses, not play my kennel keeper. He's a deuced good coachman. I don't want him taking his services elsewhere."

Portia wasn't convinced that care for his servant's sensitivities lay at the root of His Grace's cooperation. It could be mere wishful thinking, but she sensed a bond building between dog and man. She was wise enough to keep that observation to herself.

The hubbub outside faded. They'd left the busy thoroughfare behind and turned into the street leading to Lorimer Square. The carriage rolled to a stop, and she heard Phipps climb down and start shouting, presumably at the grooms.

Portia began to speak, but a quick hand on her knee kept her quiet. No man had ever touched her leg before. The contact shuddered through her like thunder. Waves of heat rippled through her. She went silent, more with shock than discretion.

Once again, she was grateful for the darkness. She doubted she could hide her overwhelming reaction.

When after about a quarter of an hour, Phipps opened the door to the coach, allowing light to flood in, she'd just about regained control of herself.

CHAPTER FOUR

hipps surveyed the coach's occupants with more of that stoical expression. "My lady. Your Grace." He bowed to Portia before addressing Granville. "I've sent them all off to the King's Head on your shilling."

His gaze fell on Jupiter, who stared back with the intelligent interest that seemed to be his default attitude. Portia had dealt with hundreds of dogs and loved every one of them. But she could already tell that Jupiter was special. The thought of him being ripped to pieces in a dogfight made her feel sick.

"Housing Jupiter turns out to be an expensive business," Granville said drily.

When Phipps laughed, Portia was surprised yet again. Not just because the duke's response hinted that he might take Jupiter.

It was clear that duke and coachman shared an easy relationship. She'd always assumed that Granville was too high in the instep to treat his social inferiors as anything except convenient underlings. She'd been wrong about this, too.

It was a bitter pill to realize how badly she'd misjudged Granville. She thought back to how disgusted he'd sounded when he mentioned people cozying up to him because of his rank. Perhaps his remote manner in society was justified. He hadn't been at all the haughty aristocrat today. In fact, he'd been a good sport, given that events hadn't gone to plan for him, from the moment he stepped forward to confront Jim.

Phipps subjected Jupiter to a thorough inspection. "He isn't what I imagined you bringing back from the docks."

The now-familiar wry smile appeared. It exerted an unsteadying effect on Portia's nerves. When Granville smiled like that, he didn't look chilly and self-righteous. He looked dangerously approachable. "He'll make a better impression after a bath."

Portia remained as unconvinced about that as Phipps. Now she took the time to consider the dog as something other than a fellow creature in need of help, it was clear that nothing was going to turn him into a beauty.

"Shall I take him?" Phipps asked.

"Yes, please."

"What do you think he is?" Phipps caught the rope dangling from the collar and coaxed Jupiter onto the ground. "There's a bit of bull terrier there."

Granville grunted with amusement. "Among other things." He stepped out of the coach and extended a gloved hand to assist her. "Lady Portia, you're the expert. What do you think?"

What she thought was that she was in serious trouble. When Granville took her hand, she struggled against the urge to clutch at him so he never let her go. It might be worth braving her father's wrath and taking Jupiter home. But since the brouhaha with Juliet, Papa had been temperamental and despotic. She'd never doubted his ultimatum about her menagerie.

Once she stood beside Granville in the huge, airy stables, she realized that she still held his hand. It shouldn't be a wrench to disentangle her fingers, but it was.

And he'd asked her a question, too. She was almost used to Granville deferring to her expertise. Almost. The arrogant prig she'd assumed him to be would never take advice from a mere woman.

She fought to keep her voice even, which was harder than it should be when her heart raced like a greyhound in pursuit of a rabbit. "The wedge head is bull terrier, but the black and white coloring is more fox terrier. There's some lurcher, too. I suspect he can run like the clappers. So please don't let him go, Mr. Phipps. We'll never catch him."

Jupiter didn't show any signs of wanting to run away. Instead, he strained at the lead to get closer to his idol. His bark attracted a frown from His Grace. "Sit!"

From a dozen stalls, thoroughbred horses poked their heads out in alarm. To Portia's surprise, Jupiter immediately obeyed, which confirmed her suspicion that he'd once lived in a household. He wasn't born one of the thousands of feral dogs that infested London.

"Let's get him clean."

"Should we feed him first?" Granville asked her, taking off his gloves and shoving them in his pocket.

"Bath, then we can give him something to eat." She cast an expert eye over him. "He's not starving. I suspect Jim wanted him in top condition for the fight."

"Very well." Granville removed his beautifully cut dark green coat – a green that matched his eyes, Portia noticed, although she wished that she hadn't. His elegant cream waistcoat followed. He laid them over the gate to an empty stall.

Portia had grown up in the country. She'd seen countless workmen in their shirts and sometimes less than that. Her heart had never shifted a beat at the sight of any of them.

But upper-class men didn't strip down to their linen in a lady's presence. She told herself that she was breathless with outrage because the duke undressed in front of her.

But something powerfully feminine inside her melted as she took in the potently male body revealed under the white cambric of his loose shirt. The arbiters of fashion admired Granville's broad shoulders and firm chest. Now she had vivid confirmation that he didn't require padding to achieve the desired silhouette.

Luckily, the object of her obsessive, if unwilling interest spoke to Phipps and wasn't paying attention to Portia. She worried that she must look like she wanted to lick him all over.

To hide her flaming cheeks, she began to unbutton her pelisse. It was the height of fashion which meant a tight fit across the shoulders. If she helped with Jupiter, it would restrict her movements. She placed it over the duke's coat.

"Will you fetch Sheriff, please?" Granville said. "We'll need him to join our conspiracy if we're to get Lady Portia out of this undetected. I'd also like him to make Jupiter's acquaintance. While you do that, we'll start making our new friend fit for civilized company."

Phipps looked shocked. "Your Grace, surely you're not really going to get your hands dirty."

Granville shrugged with a casualness that Portia had never seen him display in a ballroom. "Given Jupiter's state, it's inevitable."

She'd always considered herself a good judge of

character. How lowering to recognize how wrong she'd been about the Duke of Granville. Good heavens, she'd once told Juliet that her suitor was the most boring man in Britain! Nobody who had spent the last couple of hours with him would ever say that.

"Your Grace, I'm more than happy to wash the dog." Phipps remained aghast, while Portia battled to ignore how appealing Granville looked with a self-mocking smile curling his lips. When Jupiter whined at the fraught tone, the duke's elegant hand dropped to stroke the decidedly inelegant head.

"It's all right, boy." That deep velvety voice had all sorts of odd effects on Portia's innards. He turned back to Phipps. "It's going to need more than one person. I doubt this fellow will take to the tub like a duck to water."

"Very good, sir." Phipps must realize that he verged on insubordination, although the duke's tone remained steady and held no reproach. The coachman straightened and did his best to pretend that his noble employer preparing to wash a filthy mixed-breed dog was perfectly normal. He didn't quite succeed, but Portia commended the attempt.

"Phipps, can you please send someone with a message for my coachman? Our house is just across the square." She suspected that Phipps knew that. Servants always knew the gossip before anyone else did. Not only that, she was sure that Phipps and Rankin had shared more than one drink at the King's Head, where right now Granville's grooms caroused at their employer's expense.

"As you wish, my lady." He glanced at Granville. "I'll take it myself, if that meets with Your Grace's approval."

"Good idea. The fewer people involved in our plans, the better."

"Could you please tell Rankin I'm occupied with the dog? He'll understand."

"Meaning he's your companion in crime," Granville said drily.

"He's another animal lover. Without him, I wouldn't have a hope of doing what I must."

"Very good, my lady." Phipps bowed his head in acknowledgment.

"I'll find us a tub," Granville said.

"We'll need some warm water, too" Portia said.

"Sheriff will sort that out, my lady." Phipps turned to his employer. "Will that be all, Your Grace?"

"For the moment. Thank you, Phipps."

"You've upset him," Portia murmured, after Phipps had gone.

Another of those heart-stopping half-smiles. Blast him, she wished he'd refrain. They made her stomach tighten in a most disorienting fashion.

"I know. He only calls me Your Grace when he's in a snit. He has a much stronger sense of my dignity than I do." His hand rested on Jupiter's head. It was clear that Jupiter approved.

"I always thought you were so puffed up with pride, you were likely to burst," Portia said, then raised her hand to her lips to muffle a gasp of mortification. "I do beg your pardon, Your Grace."

A snort escaped. "For heaven's sake, don't you start Your Gracing me."

"But I was just appallingly rude."

He raised his eyebrows. "Believe me, I'm well aware that you don't like me."

A painful flush prickled her cheeks. "Did Juliet tell you?"

"No, of course she didn't."

Of course she didn't. Until she broke society's rules in such spectacular fashion, Juliet had been a pattern card of good behavior. That included her famous tact.

Portia's lips flattened. "You don't like me either."

Another soft exhalation of laughter. "You're growing on me."

"Like mildew?" Portia said before she processed what he'd said. Once she did, she regarded him in open-mouthed astonishment. "Are you saying you've changed your mind about me?"

He stared back with a blandness that once she'd have dismissed as the boring Duke of Granville being boring as usual. Now she knew that he enjoyed a private joke. His voice emerged equally expressionless, which made what he said next even more bewildering. "Despite my better judgment, I find myself rather admiring you."

"But I've done nothing but disrupt your life. You should curse that we met today."

Another of those attractive shrugs. "Perhaps someone was overdue to turn things topsy-turvy."

"Juliet did that," Portia said, before she could remind herself that mentioning his brief engagement to her sister was disgracefully gauche.

His mouth turned down in self-derision and perhaps remembered pain. Juliet had always said that Granville didn't love her and had only chosen her because she made a suitable duchess. But Portia had never been sure. Less sure now she knew that the Duke of Granville was far from the stolid lump of smugness that she'd judged him.

Juliet was very beautiful. It would make sense that the man who wanted to marry her was besotted. How very lowering to note that every fiber of Portia's being loathed the idea of the Duke of Granville hungering for her sister. Indeed, the thought made her nauseous.

"A talent for disruption runs in the family."

She twined her hands at her waist. "You should despise the name of Frain."

"Perhaps, but today you've proven yourself brave and resourceful, and I applaud the way you defended Jupiter."

"You always thought I was a complete rattlebrain," she said sourly, while the unexpected compliments swirled around her, not making sense.

"I've learned the error of my ways, my lady. Closer acquaintance reveals hidden qualities." She'd never have believed him capable of such a brilliant smile. If his half-smiles sent her silly heart cavorting, this full smile punched all the air out of her lungs and left her giddy.

She was incapable of putting two words together. When she didn't reply, Granville gestured toward the back of the stables. "Enough of this cloying sentiment. We'll be sobbing into the hay bales if I keep this up. Shall we find a receptacle for Jupiter's ablutions?"

She gulped for air and through a haze, watched him disappear down the aisle between the stalls.

A smile lengthened Granville's lips, as he dug around the small storeroom looking for an apron for his unexpected guest. He'd smiled a lot today. And he wasn't a man given to constant levity. Especially during these last months, when gossip had raged about his failed betrothal to Juliet Frain.

Given this was his second broken engagement in scandalous circumstances – both thanks to that bastard, the Duke of Evesham – his political future was now in question. People asked themselves whether a man with such a chaotic romantic history was capable of running the country. Sometimes even he acknowledged a doubt or two. His judgment was faulty when it came to choosing his duchess. Could he be trusted in other areas?

Today he'd been too busy for soul-searching. It was something of a relief.

Odd to think that the cause of his newly buoyant spirits was Portia Frain, a woman he'd always dismissed as a sentimental hen-wit. Yet recent events proved that she was far from a fluttering nincompoop. And by God, she was beautiful. She took his breath away – which had never happened before.

Juliet was lovely, a perfect cool blonde to set off the Granville emeralds. But Portia was something more. She possessed so much vitality that light shone out of her.

If anyone in England needed a light in the darkness, it was His Grace, the Duke of Granville. Since his marriage plans had foundered, life had turned rather bleak. He supposed it was inevitable that Portia's zest drew him like a magnet drew iron filings.

It meant nothing more than that.

After all, she didn't like him. Nor had she responded when he'd said that he found her stimulating company. It was depressing quite how much that had stung.

He looked down at Jupiter who had followed him into the storeroom. Devotion gleamed in the brown eyes. "It's been a strange day, my friend. And likely to become more so."

Worse than talking to a dog, he'd brought a gently bred lady to his house without a chaperone. If anyone found out, he'd have to marry the chit.

He frowned at the dog. "Why doesn't that send me screaming down the street?"

Jupiter didn't answer. He didn't have to.

When Granville emerged with a thick leather apron, Lady Portia was standing where he'd left her. "This should help to keep you dry."

The sound of his voice made her jump and blush. Her exquisitely clear skin revealed every emotion. How had he failed to notice that before? Today this woman who had hovered on the edge of his awareness for so long seemed a stranger. An alluring, intriguing stranger, who sparked too many forbidden desires.

For a charged moment, she stared at Granville as if she'd never seen him before, then she blinked and broke the odd connection. "Th...thank you," she stammered, accepting the apron with an unsteady hand. She'd taken off her gloves while he was in the storeroom.

Lady Portia wasn't a woman who stammered. Her coolness through the day's dramas had impressed him. When Jim threatened her, she'd hardly turned a hair.

Was she also caught in the grip of attraction? Then a less appealing explanation occurred to him.

He straightened. All day, he'd shown a lamentable tendency to lean toward her. "Lady Portia, I assure you that if you're afraid to be alone with me, there's no need. I'm aware of the behavior becoming to a gentleman." Whatever secret impulses that gentleman might harbor.

She was back staring at him as if he'd appeared from nowhere. "You sound all ducal again."

He frowned. "How the devil else do you expect me to sound?"

His frustration made Jupiter's ears twitch. Folding her arms, she regarded him with displeasure. "That's how you talked to me when we danced. As if you were Napoleon and I was an unpromising recruit."

Startled, he drew back. "That can't be true."

"Believe me, it is. It's how Juliet talks to me, too."

"I'm sure I was polite."

Her shiver was unnecessarily theatrical. "I'm sure you were, too. But not warm. Definitely not warm."

If only she knew how warm he felt right now. As well as the heat her presence aroused, a different heat prickled at the back of his neck. Discomfort. "I'm sorry. No wonder you don't like me."

"You've been fairly human all day." She paused. "When we've been alone for hours. I'm not frightened of you. You're considered the most upright man in England. Anyway, I'm not a fool. If I didn't trust you, I wouldn't be here. Good Lord, if I didn't trust you, I wouldn't leave Jupiter in your care."

He supposed trust provided some recompense for her dislike. Although given the ideas rocketing through his mind, she should be warier of his intentions.

"I just wanted to assure you that you're safe," he said stiffly. He hadn't much liked her snide reference to his pristine reputation.

She subjected him to another of those comprehensive inspections. He wondered what she saw. From a young age, he'd adopted a manner suitable to his dignity. He'd been a shy boy and smart enough to know that people would take advantage if they could, purely because he was the Duke of Granville. Portia was right – his public behavior tended to be very ducal indeed.

Something told him that she saw beneath the polished veneer. He'd never felt that way with Juliet. But then she defended herself against the world, too. When she jilted him for the raffish Duke of Evesham, he understood that he'd never really known the woman he almost married.

Portia was much less enigmatic. He liked that. At least today, when she wasn't bristling with hostility.

"Thank you," she said in a neutral voice, surprising him anew, because he had no idea what lurked under that tone. She shook out the apron and pulled it over her head. It was too big for her. He'd expected that. What he hadn't expected was that she'd have difficulty with the ties.

A hiss of irritation escaped her. "Could you…"

He didn't want to touch her. Actually that was a lie. He desperately wanted to touch her. Too much. But he feared that pristine reputation she derided wouldn't survive past the moment his hands connected with her body.

For a few seconds, he watched her struggle. Then smothering a growl, he stepped behind her and brushed her fidgeting hands out of the way. "Here. Let me."

"Thank you." She sounded more subdued than usual. Or perhaps the pounding blood in his ears muffled her voice.

The apron strings were more complicated than he'd realized when he'd tugged the garment off the shelf. The ties laced through a couple of eyelets to hold the apron in place. Although they weren't nearly as complicated in real life as they felt when his senses flooded with Portia's nearness. His usually adept hands turned into ten thumbs.

It didn't help that he stood close enough for her rich honey scent to torment him. His gaze focused on her nape, revealed under her upswept golden hair. He'd never before found the back of a woman's neck a source of irresistible temptation. But the sight of that pale, tender skin made him itch to taste it.

His efforts with the infernal cords became even more ham-fisted. They'd be here all day at this rate.

He tried hard to touch only the apron, not its wearer. But it was impossible. When his fingers brushed her back, he felt her vibrating tension. The reminder of her dislike should dampen his rising ardor. It didn't. In a futile attempt to clear his spinning head, he inhaled. All he got for his efforts was another wallop of that smoky, alluring scent.

"Have you...have you finished?" she asked with more of that uncharacteristic stammer.

Her husky voice made him think of a sleepy Portia in his bed. A sleepy Portia available and eager for his touch.

"Nearly," he muttered and forced himself to conquer the tangle of laces. For some reason, his hands kept getting mixed up with the filmy material of her dress.

Over his thundering heartbeat, Granville could hear the uneven rasp of her breathing. He gritted his teeth and struggled to steady his hands. He was tying a knot, not drafting a complicated piece of legislation.

For God's sake, man, you've touched a woman before. You're acting like a complete clodpoll.

At last he finished, tying a clumsy bow at the back. He hoped to hell it held. He wouldn't survive doing this again without sweeping her into his arms. "There."

"Thank you." That reedy voice didn't sound at all like the Amazon who confronted Jim and insisted he hand Jupiter over.

"My pleasure," Granville said, which was both a flagrant lie and a profound truth. Because for all his regrettable ineptitude and barely restrained hunger, he loved being so close to Portia.

She'd accused him of being cold. That was true, at least for how he conducted his life. His existence followed rules of logic and cool detachment. So how could he resist warming his soul in her radiant glow? Portia Frain was everything that he wasn't. Passionate. Emotional. Openhearted. Vital in a way that nobody else in his calm, measured world was.

Over the last few hours, she'd made him feel more alive than he ever had. Definitely more alive than he'd felt with either of his fiancées.

So it was understandable if unwise that instead of stepping away to a respectable distance like a true gentleman, he placed his hands on those straight, tense shoulders.

Her gasp sounded like horror.

Appalled at his presumption, he jerked his hands away. What in Hades was he doing, touching a woman who hated his guts?

Granville prepared to step back. Before he could, Portia whirled around in a swirl of cobalt skirts. Burning eyes met his. He braced to read hatred or anger or, worst of all, disgust in her expression. Instead, all he saw was a longing that vied with his own.

Her hands landed flat on his chest, where his heart raced fit to burst. He reached out for her arms, as her fingers curled in his loose shirt.

Then the man widely held to have no impulses at all gave in to his impulses. He kissed her.

CHAPTER FIVE

Fresh. Tangy. A little tart. With a lingering hint of sweetness. Like eating a newly picked apple. A zing of pure pleasure, as the senses flooded with the taste of summer.

That was what it was like to kiss Lady Portia Frain. Like holding a sunny day in his arms. As Granville's head filled with her evocative scent and his arms bundled her close, every rational thought evaporated under a blast of heat.

It took a mere moment to register that she stood as straight and still as a column. A moment, but still too long.

Painful understanding dampened his burgeoning arousal. She must resent him mauling her.

Granville thought that he'd seen desire in her eyes. But it was so easy to read what one wanted to see in another person's expression, wasn't it?

Feeling like he shifted a ton of lead single-handed, he prepared to let her go. Fighting every instinct, he told his hands to release their grip. He told his face to lift away from hers, to end the kiss. He told himself to step back and beg her forgiveness.

Until he kissed Portia, he'd had no idea quite how

cold his world was. He was so used to the cold, it became his natural habitat. Now he held summer in his arms, how could he forsake that for deadly winter?

But he must. He must.

Feeling like he amputated his arm, he began to withdraw.

Then the miracle happened.

Portia made a faint sound. Before he could decide whether it was a complaint, her lips moved beneath his and she raised her hands to his shoulders.

A signal that she wasn't disgusted. A stronger signal still when her rigidity flowed away and her body curved to fit his. Portia Frain was a generous creature. In nature and in form. He shuddered with delight when her full breasts pressed into a chest covered only with a light shirt.

On a muffled groan, he gathered her closer and began to kiss her with intent. The flutter of her lips against his zapped him with heat. Her grasp on his shoulders firmed, and the little hum she made in her throat conveyed surprised pleasure.

Surprise...

Granville lifted his head to stare down into her lovely face. Her eyes were closed, and he couldn't mistake her rapt expression. Her lips were full and red and parted as if she trembled on the brink of asking for more.

She was the perfect image of female desire. *Innocent desire.*

What a fool he was. What an infernally stupid fool.

"Portia, you've never kissed a man before, have you?" he murmured, hands settling on her narrow waist.

Her eyelids lifted, a flicker of thick brown lashes. He drowned in misty blue, while she stared up at him as if she lost her bearings in the real world.

"Portia?" he prompted. Then smiled at her with all the gladness that she aroused in his moth-eaten soul. "I refuse to believe I've shocked you speechless. I didn't think anything could shock you speechless."

A faint frown wrinkled her brow, and her gaze focused on his face. She no longer looked as if she wandered the far boundaries of the cosmos. "You're teasing me?"

He thought about it as he stepped back. "I suppose I am."

"You're far too careful of your dignity to tease anyone."

He hid a wince. "I don't feel dignified right now. And you haven't answered my question."

She blushed, and her eyelids lowered to hide her eyes. "When would I have kissed anyone? You know what life is like for well-bred young ladies."

"You've clearly found ways to circumvent your chaperone." Juliet had been her chaperone until last year. Since then, he had a vague memory of an aging lady accompanying her when she was out in public.

"My animal rescue?"

"Yes."

Humor quirked that luscious mouth. "I didn't kiss any of the...gentlemen who were mistreating their fellow creatures."

"None were handsome enough to tempt you?"

"Some were handsome enough. But people who are cruel to animals are also cruel to humans. I might have wanted to shoot a few of them. I never wanted to kiss them."

Her murderous impulses evoked a soft laugh. "You think I'm kind?"

He asked the question in jest. More of that teasing she found so unlikely. She was right. He rarely – *never* – teased anyone. His life was serious and purposeful. Playfulness had no role.

"You've been kind to Jupiter." Grave blue eyes examined his features. "You were kind when you rescued me from Jim. Despite it being the last place you wanted to be."

Granville shifted, awkward under her praise. "Noblesse oblige."

How he wished that he hadn't asked. He'd expected a dismissive answer. He hadn't expected genuine gratitude. Was that why she'd kissed him? Because she felt in his debt? The idea made his skin feel too tight for his bones.

Her lips flattened as if she resisted saying more. "Perhaps."

He suspected that she sensed his discomfort. Which was interesting in itself. He was renowned for hiding his emotions.

To his regret, she wasn't finished. "And you stood by Juliet during that awful scene at Afton Park after the play. I've always been grateful to you for that. You didn't have to. In fact, most people would have called you a fool for being so gallant. You were the injured party, after all."

Discomfort stung worse than ever. Because Portia raised the subject that loomed like a towering cliff over everything they did. The fact that he'd once, however briefly, been engaged to her older sister.

"She deserved better treatment than she got," he said stiffly.

"See? You're a kind man." Before he could protest, she went on in a troubled voice. "I suppose you must have kissed her, too."

Discomfort tightened his gut. "Portia, a gentleman doesn't—"

She frowned. "So you did kiss her?"

"Not the way I just kissed you."

Portia looked worried. "Why not?"

He sighed. "Because, much as I admired your sister, I didn't want her."

When she retreated from his hold, he wanted to smash something. "But you still kissed her."

He sent her a straight look, praying that one chaste peck on Juliet's lips almost a year ago didn't wreck his chances with Portia. A thousand apologies and excuses welled up, but they all smacked too much of desperation. And insincerity, when he'd never been more sincere in his life. "Only once, when she agreed to marry me. It was like kissing my grandmother."

Portia folded her arms in front of her. "You say that now."

He exhaled with impatience. "I do, and I'd say that then, because it's true."

"I'm not sure how I feel about that."

Granville didn't believe her. He could tell that she didn't like it. He couldn't blame her. "It was over in a second. A duty rather than a pleasure."

"Hmm," she said, studying him with narrow eyes.

"What does that mean?"

"It means I need to think about this."

Dear God, what would he do if she broke with him because he'd kissed her sister? "I can't change what happened, Portia. I can tell you it didn't mean anything, but only you can decide if you trust me."

The stiff line of her shoulders eased a fraction. "I suppose you didn't have to tell me."

"Yes, I did."

"Yes, you did," she responded in a dark tone.

He stared down at her in helpless fascination. "Does this mean you won't let me kiss you again?"

As they'd spoken, her blush had subsided. Now another intriguing wash of color rose. "I think before that happens, we should sort out a few things."

"If we must," he said with a hint of grimness,

before he realized what she'd said. His hands caught her waist. "Do you mean—"

She searched his face as if confirming his honesty. "I mean that you should let me go before Phipps and Sheriff discover us doing what we shouldn't."

She was right, damn it. This was neither time nor place for passionate embraces. He pressed his mouth to hers in a brief kiss that nonetheless rushed through him like wildfire.

When he raised his head, her eyes were glazed again. "What was that for?" she asked in a shaky voice.

"To remind me that I've got a treat in store."

He braced for maidenly protests. But Portia, while undoubtedly a maiden, didn't play coy games. She raised a hand to her lips as if she touched the memory of his kiss.

The gesture had an infernally powerful effect on him. It was an effort to take her hand to lead her across to the bench against the wall. They sat together perhaps not innocently, but much more presentable to an audience than they'd been a few moments ago. Jupiter trailed behind them and settled at Granville's feet.

Portia's forthright manner revived. The gaze she settled on him was pointed. "Why didn't you want Juliet? She's very beautiful."

"Not as beautiful as you are."

Her free hand waved away the compliment. Her other hand remained in his. "You don't have to say that."

"Nevertheless, it's true."

"Thank you," Portia said, but he could tell that she wasn't persuaded. "Tell me about Juliet."

"She must have told you that it wasn't a love match." As became apparent to the entire world when she married Evesham.

He had no experience of an affectionate family, but he couldn't imagine Portia and Juliet kept many secrets from each other. He'd always recognized the fondness between the sisters, even worried about it when he feared that Portia might dissuade Juliet from accepting his proposal.

Although Portia hadn't known that he'd kissed Juliet, had she? Perhaps confidences only went so far.

"Not on her part. I wasn't sure about you."

"You believed cold fish like me don't fall in love."

"Well, yes, and I apologize. If you were such a dull stick, you'd never kiss me in a stable."

"We should have met in a stable much earlier."

She frowned. "I'm not used to you teasing. Stop it."

"Don't you like it?"

The corners of her mouth, the mouth that he'd tasted for such a tantalizingly short interval, deepened. He had a feeling that she'd just about forgiven him for kissing Juliet. The relief made him feel like doing cartwheels. "You were speaking of my sister."

"She and I were going to build a useful partnership. Social reform. National influence. Children to continue the line. She was born to be a duchess."

"I know. Everyone said so. I used to mock her about it. Now she *is* a duchess. And not just because Evesham's a duke. She loves him and he loves her. She'd take him if he was a gardener's boy. At the end, she didn't give a fig about rank."

"I'm happy for her."

Portia's eyes rounded. "You are?"

"She followed her heart."

"But you hate Evesham."

Self-derision twisted his lips. "He's not my

favorite person."

"Because of Vanessa Gould."

"Yes." Vanessa was Granville's first fiancée.

"Did you kiss Vanessa?"

The question was inevitable. At least he had nothing to confess when it came to that engagement. "No. That was a family arrangement. We danced a few times and I called on her, but we were mere acquaintances. She was always very quiet in my presence, I assumed out of reticence. I had no idea that she loathed the idea of marrying me until she ran off with Evesham."

"Who you shot."

Unfortunately, not fatally. "Yes."

"I'm glad."

His grunt expressed amusement. "That I shot that devil Evesham?"

"No, that you didn't love Juliet. It makes me feel—"

"Like you're not treading on her territory?"

"Yes."

"So you're happy to do it again?" he asked with rising optimism.

It was her turn to laugh. "You know, when I woke up this morning, the last thing I imagined I'd be doing was discussing kisses with my sister's jilted fiancé."

"I'm sure." He was astonished, too. "I deserve horsewhipping."

"We're in the right place for it."

Dear God, how had he missed what a jewel she was? Right now, even the way she'd imposed Jupiter on him seemed charming.

Granville hadn't encountered a girl this enchanting since his days courting Vanessa, and he'd come to see that his interest in her had been based on wishful thinking. He'd only been twenty-one and woefully inexperienced in the ways of the world.

That was no longer true. Despite his proper reputation, he'd enjoyed a number of discreet liaisons. He understood and appreciated the lure of sensual pleasure. But nothing in those affairs compared with his craving to whisk this gorgeous creature off and have his way with her.

"I was joking," Portia said, as the silence extended.

"I know. I'm just a bit nonplussed. Kissing you wasn't even on the horizon. Now it's all I can think of."

"Me, too," she admitted with audible glumness. "You'll think I'm a complete hoyden."

He shot her a disbelieving look. "I think you're utterly magnificent."

"What?"

"You heard me. I'd consider it a privilege beyond measure if you let me kiss you again."

Although that erratic blush rose again, she was brave enough to meet his eyes. "I'd like that."

Her shy curiosity tightened every muscle in his body. Somewhere at the back of his mind, a warning clanged. She was an innocent. Even more of an innocent than he'd realized. She asked for kisses, but he had a horrid presentiment that kisses wouldn't be enough for him.

She'd grant him a glimpse of heaven while casting him into a hell of frustration.

Undoubtedly, he invited trouble. So did she, but he had the experience to guess how all this would go. A sensible man – he'd always considered himself a sensible man – would run a mile.

"You can trust me," he said, as much for his own sake as hers.

She rolled her eyes. "Even when I didn't like you, I knew you were as straight as a die. You even admitted that you kissed Juliet."

Pleasure flooded him, swamping his well-founded qualms. "You like me?"

She frowned. "I just kissed you."

"That doesn't mean you like me."

"I'm not in the habit of kissing men I don't like."

His faint snort would surprise his straitlaced society acquaintances. "Portia, you're not in the habit of kissing anyone."

It was the first time that he'd used her name without her courtesy title. Did she notice?

"No, but if I was, I'd restrict myself to people I like. I wouldn't have kissed you yesterday."

How could he resist her? He caught her chin and turned her face to kiss her again. Another blast of heady sweetness. This time, her lips moved beneath his. It was an effort to pull away without pursuing the contact. "Then I'm grateful we didn't meet yesterday."

She looked tousled and confused – and bewitching – as she struggled to focus on his face. "That was nice."

"It will only get nicer."

"Oh?" The syllable expressed a curiosity that made his blood heat.

"You know, it's going to be nigh impossible to act like a polite stranger when we meet in public."

To his surprise, she looked disappointed. "You won't dance with me?"

His lips twitched. For a man who was a novice at teasing, he was getting into the habit. "If you insist."

"I do."

"Remember to put on the long-suffering expression you always wear, or people will know things between us have changed."

She gave a quick laugh. "And you must look so bored, you're asleep on your feet."

"I'm sure I didn't."

"I'm sure you did."

He was sure he did, too. Dancing with his prospective bride's harum-scarum sister had always counted as a duty, not a pleasure. Now the danger lay in concealing how much pleasure she gave him. "Strange that one day makes all the difference."

When her hand squeezed his, the action transformed to poignant emotion squeezing his heart. How puzzling. "Strange indeed."

They stared at each other. Granville saw his longing reflected in her lovely eyes. He was on the verge of kissing her again when Jupiter's faint growl warned them that their privacy ended.

"Good boy," Granville murmured, releasing Portia's hand and rising.

He patted the dog. By the time Sheriff and Phipps appeared at the stable door, he and Portia stood several feet apart, looking as innocent as lambs. Or at least Granville hoped so.

CHAPTER SIX

S he'd kissed a man. More than once. She'd liked it. Very much. She'd promised to kiss the man again.

How astonishing.

Yet the most astonishing element of the day wasn't that Portia discovered a pastime to vie with her interest in stray animals. It was that the man she'd kissed was the almighty bore and self-righteous prig, the Duke of Granville.

Except it turned out, he wasn't boring at all. Nor was he the slightest bit self-righteous. He was kind and sweet and funny. And endearingly shy.

Which might explain his haughty manner in public.

She couldn't wait to kiss him again. His lips had been soft and warm. And they'd provided the most exciting experience that she'd ever had in all her twenty-five years. She probably should hold it against him that he'd kissed Juliet, but she believed him when he said he'd done that purely to seal the contract between them.

For the first time, she understood why Juliet and Viola had abandoned common sense and thrown themselves into the arms of unsuitable men. What did propriety matter compared to passion? Portia struggled to hide a shiver of anticipation and look as if she and the duke had been discussing the weather instead of lessons in kissing.

Phipps put down the two large buckets he carried. A tall, rather cadaverous-looking man followed him inside, also carrying two steaming buckets. "Your Grace, I'm at your service."

Granville's smile conveyed affection. "I knew you'd help us, Sheriff. This is Lady Portia Frain, who is making sure that we treat our guest right."

Sheriff set down his buckets and bowed with an impassive expression, as if finding unchaperoned young ladies in his employer's stable was an everyday occurrence. "My lady."

Granville gestured to Jupiter, who as usual pressed as close as he could get. "This is Jupiter, who's in dire need of a wash."

"Yes, sir." More impassivity, but she couldn't imagine the man approving of a mongrel dog in the household.

"Did you find a tub, Your Grace?" Phipps asked.

The tub? That was right. She and Granville were meant to search for one while Phipps fetched Sheriff.

Portia was completely charmed when Granville looked as if he'd been caught raiding the larder. Before today, she'd never imagined the duke as a boy. If anyone had asked her, she'd have said that he was born middle-aged. But the hunted expression on features that she'd once found magisterial made her want to hug him.

"I couldn't see it," he said with such obvious discomfort that it was difficult not to roll her eyes again. It turned out that he was competent with most things, except lying.

"I'll have a look." Phipps disappeared into the

room where Granville had found her apron. Within seconds, he returned bearing a tin bathtub.

Heat prickled her cheeks, although neither by word nor gesture did Phipps indicate any criticism of his employer's eyesight. To hide her fluster, Portia fell to her knees beside Jupiter and ran her hands over his dirty, matted coat. "It's all right, boy."

By the time she stood to unclip his collar, she'd recovered her composure. The men had filled the tub and fetched soap and brushes and towels. She stepped forward to lift Jupiter, when the duke brushed past. "Let me."

Once Jupiter hit the water, he made his displeasure felt – and heard. They'd hear that howl of outrage in Birmingham.

She rushed forward to hold him down, noting that even offended, he didn't snap. That was a good sign. Sometimes her rescues were so affected by their experiences, they turned savage.

Portia kneeled on the wet slate floor. "Shh, boy. It's fine. You're safe." She struggled to sound authoritative above all the splashing.

He howled again. Equine disapproval resounded from the stalls and hooves kicked against wood. On the other side of the tub, Sheriff stepped beyond the range of flying water.

"Stop it," Granville said.

To Portia's astonishment, the dog went still, although he quivered under her hands. Granville settled beside her, and she thrilled to the rub of his hip against hers.

"You'll get wet, Your Grace," Phipps protested, barely able to suppress his horror at the sight of his aristocratic employer performing such a humble task.

The smile that had such an intoxicating effect on Portia's pulse appeared. "I'm not made of icing sugar. I won't melt."

"Your Grace, I'll take the liberty of returning to the kitchens for more towels," Sheriff said, picking up two empty buckets.

"Grand idea." Granville stroked Jupiter's head with a notably calming effect. "We need more hot water, too."

"Very good, sir."

Portia missed Sheriff's departure because Jupiter began to wriggle, despite his idol's touch. "Let's do this quickly before he loses his temper."

Phipps passed her a brush and some soap. She took a deep breath, sharp with the odor of wet dog, and worked up a lather on Jupiter's coat.

"Shall I help?" Granville asked.

"Just keep talking. Your voice calms him." Hardly surprising. That deep voice stirred all sorts of forbidden longings inside her. Not that she'd describe the result as calming.

"It's all right, old man. Nobody's going to hurt you. You're safe. Good boy. You're such a good boy," Granville crooned over and over.

However the praise worked with the dog, it had a mesmerizing effect on Portia. That was a pest when she needed to concentrate on Jupiter. In her sopping clothes – the apron provided little protection against Jupiter's frantic efforts to escape – she should be cold. Granville's nearness made her feel far too warm.

"He looks clean to me, my lady," Phipps said.

With a sigh, Portia dropped the flannel that she used to wash Jupiter's more delicate areas. The water was black and scummy. "That's the best we'll do for a first bath." She scratched behind Jupiter's ears. "You've been a brick, Jupiter. A real hero."

"Shall I lift him out?" Granville was as wet as she was. His fine white shirt turned transparent, revealing the sculpted planes of his chest. In full evening dress, the Duke of Granville looked superb. But heavens above, how every debutante in Mayfair would swoon if they saw him now.

"Yes, please. I'd like to rinse him off with clean water."

Sheriff arrived with a pile of towels considerably more luxurious than the rough linens that Phipps had found in the storeroom. A gangling youth followed, carrying two buckets of hot water.

"Good man." Granville rose to lift Jupiter out of the tub. The dog whined, and his short legs scrabbled in the air. Once Granville placed him on the ground, he released a canine sigh of relief. And had a thorough shake, spreading water everywhere. Dripping wet, he was a sorry sight, even if much cleaner than he had been.

"I hope you don't mind, sir, but I've asked my nephew to help," Sheriff said with commendable dignity, given everyone else was soaked to the skin. "You can trust him to keep Lady Portia's presence a secret."

Granville directed a serious look at the boy. "Matty, you must give me your word that you will never betray our trust. This dog owes his life to Lady Portia. It would be wrong if she suffered for her kindness."

Matty, all knees and elbows, didn't seem to hear. Instead his eyes went as round as saucers. "Cor, you know my name!"

"Matty Gant!" Sheriff bleated in dismay. "That's not how to address your betters."

All day, Portia had been coming round from her dislike for the Duke of Granville. But she fell in love with him when, instead of climbing on his high horse, he laughed and clapped Matty on the back. "Of course I know your name, lad. Sheriff and I have big plans for you. Now come and meet Jupiter. You can hold him while we rinse him off."

Thank goodness, everyone was busy finishing up Jupiter's bath, because her ability to speak had deserted her. She'd seen so many examples of Granville's kindness, but his generosity to an awkward boy sliced through the last of her misgivings.

From earliest childhood, Portia had valued kindness above all other qualities. And loathed its opposite. Hatred for cruelty from the strong toward the weak, the attitude that one hurt another creature just because one could, had launched her crusade to save as many animals as possibe. The horrors that she'd seen meant she knew to value a kind heart wherever she found it.

Against all expectations, she'd found one of the kindest hearts she'd ever known in her sister's rejected suitor. A lesson against leaping to conclusions based on superficial impressions.

If this was love, it wasn't very comfortable. She felt like an ax had struck her. How had this happened? Yes, her liking had grown as the day progressed. Yes, it turned out that this man she'd dismissed as a prig and a bore turned out to be everything she admired. Yes, he'd kissed her. Too briefly, but with enough intent to hint at heavenly delights in store.

None of that should scar her heart so deeply that she feared she'd never recover. Because that was how this felt. Like Granville's image was etched on her soul forever.

And it was a disaster.

Because he remained the Duke of Granville. Influential. Elegant. Universally admired. Her sister's former suitor. The man searching for the perfect duchess.

Nobody in their right mind would call Portia a perfect duchess. Portia with her impulsive nature and outspoken manner. Not to mention her menagerie of rescued animals.

The prospect of a lifetime with Alaric Dempster struck her as paradise. Except that he'd never consider her as a potential bride. Even if one overlooked his history with Juliet, Portia could never be a great political hostess or a leader of fashion.

She was just a girl who attracted him. A girl he'd kiss then abandon. A girl he'd forget while he pursued the life that he was born to lead.

The bleak reality of her situation made her want to howl louder than Jupiter in his bath.

"He smells better than he did." Granville kneeled beside Jupiter, toweling him dry.

Lady Portia's quietness niggled at him. Nor had she taken an active part in the final steps to make Jupiter presentable.

"I should hope so." Phipps rather than Portia replied to his remark. "He was no bouquet of roses when you found him. I'm not sure the carriage will recover."

"You'll work your magic, I'm sure." He wished that Portia would say something. After their hours together, he knew that silence wasn't her natural state.

Was it Matty? While he knew the boy well enough to trust to his discretion, Portia didn't. But she'd taken the entrance of Phipps and Sheriff into their conspiracy in her stride.

Was she worried about getting home undetected? Her gown was wet, and her damp hair hung down her back in a tangle of dark gold. Anyone who saw her would know that she'd been up to no good.

Her silence tied his gut into knots. Dear God, don't let her regret their kisses. She'd seemed to enjoy being in his arms. She'd seemed eager to step into his arms again.

He wasn't used to stewing over female megrims, but something inside him was desperate for Portia to be happy. The devil of it was that he couldn't ask her what was wrong while they had an audience.

Jupiter whined and shifted under a toweling that wasn't as brisk as it had been. Granville realized that he gawked at Portia like a thunderstruck yokel visiting London for the first time.

But by God, she was lovely. Even now when she looked like a drowned rat. During his courtship of her sister, he'd always found Portia too much. Juliet was measured and calm. Portia...wasn't. She was too vivid, too passionate, too alive.

Now that electric quality struck him as perfect. She made a man recognize that he was on this earth just once, and he ought to take advantage of that fact.

She'd said that she liked him. But two fiancées had decided that he wasn't the man for them. Had Portia reconsidered her plan to kiss him again? Denial churned in his belly.

"We should feed Jupiter," she said.

In Granville's ears, her voice sounded strained. She avoided his questioning glance.

Then he wanted to kick himself for being such a dolt. The evening advanced and with it, the evening chill. "By heaven, my lady, you must be freezing. We need to get you out of those wet clothes."

Dear Lord. He wanted to kick himself even harder for being doubly a dolt. He refused to look at the servants.

Rosy color flooded Portia's cheeks. Her hands

tangled in front of the wet apron, and her eyelashes fluttered down. She must want to kill him. Despite promising discretion, here he announced his intentions to the world. Or at least three servants, one dog, and the lady he desired.

She plucked at sodden skirts that showed an unfortunate tendency to cling to the sinuous lines of her hips. He struggled not to notice. Unsuccessfully.

"Yes, that would be good," she said in a muffled voice.

Granville cleared his throat and turned to Sheriff. He strove to sound as if he remained in control of circumstances that rapidly unraveled in all directions. By God, the Duke of Granville was *always* in control. What in Hades was going on? "Do we have any women's clothes in the house?"

"Only those belonging to the female staff, Your Grace." Sheriff's distant stare hinted that he'd caught his employer's faux pas. The man had known him since he was a boy. He'd recognize that Granville's interest in Portia extended beyond the platonic. Good God, how could he not? Granville had never before brought an unaccompanied lady to this house. To any of his houses.

Phipps wouldn't miss much either. He'd served the Dempsters as long as Sheriff had.

"Enough people are aware of my presence already," Portia said.

Granville, who was having inappropriate visions of Lady Portia in a neat white apron and a mobcap, spread his hands in apology. "Mine is a bachelor household, my lady."

"I should go. I'm sure you'll find something to keep Jupiter satisfied." She regained her poise after his gaffe about taking off her clothes. "Phipps and Sheriff, are you familiar with dogs?"

"Not really, my lady," Sheriff said. "His Grace's

grandfather couldn't abide them. Called them filthy brutes. Wouldn't even let the local hunting pack cross his land."

"Exactly so, my lady," Phipps said.

"We had dogs growing up, my lady," Matty piped up.

His uncle shot him a stern glance. "Matty Gant, keep your lip buttoned until you're spoken to."

Matty's mortified flush made his spotty skin look even angrier. "Your pardon, my lady, Your Grace."

Portia looked interested. "Perhaps His Grace might make you Jupiter's guardian?"

Granville liked the idea. "Kennel master?"

Matty's chagrin vanished in a broad smile. "Cor blimey. Too right, Your Grace."

Sheriff looked like he was about to have a fit. Before he could splutter out another stinging rebuke, Granville spoke. "Then that's settled. Do you want to start by taking him for a walk in the garden while your uncle puts his dinner together?"

Before Matty could utter another "cor blimey," his uncle spoke with the voice of authority. "That's an excellent suggestion, Your Grace."

"And I should go," Portia said again, as Matty fastened the rope to Jupiter's collar.

"Not looking like that, you won't," Granville said. "I've got an idea, if you'll come across to the house."

"But I'll be seen."

"Borrow my greatcoat and hat. We need to get you out of the stables, in case my grooms remember they have duties beyond spending their employer's coin at the King's Head."

He collected his coat and draped it across her shoulders. Wrapping her in a garment that belonged to him filled him with deep masculine satisfaction. This close, he noticed her shivering. It would be nice if she reacted to his presence, but he suspected that she was just cold in her wet dress.

An impression confirmed when she clutched the voluminous folds around her. He passed her his hat. "Pull this down over your face. It should do to get us across the garden. The house's public areas should be empty at this hour."

"Thank you."

He waited for her to put the hat on, before he dared to tuck the long tail of wet blond hair under her collar. He collected her pelisse from the stall gate. "Let's go."

Taking her arm, he steered her out of the stables and across the cobbled yard to the gate in the garden wall. Granville liked escorting Lady Portia even more than he liked her wearing his coat. He didn't like that she returned to her father's house. Something primitive inside him insisted that she belonged at his side, that they should always walk together like this.

He heard a howl of protest behind him, a shout from Matty, and Phipps using language that he'd never permit in front of his employer. A scrabble of paws on cobblestones, and a black-and-white shape came barreling in their direction.

Granville felt Portia's low chuckle in his balls. Despite his wet clothes, heat rushed through him and his hand tightened on her arm.

"I'm not sure how much work your new kennel master will have to do. Jupiter wants to be with you."

As the dog skittered through the open gate, Granville gave a long-suffering sigh. "I told you he's fallen victim to my fatal charm."

"He's not the only one," Portia muttered.

"What..." Before he could respond to that astonishing remark, Matty appeared at the gate. "Your Grace, I couldn't hold him."

"He can come inside. I'll bring him back, once I've got her ladyship sorted out."

"Very good, sir."

Portia studied the stocky dog. "If you imagine he's sleeping anywhere but in your bedroom, you're very much mistaken."

Granville shut the garden gate behind them. "Are you sure?"

Her short laugh was answer enough.

He drew Portia toward the terrace along the back of the house. The idea of kissing her, now that he finally had some privacy, struck him. Or at least shifted to the forefront of his mind. The regrettable truth was that kisses had occupied his thoughts for most of the afternoon and evening.

But he was freezing and she must be, too. He'd kiss her after she was warm and dry.

On that highly satisfactory conclusion, Granville brought Lady Portia Frain inside his house for the first time.

CHAPTER SEVEN

Without speaking, Granville led her through a garden lit with charcoal braziers. They climbed stone steps to a terrace extending the length of the house. Torches at either end of the terrace and candlelight from inside outlined Granville's profile, as finely cut as a face on a new-minted coin.

Portia had always thought that he was handsome, but it had seemed a cold beauty. Now that aristocratic face stirred a tidal wave of longing. And she had no idea what to do about it.

He unlatched a glass door and sneaked her into a morning room. She took a moment to appreciate her elegant surroundings, before he opened a door to reveal a black-and-white tiled hallway and a staircase leading upwards.

His destination turned out to be his rooms on the upper floor. "Granville..." she whispered.

He lifted a finger to his lips, as he opened the door to a luxurious sitting room decorated in shades of green and cream. Jupiter trotted inside before Granville shut the door.

"You're safe here," he said in a low voice, ushering

her into the bedroom and passing her the pelisse. "But my valet will listen for my return. Go behind the screen and I'll send him on his way."

Without speaking, Portia obeyed. Granville appeared accustomed to romantic intrigue. Was it possible that the famously virtuous duke wasn't quite the pattern card of duty and respectability that he presented to the world?

As she subsided onto a wooden chair behind the screen, the suspicion that Alaric Dempster could be wicked presented fascinating possibilities. Which was mad when she was at his mercy. If ever she needed His perfectly behaved Grace to remember his principles, it was when she was in his bedroom.

A door clicked open. "Shall I help you to..." The unknown speaker faltered to a stop. "Is that a...dog, Your Grace?"

The horror in the man's voice made Portia want to laugh.

"It is indeed." Granville's airiness contrasted with his original reaction to Jupiter, when he'd sounded every bit as put out as his valet did.

"In your apartments?"

"This is Jupiter, Hobbs. I hope you'll be great friends, now he's joined the household."

Portia didn't want to like Granville any more than she already did. But her heart softened when he claimed Jupiter as his own.

"Your Grace, I must protest."

"Please don't make me choose between London's finest valet and my new best friend."

The tone was pleasant, the flattery overt, and the threat clear. Astonishment flooded Portia. Granville preferring Jupiter over his valet left her floundering.

"Very good, sir." Hobbs didn't sound happy.

Portia hoped Jupiter's charm would prevail. It had with Granville. She couldn't imagine London's best valet having difficulty finding another position, but she hated to think of a faithful servant losing his place because she'd given his employer a pet.

Granville's laugh made forbidden awareness streak along her backbone. Now that she couldn't see him, that beautiful baritone worked its magic on her unruly senses. Good heavens, if he spoke seduction, how could she resist?

"I'm in rather a mess," he said ruefully. "I doubt you'll get these rags back into a wearable state."

"Your Grace, you must be frozen. Let me help you." The man sounded overcome. When she'd hidden behind the screen, Portia hadn't expected that stifling her giggles would present the greatest danger.

"I'll look after myself tonight."

"But, Your Grace…"

"I assume there's hot water in the bedroom."

"Of course, sir."

The man sounded almost as scandalized at the idea that there mightn't be as he was at Granville's rumpled appearance. Not to mention Jupiter's presence. "But you'll require my assistance. Had you forgotten that you planned to attend Lady Plunkett's musicale?"

So had Portia, she realized with a start. When she set out this afternoon, she'd imagined that she'd rescue Jupiter with ease, then hide him in the stables before she left for the party.

"To the devil with that. I feel like a night in."

"In that case, shall I bring Your Grace's dressing gown?"

"No, I'll shift for myself. I have some parliamentary papers to check. You may take the evening off."

"But, Your Grace…" The man sounded as if he was strangling. "I'll arrange a bath at the very least."

"That will be all, Hobbs. I'll see you in the morning." The tone remained polite, but the command was unmistakable.

A soft knock announced another arrival, she guessed a footman. "Mr. Sheriff suggested Your Grace might appreciate some more hot water."

"Capital," Granville said. "Place it over there."

"I'll take it through to the washstand," Hobbs said.

"No, I don't wish to be disturbed."

"As you wish, sir," Hobbs said with reluctance.

Portia only took a full breath after she heard both doors shut. When Hobbs offered to bring in the hot water, she'd almost had an attack of the vapors. All urge to laugh had vanished. Granville said his staff was loyal, but she feared that the tale of grimy, wet Portia Frain hiding in the Duke of Granville's apartments was too juicy not to spread.

Granville came around the screen, Jupiter at his heels. "A man's servants can be too conscientious."

She lowered the trembling hand pressed to her racing heart and mustered a shaky smile. "Goodness, that was close."

"Hobbs wouldn't betray us."

"I can tell he's devoted to you." Like all the servants in this house. It spoke volumes for what sort of master Granville was. Today had been full of surprising discoveries. Rather wonderful discoveries.

Self-preservation insisted that she get out fast. Not just to save her good name. She'd already fallen too far under Alaric Dempster's spell. She needed to break away and pray to heaven that her heart forgot the duke.

As she rose on shaky legs, her voice emerged unnaturally high. "I can't stay here."

He made a conciliatory gesture. "You have my

word that you're safe."

Portia linked her hands together at her waist. "I still can't stay. Papa lives in his own world most of the time and Aunt Mabel isn't the world's most diligent chaperone, but at some stage, they'll both realize that I haven't come home."

"You need to change into something dry."

"A maid's dress?"

"I'll lend you some clothes, then see you safely across the square. If we stick to the shadows, a coat and trousers and a hat will do the trick. Nobody will look twice to see me out with another man."

Jupiter sat and watched Granville, as if he couldn't imagine him concocting a plan that was less than brilliant. Portia had a suspicion that it would be simple to entrust all decisions to the duke, but it wouldn't do. She'd fought hard to carve some independence for herself. Just because his smile made her knees weak didn't mean she turned into a clinging vine.

"That might work." It was clever, she had to admit. And she was more than ready to get out of the filthy, clammy frock.

"Can you get back into your house without being seen?"

"I'll get Rankin to send for Betty, my maid. We'll manage."

"Let me help with the apron. Then you can wash, while I find you something to wear."

"Thank you." She appreciated him sticking to practicalities.

Nonetheless, the promise of more kisses hovered. Portia was generally even-tempered and unshakable, but her iron nerve failed at the thought of what might happen in this room. A magnificent mahogany bed dominated the chamber. She wouldn't be human if thoughts of sharing that bed with its owner didn't tiptoe across her mind.

She presented her back, struggling not to remember what had happened when he'd helped her to put the apron on. To her relief, he was quicker this time. He slid the apron off and tossed it over the top of the screen.

"I think...I think you may need help with your dress." His voice held a husky note.

She licked dry lips and cursed her choice of gown. She had plenty of dresses that fastened up the front, but this wasn't one of them. She'd been coming home from her old governess's house when she caught sight of Jim and Jupiter disappearing down a side street and she'd set off in pursuit.

Portia wanted to tell Granville that she'd stay in the wet dress after all. But those weren't the words that emerged. "Do you mind?"

His voice turned even gruffer. "Of course not."

She raised her arms to shift her hair out of the way. The movement lifted her breasts. Breasts that ached for a man's touch. For Granville's touch.

Dear Lord, she didn't recognize herself. Over the years, she'd dealt with hundreds of men. Apart from a brief unrequited penchant for the vicar's son when she was fourteen, none had made her heart race. Today, the merest sight of Alaric Dempster set her heart galloping like a wild horse.

The man who had almost married her sister. The man she'd once called the most boring gentleman in England.

Right now, she was anything but bored. Compared to this turmoil, boredom would be a blessed relief.

"Th...thank you." She hated the betraying break in her voice. She was used to being in control of her feelings. When it came to Granville, feelings took over. Everything was too raw and new for her to know if she could trust what was happening.

The delay must only have lasted a couple of seconds, even if it felt like an eon. Then Granville touched her neck as he released the top hook and eye. At the brush of his fingers, heat flared under her skin. A faint gasp escaped her.

"Are you all right?" He didn't sound too steady himself.

"Yes," she said, although it wasn't true.

As his hand moved to the next fastening, she gulped air into her starved lungs. In twenty-five years, she'd never needed to remind herself to breathe. It always came naturally. Not today. Not when Granville touched her.

He stood so close that his unsteady breath was hot on her nape. It was bad enough when he'd touched her in the stable. Then they'd both known that an interruption was due at any time. In his bedroom, nobody would barge in to shatter the physical awareness rising between them.

The urge to turn around and beg him to kiss her again was nigh impossible to deny. But if she went into his arms right now, she'd be in his bed soon after. Everything she'd been taught, everything she'd always believed told her that a girl who gave away her virtue too lightly invited more trouble than she could handle.

Portia curled her hands in her skirts. She clenched her teeth until her jaw ached, as this torture in the guise of helpfulness continued. Surely it couldn't go on much longer.

Her bodice sagged as he released the lower hooks. Her undergarments would be visible. No man had seen her unclothed. Even as unclothed as she was now, with a corset and a shift concealing her back. The thought turned her legs to water.

Granville released a sigh of relief. The ordeal was

over at last. "There," he said in a raspy voice that she hardly recognized.

She staggered as she turned. With her bodice clutched to her breasts, her eyes met his. She wasn't sure what she'd see. Salacious interest? But he looked on edge. Feverish color marked those perfect cheekbones.

"For God's sake, don't look at me like that, Portia, or I won't be responsible for my actions. I'm struggling to remember the duty I owe you."

She licked dry lips again, then wished she hadn't when he groaned and closed his eyes in visible agony. "I'll leave you to undress."

The word "undress" thundered through her like cannon fire. She was far too aware of how few steps they needed to take to reach the bed.

Then nothing would stop them until she was a virgin no more.

Right now, she wasn't sure that she cared.

Thank heaven, Granville opened his eyes and moved back. "Can you manage now?"

She bit her lip and told herself to calm down. Not that it worked. She took her own step backward and in her fluster, blundered into the screen. "Oh!"

Granville caught her arm to save her from falling. Behind her, the screen rocked without falling. She was already in a lather of heat. His touch set that heat ablaze.

"God give me strength." He released her as though she scorched him.

Without looking at her, he stumbled past the screen. Through the pounding of blood in her ears, Portia heard a door shut.

It took Granville several seconds before he saw clearly enough to make out the clothing stacked on open shelves in the dressing room. Even so, when he reached to choose a couple of shirts and pairs of trousers, his hand shook.

He was renowned for his coolness under pressure. Nobody who saw him now would call him cool. He was burning up.

At his side, Jupiter gave a soft whine. He glanced down and, despite everything, smiled. The dog wouldn't win any prizes for looks, but the animal's sturdy form and wedge-shaped head pleased him. "It's all right, boy."

Except it wasn't.

He needed his head examined. Why the hell had he brought Portia to his private apartments? Apart from the improper but irresistible yen to get her into his bed.

He should have taken her to a guest room to wash and change. Except that would betray her presence to the staff and a bed would still be far too close at hand. He was damned whatever he did.

Jupiter padding beside him, he took the clothing through to his room. "How are you managing?"

"Well, thank you."

He stepped up to the screen and struggled to ignore the blue gown flung over the top. Because if he thought about it, he'd picture Portia wearing nothing. That peachy skin wet and shining as she washed. "I brought you a shirt and some trousers to try on. The shirt should fit. I'm hoping the trousers do, too."

"Thank you." Her voice sounded muffled. Water splashed as she washed. He smelled the soap that he always used. Cedar and sandalwood, transformed into the most alluring scent on earth, now Portia used it.

It was all too bloody intimate for words, damn it.

"I'm going to wash and change in the dressing room. I'll see you in the sitting room when you're ready." Not the bedroom. He desperately needed to get her out of the bedroom.

Granville retreated before the urge to stay overcame him. He picked up the fresh hot water from the sitting room and carried it into the dressing room.

It was a relief to change into something dry. The interval on his own offered a much-needed opportunity to remind himself that he'd promised Portia her safety. He couldn't jump on her and have his wicked way.

His good intentions lasted precisely ten seconds after he entered the sitting room. In male attire, Portia looked completely scandalous and completely desirable. His pulse, which had almost settled back into its usual steady beat, surged into a dizzying rush. Every drop of moisture dried from his mouth, as he took in the delectable sight.

He hadn't expected the loose shirt to spark lascivious thoughts. But when he'd chosen the garment, he'd given no thought to how a generously curved woman might fill out a shirt designed for a man's angular shape.

The soft linen revealed too much of the body beneath. Her breasts were luscious trussed up in a corset and concealed under a modest frock. Now they pressed against the clinging material in unconfined glory.

She turned at an angle to tuck the shirt in, revealing graceful hips and a richly curved rump. By God, he'd been right about her legs. In narrow trousers, her legs were works of art.

Portia wasn't paying him any attention as she faced him again. Instead, she was plucking at the buttons on the trousers. "They won't do up. I'm the wrong shape."

"I wouldn't say that," escaped before he could stop himself.

She glanced up and blinked. "Stop it. I'm trying to do the right thing here."

Surprise held him still. Surprise and pleasure. "You're not frightened?"

"I'm nervous. It's not the same." She tugged unhappily at the braces holding the trousers up. The long shirt covered her stomach and protected her modesty. It was his problem that he couldn't help thinking about what lay under the linen. The path to paradise. A path he couldn't follow without a parson's blessing. Not to mention Portia's consent. "I really shouldn't be here."

"Blame Jupiter," Granville said, happier now he learned that he didn't suffer alone.

The dog glanced up at the sound of his name. Then as if realizing that nothing of interest occurred, he stretched out near the fire.

"I hope you don't mind, but I used your hairbrush. I had just about enough pins left to put my hair up."

She'd plaited her golden hair and wrapped it around her head. She looked like a saucy milkmaid. In his clothes.

"You're welcome to anything I have." He meant every word.

When she dismissed his comment with a wave of her hand, her breasts shifted against the linen. "Thank you. But I can't cross the square like this."

Granville's hands curled at his sides as if he shaped that lush flesh. "Come through and choose a coat and hat. That will cover a multitude of sins."

Even if he couldn't stop thinking about sin. In conventional clothing, Portia was a temptation. In masculine attire, he saw far too much of her body. Desire threatened to snap the tight rein that he placed on it.

He held the door open to allow her to precede him into the narrow room. She passed close enough for him to catch her scent. Portia, with a hint of sandalwood and cedar. His soap never smelled that good on him.

Granville gestured to the row of coats hanging on pegs along the wall. "Royal blue will bring out the color of your eyes."

She shot him a questioning glance, as she rolled up her sleeves to uncover slender wrists. Dear God, he really was in a bad way if the sight of a woman's wrists put him into a fever of lust. "You've noticed the color of my eyes?"

His snort was derisive. "Of course I have, Portia. Even before kissing you became my new obsession."

"Oh," she said. He waited for more, but she stared at the coats. "P...perhaps we should finish getting dressed."

"Yes, perhaps we should." At the very least, he needed to get her out of this confined space before he did something he shouldn't.

He dragged down the blue coat and a black one for himself. Then he tugged a couple of hats from the upper shelf.

Stepping back into the sitting room should feel like a relief. But Portia's allure remained just as strong.

"Let me help you into the coat," he said in a thick voice. At least the coat would cover the jiggle of her breasts.

"Thank you." She turned to allow him to slip the garment over her shoulders. Why did everything involve so much touching?

He was built on larger lines than Portia. The

shoulder seams sagged down her arms and the cuffs covered her hands. But when she faced him, he felt optimistic. In a ballroom, she'd create an uproar. Crossing Lorimer Square by lamplight, the outfit might just get her home undiscovered.

In the dark and at a distance, the illusion of her being male might hold. Although Granville remained far too aware that she was a woman. A delectable one at that.

"Here." He passed her a hat.

An ornate mirror was set above the sideboard. To his relief, she stepped out of reach and concentrated on setting his low-crowned beaver hat on her head at a convincingly masculine angle.

Unfortunately for his nerves, Portia's dashing appearance went straight to his balls. There was something so racy about a voluptuous female kitted out in severe male clothing. When she wore her bedraggled blue gown, he'd wanted her like the very devil. This was a thousand times worse.

Right now, he was on fire. Who knew trousers on a woman could have this incendiary effect?

She met his gaze in the mirror. "Granville?"

"I was right. The coat brings out the color of your eyes."

She flushed, and her eyelashes fluttered down. He knew that she didn't mean to be flirtatious, but the effect was the same, blast it.

He struggled to settle down. But how could he, when he ached to touch her? It took far too long to put on his coat and not just because it was a snugger fit than Portia's on her.

"Let's go," she said.

He managed to smile at her. "You'll emerge unscathed from your adventure."

"Yes."

That couldn't possibly be disappointment he

heard. "You can't have wanted to be discovered?"

"No, of course not."

"You sound downhearted."

"Not about that."

He frowned. "What then?"

She licked her lips and glanced at him. "I'd...hoped for more kisses."

Thunderstruck, he stared back before, ignoring conscience and propriety, he crossed the small distance between them and caught her in his arms.

CHAPTER EIGHT

*T*he moment Granville hauled Portia up to meet his descending mouth, she melted. The sensation was extraordinary, as if every bone in her body dissolved to honey.

Through the furious pulse of her blood, his groan echoed in her ears. His mouth was so hot on hers, a wave of ecstatic dizziness engulfed her. Instinctively she curled her arms around him. That hard muscular form was all that stopped her from collapsing to the floor in a puddle of feminine longing.

Instinct, too, made her move her lips. She felt the same tingling heat. More. As if a charge flashed from him to her, setting her alight.

This kiss wasn't like the last one. That had felt wild enough to a woman who had never been kissed. Only now did she realize how he'd held himself back. This kiss was hotter and harder. It didn't ask. It demanded.

And willful, independent Portia Frain surrendered with wholehearted fervor. The rest of the world evaporated to nothing as she clung to Granville. All that remained was the pressure of his lips, his rich, woodsy scent, and the warmth of his body crushed against hers.

Then everything changed. Even this miraculous response receded under a new onslaught of sensation.

His tongue flicked against her lips. The action surprised her into a gasp. She caught his taste. Without thinking, her tongue ventured out to test the flavor. Another of his growls of pleasure reverberated through her like soft thunder.

To her astonishment, his tongue slipped between her lips. The feeling was unlike anything that she'd ever experienced. Fear of the unknown pierced the mists of pleasure, and a faint protest escaped.

Then she wished to glory that she'd kept silent.

He ended the kiss. Which wasn't her intention at all.

"Portia?" The murmur sounded like an endearment. "Should I stop?"

The obvious – the proper – answer to that was yes. The answer that twenty-five years of training insisted upon. The answer that ensured her safety, because Granville said she was safe and she trusted him.

Today, she stepped into a dangerous new world that could leave her wretched and ruined if she wasn't careful. But Portia wasn't by nature careful. She wasn't careful, rescuing her fellow creatures from untold suffering. She wasn't careful now, when if anyone needed rescuing, it was Portia herself.

She examined Granville's features, wondering how within mere hours, they'd become the dearest sight that she knew. "What you did, it—"

"Frightened you?"

"No." Which wasn't entirely true. "It surprised me." That was definitely true. "Is that how you kiss someone you...want?"

The tenderness in his smile made her susceptible

heart cramp. "Yes."

He didn't deny his desire, she was pleased to hear. Then chided herself for relishing the risks that she took. "It was strange."

"Too strange to try again?"

"You like this?"

"I do. If you allow me to try again, I'll wager you'll like it as well. A whole world of new experiences awaits. I hope you'll enjoy them all."

Her hand was buried in his soft linen shirt. It clenched into a fist as secret muscles inside her clenched, too. Thanks to Juliet, she knew the basics of what men and women did in bed. But something in Granville's tone told her that he referred to more than basics.

The feeling when he'd licked her lips was odd. But far from repellent. Too far from repellent for a woman determined to retain her chastity. She was close to losing her virtue. That should send her running for her life.

She didn't budge an inch.

Granville slid his hands under her coat. Only a thin shirt separated her skin from his touch. Female garments were more substantial, with layers of fabric to protect the wearer from recalling that a warm human body lurked beneath the formal garments. Her present outfit offered no such reassurances.

It was impossible to ignore the physical reality of the man who touched her. She'd never felt like this when they danced together. Although after today, he could touch her through a suit of armor and she'd go up in flames.

"Would you like to try again?" she asked in a thin voice.

His smile intensified. "I'll take it slowly."

"Maybe you should."

"I've never kissed anyone wearing trousers, so it's a novel experience for me, too."

Portia should be too nervous and stirred up to laugh, but his teasing elicited a huff of amusement. "I've never kissed anyone in trousers before today either."

His expression flared into urgency. Then he was kissing her again, tugging her close until her pelvis met the proof of his excitement. Another gasp escaped her, although she didn't move away. Nor did she pull back when his mouth opened over hers. Although what he did was even more shocking than that first intimate kiss.

His tongue slid into her mouth and lingered for a thorough exploration that set her already racing heart skittering out of control. When she dared to move her tongue against his, a thrill ripped through her and settled between her legs in a most disturbing fashion.

A shift of her hips made him groan again, more in pain than appreciation. "Perhaps don't do that. I'm tempting fate as it is."

Tightening his grip, he returned to kissing her. This time, he sucked her tongue into his mouth. Tentatively she imitated what he'd done with the intimate kiss. His murmur expressed encouragement. Amazing just how much he conveyed without words.

The kiss deepened, swept her away to a place where sensuality ruled. Where lips meeting lips sparked lightning. She leaned closer, blind to peril. All she wanted was more. More kissing. More touch. More Granville.

Jupiter whined. She almost told herself to ignore it. When she'd never in her life ignored an animal in distress.

Granville lifted his head. His breath was

irregular, and his hands were hot on her hips. She was shaking.

What she found profoundly moving was that he was shaking, too. He leaned his forehead against hers. Even without kissing, they shared the air between them. It seemed almost as intimate as having his tongue in her mouth.

Jupiter whined again. He'd been snoozing in the corner. Now he sat just behind Granville.

"Our chaperone has spoken," Granville said with such wry affection that she fell in love with him all over again.

"He's hungry."

"So am I." The yearning in his voice tightened those unruly muscles inside her. He raised his head and sent her another one of those fatally attractive half-smiles. "Who knew that trousers would make you irresistible?"

What could she say to that? "We should go."

If she and the duke didn't make an appearance soon, it would be obvious that something was happening in the upstairs bedroom. She felt no shame for kissing Granville. But that didn't mean she wanted people sending her knowing glances.

"We should." The audible regret in Granville's sigh echoed her own improper feelings.

"Papa will be having all sorts of fits."

"Yes, we've taken enough risks, and I still have to get you home safely."

When Granville released her to stand on her unsteady legs, Portia had to stop herself from clinging to him. Parting from him sliced like a knife. Some reckless element inside her wanted to stay. For more kisses. For more than kisses.

Which meant it was past time to leave. Before that reckless side spurred her to do something completely *outré*. Something that left her life in shreds. "Yes."

To her surprise, Granville touched her cheek. "Next time I kiss you, I'll make sure the dog's been fed and nobody's waiting."

"I ought to say that's a bad idea, Granville." It *was* a bad idea, even if right now it sounded like an invitation to heaven.

A frown drew his golden eyebrows together. "Can you bring yourself to call me Alaric?"

"I've always thought of you as Granville." It seemed mad that after she'd been in his arms, using his Christian name felt like such a concession. Somehow it did.

That expressive mouth quirked into a self-deprecating smile. "You've always thought of me as the dullest dog in creation and too puffed up with my own consequence to admit to the slightest failing."

"You've grown on me since." Portia blushed. Which was just as mad as balking at calling him Alaric. "Anyway, I like dogs."

He caught her up and kissed her. It was over within seconds. She was back struggling to balance on her rubbery knees before she could respond. Which didn't mean the kiss lacked effect. Far from it. She battled to breathe. "What was that for?"

"Just confirming you like me now."

"You didn't like me either."

"I've changed my mind about that."

"We've been fools."

"Yes, we have." He paused. "I'm very glad I didn't marry your sister."

He caught her on the hop again. Before she could come up with an adequate reply to that – as if there was an adequate reply to that – he collected his hat and Jupiter's lead and marched out of the door.

Biting back an inappropriate desire to laugh, Portia retrieved her hat from the floor where it had fallen during those earth-shattering kisses and followed.

Getting Portia back to the house that her father leased on Lorimer Square should have been a straightforward process. On a cold April night, nobody was out taking the air. Most residents of the square were busy preparing for the night's entertainments. The balls, routs, musicales, and operas where he'd encountered Portia over and over, yet somehow remained blind to who she really was. After today, that seemed impossible to believe.

In the stables, Granville consigned Jupiter to Matty's care, while Portia lingered outside in the shadows. Within seconds, Jupiter was wolfing down a dinner of what looked like fillet steak.

Granville took her arm and led her down the short, cobbled lane out of the mews. Touching her was a bad idea. It made him want to take her into his arms again.

Then a genuine problem raised its head.

Before they reached the street, Jupiter started to howl.

"Oh, dear." Portia's dry tone only made him recall how breathless and delectably confused she'd sounded when he kissed her. The Duke of Granville could cross a public square in another gentleman's company. If he seized that gentleman in a passionate embrace, eyebrows would rise.

"What the deuce is the matter with the animal?" He had just enough sense left to keep his voice to a murmur.

"He misses you."

Obviously. The howling became more frantic by

the minute. "I can't spend the rest of my life playing nursemaid to a dog of indeterminate parentage. I have parliamentary duties and social obligations. If Almack's refused to admit Wellington because he had the temerity to turn up in trousers, they won't admit me with a scruffy hound who doesn't have vouchers."

"So you *are* going to keep him?"

He should have known that she'd ignore his jocularity and fasten on the one piece of salient information. "Haven't I said so?"

"Not in so many words."

He sighed. "To Hades with you, Portia Frain. You knew I was going to adopt that dog the minute you asked me. Don't turn all coy on me now."

That husky chuckle always made him think of bed sport. "I hoped."

"You did more than that, and don't pretend you didn't."

She didn't bother denying it. "He'll settle in, once he gets used to Matty and the rest of your household. He's been through a lot today."

"He's not the only one," Granville muttered.

"You need to go back before people start banging on your door."

"I need to see you're safe first."

He didn't want to leave her yet. Hell, he didn't want to leave her at all. It seemed that Jupiter wasn't the only one avid to remain with the object of his affections.

He shouldn't mind that she suffered no qualms about leaving him.

"I'll be fine. It's only a few yards."

"But..."

But I don't want to let you go. I don't want to sleep alone without you tonight. I don't want to wake up without you at my side tomorrow.

He couldn't say any of that, damn it.

"My lady?" A male voice emerged from the hedge edging the garden in the center of the square.

"Rankin?" she asked in a whisper, although with Jupiter's caterwauling, they could have a coloratura soprano out here and nobody would notice. "Is that you?"

"Aye." A burly man emerged from the greenery. "I thought you might need help getting back into the house."

"God bless you," she said. "Yes, please."

"What is that unholy racket?" the coachman asked.

"That's the dog we rescued today. He's missing his master."

"That stinker Jim Jones?" Rankin asked in astonishment.

"No, His Grace, the Duke of Granville."

Rankin only now seemed to realize that Portia wasn't alone. He straightened and bowed. "Your Grace." The formality in his voice contrasted with his ease with Portia.

"Has Papa been on the rampage?"

"His lordship hasn't returned from his club, my lady."

"That's a relief. I should manage to get inside without running into him."

"You usually do, madam."

Granville could believe it. He noticed that Rankin made no comment on Portia's clothing. He didn't even seem particularly surprised. Her allies in the household must be inured to antics that would make her a social outcast if they became public.

She turned to him. "You'd better go before Jupiter gets any louder."

Granville gave her a brief bow, the formality striking him as absurd, given that he'd kissed her to the stars and back. "Your servant, my lady."

"Good night, Your Grace." She still hadn't called him Alaric. That was something they needed to sort out tomorrow. "Thank you for taking Jupiter. And for...everything else."

By Jericho, he cursed the coachman's presence. He wanted to talk to her about the day's adventures. He wanted to kiss her again. Devil take it, he just wanted her.

But it was past time that she was back in her own home and more than past time that he took control of Jupiter. The dog's uproar provided an earsplitting counterpoint to their conversation.

"My lady?" Rankin said, when Portia seemed as reluctant to go as Granville. He saw her give a small start, then without a backward look, she and the coachman disappeared into the shadowy gardens.

Granville shouldn't feel bereft. He'd see her tomorrow. But the minute she left his presence, her absence became an ache.

Jupiter didn't care about his humans' romantic entanglements. Granville had to get back before every servant in his employ walked out in protest. So far, his staff had taken Jupiter's arrival in reasonably good spirit. He wanted that to continue.

Because despite his original refusal, his definite reluctance, and his complete lack of qualifications to take custody of a living creature, Portia's wishes had prevailed. For the first time in his life, the Duke of Granville had a dog.

When he reached the stables, Jupiter immediately stopped howling and broke free from Matty to rush over and jump up at him. The situation should infuriate him. It didn't. The faint smile that he'd worn on his short walk home broke into a full grin. Nobody had been this pleased to see him since...since forever. And that included his two fiancées.

"Come back, Jupiter!" Matty lunged after him to catch the trailing lead.

"Down!" Granville said.

Yet again, the voice of authority performed its magic. Jupiter subsided onto his haunches, those clever eyes fixed on Granville's face.

"He got away from me, Your Grace," Matty said in a subdued voice, looking terrified that he'd be blamed for this chaos.

Granville could only blame one person for his current circumstances. Given that he still wanted to kiss her, he wasn't feeling too resentful.

Sheriff was nowhere to be seen. Phipps sat beneath a window, smoking a pipe. "He started carrying on as soon as you left, sir."

When Granville gave Jupiter a scratch behind the ears, the dog closed his eyes in ecstasy. "So I heard." He glanced across at the half-full dish of meat. "He didn't finish his dinner?"

"He will, now you're back, Your Grace." Matty sounded more at ease. He must have realized that Granville wasn't angry.

Granville crossed to pick up the dish and set it before Jupiter. "Go on, boy."

Stubby tail wagging, the dog set to his meal. Granville looked at Matty. "He needs to get used to you. I can't take him everywhere I go. We can start training him tomorrow. Lady Portia will help, I'm sure. I'll take him up with me tonight."

"That's wise, Your Grace, or nobody in Mayfair will get a wink of sleep," Phipps said.

"Are the grooms back from the King's Head?"

"Not yet. Should I go and chase them home?"

"You probably should. Or they'll have sore heads tomorrow."

"I'll do that straightaway." Phipps knocked out

his pipe and stood up. He sent Granville a leery glance. "Has Mr. Hobbs encountered our new arrival?"

"Yes," Granville said. "So far he hasn't complained."

Which didn't mean that he wouldn't. In fact, he was probably composing applications right now to the many noblemen who envied Granville his accomplished valet.

"I see," Phipps said, clearly also unconvinced that the arrival of a dog off the streets would meet with the starchy valet's approval.

Hobbs would have by now dealt with the mess upstairs, Granville assumed. He'd listen for the sound of the duke going out. That mess upstairs that included…

All the blood drained from his head.

Dear God, Portia's clothes were still draped over the screen.

Those damned drugging kisses had done for his brain. After all their trouble to conceal Portia's presence, they'd made an egregious mistake.

Not to mention that Granville hadn't cleared away the signs that two people had used his apartments. Two sets of wet towels. Two bowls of dirty water.

"I have to go," he said urgently, already heading for the door. "Thank you both for being so good with Jupiter."

He took to his heels with the frail hope that Hobbs, the world's most punctilious valet, hadn't tidied the ducal chambers, the moment he got the chance.

Scampering across the cobbles behind him indicated that Jupiter followed. By the time he pushed the garden gate open, the dog was at his side.

Granville clattered up the steps two at a time. He

reached his room and flung open the door. And drew a great breath of relief.

Relief, but also puzzlement.

Nothing had been touched. The crumpled blue dress draped over the screen. When he checked the dressing room, it was similarly untidy with his discarded clothing and a heap of wet towels. The soapy water hadn't been removed either.

Hobbs mustn't have set foot in here since Granville sent him on his way. Perhaps he'd taken advantage of his evening off to go out, but that was unlike him. To Granville's knowledge, the fellow had no life outside his master's requirements.

But a man shouldn't look a gift horse in the mouth.

He and Portia had dodged a bullet. Or a serving of spiteful gossip at the very least.

By God, he wasn't used to all this intrigue. He'd better get smoother at covering his tracks quick smart. Because while a respectable man would decide that he must never again be alone with Portia, the very proper Duke of Granville had other plans. Plans to spend as much time alone with his beautiful neighbor as he could, and be damned to conventional morality.

CHAPTER NINE

*E*arly on a drizzly April morning, riders in Hyde Park were thinly spread. A thick mist emphasized the atmosphere of isolation and mystery.

That suited Portia fine. She was out for a morning canter with Rankin in the hope that she'd run into the Duke of Granville, who always rode in the park before settling down to the hard work of governing his estates and the nation. She told herself that she wanted to find out how Jupiter had fared overnight. But she knew at heart that while she cared about the dog's welfare, for once her interests were much more selfish.

She wanted to see Granville. She wanted to learn whether he planned more kisses. And if he did, when and where.

Oh, those kisses…

She usually slept like a log. She was a healthy, active woman with a clear conscience. Last night, she'd stared into the darkness for hours. Strange feelings kept her awake and restless. Those extraordinary kisses had turned her whole life upside down. She'd never experienced anything to match them.

The memory of Granville's lips on hers stirred a pleasurable tightening in the place between her legs. She shifted in the sidesaddle to ease the sensation.

No longer did she marvel at her sisters going dotty when they fell in love. She'd always been puzzled that proper Juliet and shy Viola threw wisdom to the winds when they met the men they'd since married. Although it still left her reeling that the man who sent her demented was that supercilious prude, the Duke of Granville. Who turned out to be the sort of man she'd dreamed of, before she'd matured enough to understand that no husband would allow her to pursue her crusade.

So far, there was no sign of the duke. Could he be having second thoughts about an entanglement with another Frain woman? Yesterday he'd spoken of Juliet without resentment, and Portia believed him when he said that he hadn't loved her. But his unhappy history with her family remained an obstacle.

She wasn't subject to nerve storms, yet this morning she felt as jumpy as a scalded cat. Her horse, Cleo, a mare as even-tempered as her mistress, picked up on Portia's edginess and shied at every shadow.

"Cleo, settle down," Portia murmured, as the mare jumped at a harmless bush poking out of the murk.

"She's in a state, that's for sure," Rankin said from behind her.

Her groom criticized the rider rather than the horse. Rankin never blamed an animal, only the humans around it. With her rescues, Portia had taken that lesson to heart.

She told herself to calm down, but that was easier said than done. Although she had a grim presentiment that she'd put Rankin, Cleo and herself through this chilly torture for no purpose.

The duke might have decided that he preferred to keep Portia at a distance. Heaven knew it would be easier. In less than a day, her life had become vilely complicated. He must feel the same.

The idea that those knee-shaking kisses might be her quota left her in such a funk, she didn't notice the tall man on the path ahead. Only when Jupiter barked a welcome did she realize that she'd stumbled upon His Grace of Granville at last. Not on horseback as expected. Instead he was on foot, walking his plebeian dog on a leash.

Unfortunately, a barking dog placed the seal on Cleo's woes, although if any horse in England was used to dogs, it was her. She reared on her hind legs and neighed. Which only set Jupiter barking anew.

"Cleo, stop!" Portia said breathlessly, struggling to keep her seat. "It's fine, darling. Nothing to worry about."

Rather than presenting a cool and elegant image to the duke, she found herself clinging to Cleo's neck and praying that she didn't end up flat on her face.

Before Cleo could bolt, Granville caught her bridle. "It's all right, my beauty. No need to worry. Only a dog. Only a dog."

The singsong tone brought Cleo back onto four legs. Portia felt her trembling, but at least she wasn't about to bolt. Jupiter, bless him, now sat in silence.

Alaric's croon had an incendiary effect on Portia. With difficulty, she forced herself to stay in the saddle, when all she wanted to do was spring to the ground and fling herself into his arms.

To hide her reaction, she collected the reins in one gloved hand and straightened the black high-crowned hat that finished off her riding habit. This morning, she'd taken a ridiculously long time dressing. She'd never been someone who preened and primped, but she'd definitely primped today.

"Thank you, Your Grace." She hoped Rankin wouldn't hear the unnatural note. The duke, she was sure, did. After yesterday, she'd never again dismiss Alaric Dempster as less perceptive than the average block of wood. Not much escaped those gleaming green eyes.

Gleaming green eyes that focused on her. When she met his intent gaze, color rushed into her cheeks. He looked concerned, not bent on seduction. But seeing him again revived last night's fevered fantasies.

His smile asked so many questions, most of them inappropriate for casual acquaintances meeting in Hyde Park. "Are you all right, Lady Portia?"

No, I've turned into a complete wanton, and I don't know what to do about it.

"Yes, thank you, Your Grace." She was conscious of Rankin behind her, listening to every word. She settled on a less fraught topic than her unsuitable desires. "How is Jupiter this morning?"

"In fine fettle. I'm not sure I can say the same for myself."

"Oh?" She was pleased to note that he sounded amused, almost fond. Any fears that Jupiter might wear out his welcome faded.

"There was something of a battle last night over who would occupy my bed."

Portia laughed, although she really didn't want to think about Granville in bed. Thinking about Granville in bed made her think about joining him there. "Who won?"

"I did, but it was a close-run thing."

"I commend your grasp of strategy. My money would have been on Jupiter."

The dog stood beside his new master, wagging his

tail. He knew that they were talking about him. "Would you like to come down and say hello and perhaps walk a little way with us?"

"I would." She struggled to keep her voice even, almost impossible when she felt like she contained a sky full of fireworks. "Rankin, will you please hold Cleo?"

"Aye, my lady," her groom said in an uninflected tone. He must guess that this rendezvous wasn't accidental, but he'd cooperate as he always did.

"Let me help you." Granville stepped forward, regarding her from under the brim of his stylish gray hat.

The moment that she looked into his eyes, her insecurity vanished. They were warm and interested and alight with admiration. She hadn't imagined the rapport that she shared with him.

Portia noted, now that she wasn't likely to end up on her bottom in the mud, that all of him looked stylish in a silvery gray coat and darker gray breeches. Had he taken similar trouble over his appearance? She'd like to think that he had.

Her heart giving a happy skip, she smiled down at him with a sunniness that shamed the gloomy weather. "Thank you."

When he caught her waist, his eyes widened. For a blazing instant, the social mask slipped. She saw that he hungered like she did.

The breath jammed in her lungs. His hands tightened, and she automatically reached for those impressive shoulders.

After a charged instant, he lifted her to the ground. Thank heavens, he kept hold of her a fraction too long. Her legs were too wobbly to support her.

She still stared into Granville's face when Rankin cleared his throat. "Shall I take Cleo, my lady?"

The real world rushed in with painful force. Portia stepped back, bumping into Cleo's warm flank. "Yes. Yes, please."

She sounded flustered. She couldn't help it.

"Very good, ma'am," Rankin said in a stoical voice, coming forward and collecting Cleo's reins.

The horse had settled. Most creatures felt safe in Granville's company. Dear Lord, even Portia did, when safety was the last thing that His Grace offered.

"Shall we proceed?" While the duke did a better job of hiding his agitation, she was close enough to hear unaccustomed huskiness in his voice and see a muscle dancing in his lean cheek.

"Yes." When he extended his arm, she clung as if she was drowning and he'd flung her a rope. Except she feared that they were both lost in a strange ocean and likely to sink beneath the waves.

Granville let Jupiter off the lead before they began to stroll along the path. Behind them, she heard the horses' hooves clopping on the gravel. Rankin, bless him, hung back to grant her and the duke a moment's privacy. It might make her groom a terrible chaperone, but it did make him a dear friend.

"Did you have any trouble getting back into the house last night?" the duke asked in a low voice. The question wasn't suggestive, yet a ripple of forbidden awareness warmed Portia. The murmur was a powerful reminder of how he'd sounded when she was in his arms.

"Portia?"

By now, she should be used to blushing. She'd drifted off into enthralling memories of his kisses. "No. It was fine in the end. Rankin smuggled me into the stables, where I keep a few dresses in case I need to change. Rescuing dogs can be dirty work."

"I know," Granville said with such feeling that she

laughed.

"Papa ended up dining at his club and has no idea how late I was out."

"Rankin was the only one to see you in trousers?"

"Yes." She paused. "And you."

"The world missed a treat. The sight of you dressed as a man was rather...piquant."

She was back to thinking about kisses. Her voice shook when she replied. "I need to return your clothes. At the moment, they're bundled up under the window seat in my bedroom."

"Yours are in the bottom drawer of the desk in the library. And there's a very pretty little pistol in there as well. You left it in the pocket of your pelisse."

"Oh, I forgot my gun. Shall I send Rankin over?"

"I'd rather you came yourself."

She stumbled slightly, and it was nothing to do with the mist. "For Jupiter?"

"For me."

"Granville..."

"Alaric."

Stupid to feel that using his Christian name was a step too far, when he'd already kissed her as if he wanted to devour her. Nevertheless her voice stumbled as her feet did when she answered. "Alaric, are we...are we going to pursue this?"

His expression turned somber. "I'd like to, but the decision must be yours. I swear on my life I'll do everything in my power to protect your good name, but I don't need to tell you the risks."

"No, you don't," she said soberly. Her heart lurched like a drunkard after a Saturday night spree. "I've taken risks before."

"To save your animals."

"Yes."

"This goes beyond your previous adventures." His voice was a low rumble. "When you hear my proposition, you'll be within your rights to slap my face."

Her heart began to race. "You want me to visit your house?"

Alaric shook his head. "Worse than that."

"Worse?" Although she could already guess, and what she guessed filled her with a roiling mixture of terror and excitement.

"Much, much worse." Urgency darkened his tone. "I don't want to see you for a few hours here and there. I don't want to worry about interruptions. I want you to myself. I want you in my bed. I want us to go away together and see where this attraction takes us."

Dear Lord, she *should* slap his face. He was talking sin, the sort of sin that any decently-raised girl would run a mile from contemplating. If Portia said yes to what he suggested, her life would change forever. *She'd* change forever. So far, they'd skirted the edges of wickedness, but if she became Alaric's mistress, she violated society's every code. If she was found out, she'd be a pariah.

Nervously she glanced behind, but Rankin had fallen further back. At least he wouldn't overhear this improper conversation. He might be her regular co-conspirator, but he'd never cooperate with what the duke suggested.

She licked parched lips, as herds of elephants performed somersaults in her stomach. "If the world learns we're lovers, the scandal will eclipse anything I've done in my rescues."

"I'm aware of what I'm asking. I'm aware of what it could cost you." He sounded as serious as if he proposed a parliamentary motion. "Do you want to slap my face?"

Her hands curled in her skirts, not because she wanted to hit him, but because she wanted to reach out and touch him. It seemed that she wasn't running a mile. "Not...not straightaway."

"I want you, Portia." The strength of his feelings vibrated in his declaration. "I want you more than I've ever wanted another woman. I didn't get a wink of sleep last night for thinking about what I want to do to you."

"I didn't sleep much either," she admitted in a wisp of a voice. Alaric's frankness made her heart flutter like a trapped sparrow. That and fear that she might *– she just might –* agree to his shocking invitation. She steeled herself to respond with equal candor. "I loved your kisses. I'd like more of them. I'd like...more."

It wasn't surrender, but it put her on the path to surrender. They both knew it.

"So would I." His laugh held the self-mockery that had surprised her yesterday. "I'm as astounded by all this as you are, believe me."

"But how on earth would we manage it?" She tried to tell herself that she asked out of curiosity, not because she really considered doing this rash thing.

"I have a hunting box in Surrey. We could go there."

Was that where he took his other women? "It's easier for you."

"Yes, it is. Although make no mistake. I'd receive my share of disapproval if the beau monde knew I'd seduced my former fiancée's virginal sister."

He was right. His engagement to Juliet would add extra spice to any gossip about his entanglement with Portia.

She struggled to hold onto rapidly disintegrating prudence. Once she would have asked herself what Juliet would do. But these days, Juliet provided no example of how to avoid a scandal. "You'd remain a duke and rich and a man of influence. You could still marry."

"The high sticklers wouldn't touch me, and my political career would be in tatters, duke or not. What we do holds dangers for me, too. I don't want you to feel like I'm asking you to make all the sacrifices. I have my own stakes in this game. But yes, I could still marry. The risks weigh heavier on you."

Alaric was tireless in his parliamentary work. He didn't have to tell her how much it meant to him. A sensible woman would wonder why they even discussed such a dangerous step. Discovery promised ruin for both of them.

Portia swallowed to shift the solid lump of trepidation blocking her throat. "You know, I can't see I'll ever marry."

"I wondered if you'd made some such decision. You're too beautiful not to have received a hundred offers. A few of those men must have been eligible."

Grim humor turned her lips down. "Not quite so many offers as that."

He didn't smile back. "Nonetheless you're in your mid-twenties and unattached. That hints you're unmarried by choice. Juliet was in mourning for her late fiancé, but you've never even flirted with anyone."

"You listen to society tattle?"

"Doesn't everyone?"

"I had no idea you'd paid such attention to me."

His short laugh was rueful. "Devil take it, neither had I. I'm gladder by the minute that I didn't marry Juliet."

Horrified, she stopped to stare at him. "Dear Lord, what if I developed a passion for you when you were my brother-in-law? It hardly bears thinking about."

He met her eyes. "Have you developed a passion

for me?"

Her cheeks heated again. "I…I suppose I must. I wouldn't have kissed you otherwise. For pity's sake, how did this happen?"

Alaric concentrated so hard on her that her nerves spiked, even as her stomach churned with perilous longing. Fear and yearning tore her apart, as she wrestled with what she should do and what she wanted to do.

"By God, you have no idea how much I want to kiss you right now." His voice was low and savage. It made her very bones ache with hunger.

She sucked in an unsteady breath and struggled to recall that they were in a public space, her groom was within calling distance, and the mist supplied inadequate cover for an embrace. "You can't."

"I know," he said in a flat tone. "But that doesn't stop me wanting."

Or her, heaven forgive her. "We should…we should keep walking, or Rankin will catch up."

"Jupiter," Alaric said. The dog had taken advantage of his master's distraction to sniff around the base of the yew hedge lining the path. As he trotted ahead, Alaric returned his attention to her. "Why don't you want to marry?"

"Isn't it obvious? A husband would keep me from my rescue work."

"Did you explain that to any of your suitors?"

"Of course not. But I know how the world works. A man wants a wife at his beck and call. He doesn't want her running around who knows where, taking in mistreated animals. He wants a chatelaine for his house, a smiling, gracious hostess, a mother for his children."

"Don't you find any of that appealing?"

Oh, dear, she thought that she'd long ago come to terms with life as a lone crusader. She had until, plague take him, Alaric decided to show her what she missed out on. But the reasons for refusing her other suitors counted double with Alaric. A duke with political ambitions needed a hostess and a helpmeet. He needed a suitable duchess. That was never going to be Portia Frain.

He must feel the same, because he suggested an affair, not marriage. Just as when he spoke, the topic was desire, not love.

"You can't have everything." She hated the wistfulness weighting her answer.

"You're giving up a lot for your animals."

Portia squared her shoulders and told herself not to be such a wet hen. "My animals have no other advocate, whereas society is full of pretty, biddable chits who would – and do – make perfect wives for conventional gentlemen."

"Perhaps you underestimate the gentlemen. If a man really loved you, he'd want you to be happy. It's clear that helping animals makes you happy."

She wished with all her heart that was true about the Duke of Granville. How easily he spoke of love. It hurt to hear the word on his lips and know that he'd never love her.

"Perhaps," she said, knowing no such tolerant gentleman existed. "But it's a risk I can't take. Single, I have more freedom than most women. I have a fortune of my own, so I needn't wed for security. I'm in a unique position to make a difference."

He remained silent. And the silence bristled.

"Have I appalled you?" she asked eventually.

"No," he said. "It makes sense."

"But you don't approve?"

"It's not for me to approve or disapprove." He frowned. "But it's a lonely life you're talking about. I know you'll have dogs and cats and horses. But it might be nice having some human love in there as well. Someone to cuddle who isn't covered with fur."

"I have my sisters." Portia wished that she didn't sound defensive. She didn't need to justify herself to Alaric. He had no power over her decisions, except the power that she granted him. Although she had a sinking feeling that in loving him, she granted him more power over her than any man had ever wielded. "I'll be aunt to their children."

"That's something." He didn't sound convinced.

She couldn't blame him. Right now, her plans sounded dismal to her, too. Blast Alaric. Before she'd tumbled into love with him, her independence had always seemed rather dashing. Yet again, she told herself to perk up.

"But my unusual circumstances offer some advantages." She hoped that he didn't hear the false brightness in her tone.

He cast her a wry glance. "That you can do as you like?"

"As you must know, I try not to scandalize society. That would upset Papa. Especially now. He's had a difficult year."

"Very good of you."

She hadn't mistaken his grumpiness. She supposed like most men, he didn't appreciate women striking out on their own and choosing a path that didn't rely on male endorsement. "You're not following me."

"Yes, I am. You've decided on a future without husband or children or company, beyond a menagerie of stray animals."

She couldn't help laughing, when her intentions should have her hanging her head in shame. In fact, any right-thinking woman would get back on Cleo and gallop home to Lorimer Square to scour the library for a book of improving sermons. "You make it sound so eccentric. Plenty of women don't marry.

Plenty of women have pets."

He didn't smile. "Not women like you. Not women capable of passion like you."

Portia delayed before answering. Once she set this course, the path that she'd imagined her life taking would diverge into an unfamiliar and precarious wilderness. She waited for conscience or cowardice or even good old common sense to speak up. All maintained a deathly silence. Instead, her imprudent heart cavorted with drunken joy at knowing that she would at least have this much of Alaric.

She licked her lips, straightened her spine, and spoke the fatal words. "I'm hoping you can supply the passion."

He stopped as if he'd slammed into a pane of glass. Which meant that Portia stopped, too. After a charged moment, he stepped in front of her. His eyes blazed in his face, and that muscle danced in his cheek once more. "Are you saying what I think you are, Portia?"

She very much feared that she was. Not sure if she was intrepid or unforgivably rash, she raised her chin and met that intense gaze. "I'm saying that I don't need to be a virginal bride for some unknown gentleman. I'm saying that if we can arrange things, I'd like to be your lover, Alaric."

Granville stared at Portia as if she'd appeared out of nowhere. In so many ways, she had. Despite being in plain sight for years.

He caught her gloved hand in a firm grip. Inside his chest, his heart sang with elation – and primitive anticipation. "It's torture not being able to kiss you."

She tugged her hand free. "We have to be careful. More than ever now."

Now that they were about to start an affair, she meant. "I swear you won't be sorry."

"We need to make plans."

"Yes."

Portia looked troubled and ruffled. And glowing, as if someone had lit a candle inside her. Her gaze sought his. "Not now."

Slow hoofbeats approached. Rankin was nearly upon them. Not to mention that the morning advanced. For the moment, they were unobserved. Granville would prefer not to be seen with Portia, despite a walk in the park with a chaperone being acceptable. He was the famous – and famously unattached – Duke of Granville. People were always too quick to speculate about his marriage plans. Portia's connection to Juliet would only feed the interest.

"I'd ask you for a drive, but—"

"But we don't want to attract notice."

"Can you meet me in the square tonight? It needs to be late. I've committed to a box at the opera with the Lumsdens."

"I'm dining with the Tierneys. Shall we say midnight?"

He caught her hand and squeezed it. "Midnight."

Staring down into her face, he reminded himself once more that he couldn't kiss her. How he longed to get her to himself, somewhere he needn't worry about wagging tongues and curious eyes.

"Don't look at me like that," she said in a tormented tone.

"I can't help it." He released her hand with reluctance. "You're just so damned beautiful."

Rankin emerged from the thinning mist. He dismounted and led the horses up to Granville and

Portia. Hopefully the fellow thought that they'd been talking about Jupiter. Which reminded him…

"Jupiter!"

In an ebullient mood, the dog bounded out of the shrubbery. Grenville gagged, as he clipped the lead to his collar. "Good God! What have you been rolling in?"

Portia laughed. "You'll need to give him another bath when you get him home, Your Grace."

"Without your help this time." He turned to the dog. "Sit, you troublesome hound."

While Jupiter obeyed, Granville advanced on Portia. "Let me help you into the saddle."

It was a chance to touch her again. He didn't want to let her go, just as he hadn't wanted to let her go last night. It seemed wrong that she should be anywhere but at his side.

She nodded. "Thank you."

Granville caught her by the waist, taking a moment to appreciate her vivid presence. Soon all that spirit and vitality would tumble into his arms and he'd be in heaven.

Intoxicated with the untold joy that extended before him, he tossed her onto the gray mare's back. She gathered the reins and settled in the saddle with a wriggle that beggared his good intentions.

Impatience came close to overmastering him. He wanted her now. He hated to wait.

But he must play the game. The stakes were too high now to abandon strategy. So he kept his voice light, while his desire for her coiled tight as a spring.

Her lips twitched, as she regarded him. "I've enjoyed our conversation, Your Grace," she said with a theatrical formality that made him want to laugh.

He wanted to laugh anyway, he was so bloody happy. She was a minx, and he loved it. Nobody ever teased him. Except Portia. "As have I. I wish you good morning, my lady."

Granville stood on the path with Jupiter beside him and watched Portia canter away. Now the mist dissipated, he realized that the park was jammed with riders.

"Shall we continue our walk, old man?" he asked Jupiter.

A twitch of a tail expressed approval. Yesterday Granville's life had changed. Forever. Not just because he'd finally recognized Portia for who she was. He'd also gained a canine friend who, in the space of less than twenty-four hours, had claimed a place in his heart.

"By Jove, Granville, what have you got there?"

The mocking voice emerged from another universe. Granville raised his head to give Lord Colville a jaunty smile. "Come and meet my new friend, Jupiter."

Colville rode with his wife, the once-scandalous Lady Verena Gerard. The couple had been married for two years and remained inseparable. Society had predicted disaster for the union of the wild duke's daughter and the punctiliously correct viscount. So far, Lord and Lady Colville had proven society wrong. Good heavens, the Colvilles were almost as ill-suited as he and Portia.

"I've never seen you with a dog before." Verena dismounted and approached Jupiter with her gloved hand outstretched.

"Are you sure that's a dog?" Colville asked.

"A very fine one, I'll have you know. Looks aren't everything."

"Don't listen to him, boy," Verena said, as Jupiter sniffed her hand. "I think you're very handsome."

"What do you know?" Granville asked. "You think that your husband is handsome."

He liked the Colvilles. Eliot Ridley's pristine

reputation rivaled his own. Or at least it had, until he'd married Verena. Looking at a couple so obviously relishing each other's company, Granville couldn't help thinking that Colville had made the right choice.

Verena laughed and sent her husband a sultry glance. "Colville's handsome enough for me. And so is this excellent fellow." She scratched Jupiter behind the ears until he closed his eyes in pleasure.

"He's a bit smelly." Granville's understatement bordered on an outright lie.

"He's not too bad," Verena said. "Where did you get him?"

"A friend gave him to me."

Colville's searching look made Granville's cheeks heat. He braced for questions about the friend's identity. When they didn't come, it was almost more worrying.

"You'll be caricatured in the papers," Colville said in a neutral voice. "You know how the press love to point out eccentricities in the great and the good."

Granville supposed he was right. He just hoped to hell that nobody linked Jupiter's arrival to Portia Frain and her penchant for strays.

CHAPTER TEN

*P*ortia had sneaked out of the house at night before. Back in Wiltshire, she often went out to collect a hurt or mistreated animal. Always with one of the servants. Usually Rankin. He came in handy if she encountered any ruffians, although around Afton Park, her status as Lord Portdown's daughter was protection in itself.

Never before had she sneaked out to meet a lover.

Not that Alaric was her lover yet.

Her heart raced like a runaway horse when she hurried across to the grove of trees in the center of the square. She hoped to heaven that Alaric was there already. She was nervous tonight in a way that she hadn't been nervous on her previous nocturnal adventures.

When a hand caught her arm, a squeak of terror escaped her.

"It's me," a familiar voice murmured, as he drew her into the shadows. Mere days ago, that voice would have left her unmoved. Now it made her wayward heart falter, before it set off on another headlong gallop.

"Thank heaven," she whispered jerkily. "I mean, I

wasn't expecting anyone else, but it's so quiet and dark, and my mind was playing tricks on me so everything looked like someone lying in wait, then I..." She waved her hand in an apologetic gesture that he wouldn't see. "I'm sorry. I'm babbling. It's just that—"

"You're on edge."

"I am." She sucked in another breath as panic subsided, which was mad when it would be worse to be found with the Duke of Granville than on her own.

He drew her deeper into the copse. "Pretend I'm a lost dog."

That made her stifle a laugh. "For a man with no sense of humor, you're pretty funny."

"I'm not sure if that's a compliment or an insult," he said ruefully.

"Neither am I." When something bumped against her skirts, she gave a muffled gasp. "You brought Jupiter?"

She gave the dog a welcoming pat, as she listened to Alaric's fond sigh. "He still won't leave my side. Matty is having an easy time of it."

They'd stopped in the darkest part of the grove. She could barely make out either Jupiter or his master, although she was far too conscious of the duke's nearness. The square was deserted. Most of the parties and balls wouldn't finish until around two.

"Let Matty feed him for a few days while you watch on. It will confirm that Matty's part of his pack. Part of your pack, too. You are, after all, the top dog."

That made him laugh. She thought it would. "If you say so."

"Dukes are the top dogs in society, too."

"I don't want to talk about Jupiter."

Her stomach knotted with wicked yearning. Her

breath jammed in her throat, although if she was honest, she didn't want to talk about Jupiter right now either.

"What would you like to talk about?" she asked in an unsteady voice.

When his grip on her arm tightened, a thrill rippled through her. "I don't want to talk at all."

Portia swayed closer to catch the intriguing drift of spicy masculine scent. "What would you like to do instead?"

"This."

Portia couldn't pretend to be surprised when he lashed his arms about her and kissed her. She'd teetered, trapped on the edge of tumbling over a cliff, ever since he'd kissed her in his bedroom last night.

Now the heat of his lips set her free to soar. She made a faint sound of surrender and twined her hands around his neck. Her fingers raked through his silky hair and dug into his scalp to bring him closer.

This kiss conveyed no hesitation. When his tongue slid between her lips, she sucked on it. He gave a soft growl of approval. Strange how much these animal sounds could express. Pleasure. Surrender. Desire.

Portia arched, pressing her aching breasts to his powerful chest. She wanted him to touch her there. A blameless lifetime had crumbled to nothing over little more than twenty-four turbulent hours.

She wanted him to touch her everywhere. Especially where heat pulsed between her legs.

Their tongues shared a frenzied dance that made her senses reel. He stroked her back, venturing lower until he caught her buttocks and lifted her against him. She gasped into his mouth, as his hardness rubbed against her stomach.

After measureless bliss, he lifted his head without

moving away.

"How do you do that?" she whispered.

"Kiss you?" She couldn't see him smile, but she knew he did. "All too easily, I'm afraid."

"No." She struggled to express his extraordinary effect on her. "I mean the way you touch me and the whole world disappears. There's nothing but you and me and what we do together."

She heard his breath catch, before he proved the truth of what she'd said by kissing her again. With a passion that made her head spin and her knees quake. She clung to his broad shoulders and rode the storm.

"Alaric..." she sighed, then nothing more. He'd stolen her capacity to link words into anything that made sense.

"I know," he murmured before sending her into another spin with a quick kiss.

When he raised his head, she couldn't contain a whimper of disappointment.

"I want to kiss you and kiss you." The declaration's softness didn't conceal the depths of his frustration.

"But we're not safe here." As if to confirm the fact, a carriage rattled into the square and stopped in front of the Comerford house. When she shifted closer, Alaric's arms tightened in a wordless gesture of protection. She shouldn't feel safer, but somehow she did.

The air she breathed was tinged with his scent. Leather and soap and some mysterious essence that was purely him. For a delicious moment, she buried her nose in his shirtfront.

"No, we're not," he said, sounding somber. He rested his chin on top of her head. "Which is why I want you to myself."

"Can we manage it?" She didn't try and hide her

eagerness.

"Can you get away?"

"I've been thinking." That was an understatement. Her mind had been in a furore since she'd seen Alaric this morning in the park.

"Can Rankin help?"

"It's fairer to keep him out of this."

"You're asking him to do more than drive you around London while you look for stray dogs."

"Much more. He's been with the family forever, but even so, he'd lose his place if Papa found out that he'd taken me to meet a lover. And honestly, I'm thinking of Papa, too. It would kill him to weather another scandal."

"I also promised that I'd keep you from harm. As far as I can."

That proviso was very like Alaric. After those ravishing kisses, she had no doubt that he wanted her. But he wasn't concealing what an affair could end up costing them.

Portia made herself bring up a topic that she never thought she'd need to discuss with anyone, particularly her sister's former suitor. "I don't...I don't want to have a baby."

She was ashamed to admit that was a blatant lie. The idea of carrying Alaric's child was all too tempting. But she couldn't endure the thought of bearing a baby out of wedlock.

"I'll do my best." His voice rumbled out of his chest.

"There are ways?"

However much Juliet had told her about copulation, much remained a mystery. Even knowing the basics hadn't given her the first idea of how overwhelming it felt to desire a man and have him desire her in return. Her imagination couldn't extend to how she'd feel when Alaric joined his body to hers. Which didn't stop her muscles cramping with excitement.

"Yes, there are."

She tried to see him, but darkness defeated her. "Ways that will still give you pleasure?"

"Yes." He sounded sure.

"I'm glad. I want to give you pleasure."

"You will. You do. Oh, hell." He kissed her again with more intent. By the time they drew apart, Portia struggled to stand. She was grateful for Alaric's hands on her waist.

"Are you cold?" he asked.

"Not when you kiss me."

With a chuckle, he shifted behind her and wrapped his arms around her. "We're both going to get pneumonia, if we keep meeting like this."

Portia smiled, even as she was appalled at how little genuine horror her impending ruin stirred. She leaned back into his body. She was a tall woman, but Alaric was taller, so she fitted perfectly against his long, powerful body. "We can't have that."

"No, I have a country to run. And a dog to walk."

Jupiter had disappeared into the bushes. Occasional rustles from the undergrowth said he hadn't gone far. Of course he hadn't. He was almost as besotted with the Duke of Granville as she was.

She stared into the night, as the effect of Alaric's sizzling kisses receded to a lazy tide. "My old governess covers for me when I go out on rescue missions."

"Will she countenance you taking a lover? Would she help us?"

Portia frowned as she considered Mary Hudson. She'd been a strict but affectionate teacher, and she was independent-minded enough to approve of Portia saving neglected animals. Would she conspire in her former pupil surrendering her maidenhead to a man to whom she wasn't wed? Portia very much doubted it.

"Does she have to know? If I tell her I'm leaving town for a few days to collect a dog, she'll believe me. It's happened before."

Mary would believe her because Portia had always been honest. She hoped to goodness that she turned into a convincing liar in the next few days.

She snuggled closer. "When I stay with Mary, I never take Aunt Mabel or my maid. There's no room for them. Mary won't question why I'm sneaking out. She'll assume I'm meeting Rankin somewhere discreet."

"That might work."

"It can only be for a couple of days." Regret edged her voice. "Even Papa would start asking questions if I disappear for too long."

Alaric settled her more comfortably. There was something so pleasurable about having a man's warm arms around her on a cold night. "I promised I'd look after your reputation. If a few days are all you can manage, that's what we'll do."

He didn't sound as if he minded. That stung, when she already knew that their time away would rush by.

Or perhaps he planned on more than one tryst. The thought made her boggle. She'd been in such a commotion that she hadn't thought beyond going to his bed the first time. Was she entering a life of continuing intrigue? "When?"

The word brought their negotiations into stark relief. Was she really going to do this outrageous thing?

Alaric, too, must realize that they reached a crossroads because his hold firmed. "I'm at your disposal."

She licked her lips, as nerves pinged and

ricocheted in her stomach. "I think…I think you need a few days to get Jupiter settled in Matty's care."

"We don't want him howling down the house again."

She gave a horrified gasp of laughter. "No, we do not."

"Tuesday?"

That gave her almost a week. "I need to be back for Friday night. I promised I'd attend the Bilsons' ball."

"I've accepted an invitation to that, too."

Another shaky laugh escaped. More the result of burgeoning dread than amusement. "We'll have to make sure that nobody guesses we no longer dislike each other."

"No kisses on the dance floor?"

She gulped back a giggle. "None."

"How will I survive? Will you at least dance with me? A waltz?"

"I'll look at you like Jupiter does."

"While we're away, you can practice looking bored to tears."

This time the giggle escaped. "Anything else will set tongues wagging."

Another carriage rolled into the square and stopped in front of the house that her father had rented for the season. "I have to go, Alaric. That will be Papa, which means the house will be locked up in the next hour."

Alaric's arms tightened. The voice rasping in her ear betrayed a frustration that might even outstrip hers. "I don't want to let you go."

"I don't want to go. Ooh!"

He'd run his teeth along a nerve in her neck that until now she hadn't known was there. Sensation whipped through her and made her toes curl. "You must, damn it."

She struggled for breath. "Will I see you tomorrow morning?"

"Yes. I hope it's foggy again."

"So do I."

It was time to go. More than time. She needed to be careful until Tuesday, just in case Papa decided to pay more attention than usual to her activities.

But it was the same as last night. She and Alaric planned sin, but the greatest sin seemed to be parting from him.

"Kiss me, then go," he said in a gruff voice. "Or else, heaven help me, I'll sweep you away to my bed and to the devil with propriety and papas."

Blindly, Portia turned in his arms and pressed her mouth to his. The first time that she'd kissed him off her own initiative. Immediate heat and desire swamped her. A promise of wonders to come next Tuesday.

CHAPTER ELEVEN

*E*ven if it hadn't meant a chance to dance with Alaric, Portia wouldn't miss Lady Shelburn's ball. Not just because she and the Shelburns were now related by marriage, either.

Kate Anstey, Lady Shelburn, and she had become firm friends since the unconventional countess's marriage and entry into society two years ago. Perhaps the fact that at heart they were both outsiders drew them together, or perhaps it was their incurable independence. The friendship had thrived, as Kate had helped her find homes for many of her rescues and had even taken in a couple herself.

This was the first time Kate had held a ball at Anstey House in Grosvenor Square. The prospect of hosting the cream of society had thrown the usually imperturbable Lady Shelburn into a complete flap. But an hour into proceedings, she seemed to have accepted that despite her predictions of failure, the event proved a raging success.

Portia had just danced a quadrille with Ivor Bilson. Now she stood with her host and hostess, surveying the extravagantly dressed crowd filling the ornate ballroom. "You need to accept it, Kate. You're about to become a famous hostess. You'll have to hold a ball every year and fight back hordes of encroaching mushrooms, clamoring for invitations."

"Heaven preserve us," said Lord Shelburn, rolling his brilliant dark eyes. "They won't call us the eccentric Ansteys anymore."

His wife's smile conveyed the love that Portia had always envied. The Shelburns' teasing give-and-take had always seemed to her the best way to be married. "Face it, my darling, you're no longer the worst lord in London. Despite marrying a peasant like me."

He caught her hand and kissed it. "Now I'm thinking about frolics amongst the haystacks."

It was time for Portia to roll her eyes. "Stop it, you two."

"Yes, stop it, Leighton. You're embarrassing our friend." Kate's voice betrayed her enjoyment of the flirtation.

Portia had known Lord Shelburn since her first season, and Kate and she had bonded from their first meeting. But only now after falling in love with Alaric did she sense the sexual spark between the pair. She wondered how she could have missed that crackling heat.

Shelburn smiled at her. "Perhaps our friend will give me this waltz?"

This morning, when they'd discussed the ball, Portia had promised the first waltz to Alaric. But she hadn't caught sight of him. Although it was safer not to be seen together, she'd had to swallow bitter disappointment. The last few days of brief meetings in the park had whetted her appetite for his company.

"I'm sure you'd rather dance with Kate," Portia said. "She deserves it, after putting this wonderful party together."

"In any case, Lady Portia has promised me this

dance," a beloved voice said from behind her.

Portia told herself that on no account must she light up like a Roman candle. Especially when the Shelburns knew her well enough to be curious about her reaction to a man she'd always disliked.

But dear Lord, it was difficult not to smile as if Alaric filled the whole world with sunlight. Struggling to keep her expression blank, she bobbed into a curtsy. "Your Grace."

The orchestra played the waltz's introduction and couples gathered to begin the dance. Alaric offered a brief bow to the Shelburns. "My lady. My lord."

"Your Grace. Thank you for coming to my ball." Kate's voice didn't give much away.

Alaric's expression remained serious, almost stern, as if that flibbertigibbet Portia Frain was beneath his lofty notice. Once that expression had made her want to kick him. Tonight, it made her want to laugh. And kiss him.

Wouldn't that set the cat among the pigeons at Kate's first ball?

"Shall we?" When he extended his gloved hand, Portia took it without thinking. The surge of connection made her jump. His grip tightening, he drew her onto the dance floor.

"Oh, dear." Portia turned to him. "I'm not sure how well that went."

She'd avoided meeting his eyes. She didn't trust him to maintain his sangfroid if she gazed up at him like a lovestruck ninny. But his faint snort of amusement made her take a peek. The somber air lingered, but the line of his mouth hinted that he was having trouble not laughing. If Portia Frain made the famously austere Duke of Granville laugh, the game would be up in a second.

"Leaping about like a frog on a lily pad when I take your hand doesn't help." He didn't sound annoyed. He sounded as if he liked her. The warmth in his tone made her silly heart caper with joy.

He slid his arm around her waist. Since her debut, she'd waltzed hundreds of times. This was the first time that setting her hand on a man's broad shoulder made her heart kick with excitement. She hoped to heaven that she wasn't blushing. "Perhaps Kate and Leighton will blame my edginess on dislike."

"Try and look as apathetic as usual." The waltz began, and Alaric swept her into a dizzying turn that had her clutching at him to keep her balance. His nearness always had the most calamitous effect on her knees. "That might help."

She'd danced with Alaric often in the past, although not this season after last summer's scandal. Never before had the dance become a flight through the heavens.

She had a sharp word to herself. Too much was at stake for her to surrender to tipsy wonder. The world must never speculate about whether the Duke of Granville had turned his attention to the younger Frain sister.

Around them, couples spun in time with the music, but for Portia only one person in this glittering ballroom mattered. Only one person seemed real. "We've never danced like this before."

His expression turned long-suffering. "You've always been as stiff as a board."

Portia muffled a laugh. She couldn't reveal how much fun she was having. Which was plaguey difficult when her heart danced faster than her feet. "Now I want to drape myself over you like a silk scarf."

"Stop it, Portia." That telltale muscle flickered in his cheek. "I'm having enough trouble as it is, not dragging you into the gardens to get you to myself."

She liked hearing that. She liked even more

hearing the agonized frustration in his voice. If she had to behave herself in public, he could suffer as well. "It's pouring out there."

"I don't care. I want to kiss you."

"Soon you can kiss me as often as you like." She chanced a quick glance up into burning eyes. The heat lit a fire inside her, and she bit back a murmur of longing.

"Tuesday seems an eon away."

It did. Her hand tightened on his shoulder. "Oh, Alaric…"

His grip on her waist firmed, bringing her nearer. "This is torture," he snapped out through straight white teeth.

It was. It was also the most glorious pleasure. Her feet flew across the floor, and her body responded to his subtlest signals. Soon her body would respond to his signals in a bed. The carnal thought made her sight dim, and she'd have stumbled if Alaric wasn't holding her so securely.

"Portia…" he growled. He didn't need to say any more.

"You're holding me too close," she said in a strangled voice. That seemed like a foul lie. She wanted him to hold her closer still. So close that she felt his heart beating with the same excitement that made her feel like she was ready to burst into flame.

She sensed his reluctance, as he loosened his grip. With difficulty, she schooled her features into what she prayed was a lack of interest. She glanced around the room as if desperate for the waltz to end.

Which was another foul lie.

She wanted to twirl around in Alaric's arms until the sun came up.

To her discomfort, curious glances arrowed in on her and Granville. Everybody would be thinking of how he'd courted Juliet and been found wanting.

The events at Afton Place had fueled nearly a year's worth of tattle. The peccadilloes of not one, but two dukes, and the lady once considered the doyenne of propriety had been irresistible fodder for the gossips.

Portia caught Kate's eye across the room. From where they danced together, Kate and Leighton observed her with a concern that flooded her with dread. It could be that they were aware of the stir of curiosity in the room. It could also be that they sensed some connection between Portia and the duke.

That would be a disaster. Nobody – *nobody* – could ever know that Portia had developed a penchant for Juliet's jilted suitor. Not even close friends like the Shelburns. But dear Lord, it was difficult pasting on a disdainful expression. She sent her friends a wry smile that she hoped conveyed the wish to be anywhere else but here.

Kate's smile wasn't convincing. Frowning, Portia focused on Alaric.

"That's better," he said. "You look unhappy."

"I am unhappy," she muttered. "Lady Shelburn suspects something."

Alaric angled his head toward the Shelburns. "They're not looking at us."

No, Kate would have the sense to know that if she stared at Portia and her partner, other people might notice and ask questions of their own.

Portia's heart sank as she realized that she took too many risks tonight. Good heavens, if word reached Papa about her making sheep's eyes at the duke, there would be the devil to pay. He'd start promoting a marriage, however unsuitable the union. And Papa never did anything low-key.

"We shouldn't have danced together," she said in a bleak voice.

"Yes, we should. If only to save me from losing my mind."

For a forbidden second, she let herself sink into his gaze. His eyes conveyed everything that she struggled to hide. Hunger. Need. Desire. "I'm having the most awful trouble pretending you mean nothing to me."

His smile was swift, gone in a second. Even so, it bolstered her faltering courage. "I like that."

"When we get back to London after our…tryst, we can never be in the same room or everyone will guess what we've done." She stared over his shoulder to where Elizabeth Tierney danced with Ivor Bilson. It was safer not to look at Alaric. Partly because when she did, she didn't want to look anywhere else. "How will we go back to being polite strangers?"

Another huff of amusement, although his expression remained grave. "When were we ever polite?"

"I always said what a lady should."

"Yes, you did. Even if the tone shrieked 'damn your eyes.'"

"You're trying to make me feel better."

"I am."

When she chanced a glance at his face, he looked particularly ducal. "Aren't you worried about what happens, once we do this outlandish thing?"

"It will all work out."

She stifled a surprised laugh. "That doesn't sound like you. You always plan ahead, do the sensible thing. You chose Juliet because she'd make the perfect duchess, not because you loved her."

Portia saw that he didn't like hearing her mention her sister. "Perhaps I've learned from my mistakes and stopped trying to control every moment."

She'd forgotten not to look at him. "Gossip wouldn't annoy you?"

His jaw set in a determined line. "I don't want anybody speaking ill of you. That's as far as my concern reaches." He paused. "Now you need to stop looking at me like that, or else I won't be responsible for my actions and people really will talk."

Portia was horrified to recall that they remained in the middle of a crowd. A nosy, scandal-obsessed crowd. She straightened. Her body showed a lamentable urge to lean toward the duke. "I can't wait for Tuesday."

"Me either."

He gave her an extravagant twirl as the waltz ended. The dance had been all too brief. Portia wanted to beg the orchestra to play the waltz again.

Since she was a little girl saving the village's mistreated animals, she'd chafed against the restrictions placed on females. Never had the rules struck her as so suffocating as they did now. Why couldn't she dance with Alaric all night? Why couldn't she kiss him when she wanted? She was an adult woman, yet society treated her like an incapable child.

For a charged moment, they stood staring at each other, before he looked away and took her arm. He led her through the throng to the far end of the room, where the Shelburns waited. Portia braced for parting from Alaric.

"Thank you, Lady Portia. May I fetch you some refreshment? Champagne? Orgeat? Lemonade?"

Under Leighton and Kate's inquisitive gazes, it was more circumspect to refuse. "That's very kind, but no, thank you, Your Grace."

"In that case, I wish you well."

"Good evening." She dipped into a curtsy.

He bowed and left her side. She was stupid to feel bereft. But she did. It took the greatest effort not to follow his progress through the crowd with covetous eyes.

"Portia?" Kate's tone brought her back to earth with an unpleasant thump.

Unwillingly, she met her friend's searching regard. "Yes?"

"I thought you didn't like Granville."

Oh, no. She'd done her best to hide her attraction to Alaric, but it hadn't been enough. "I don't."

She hated feeling like that assertion betrayed both Alaric and herself. She hated lying to Kate, especially when it was clear that her friend didn't believe her. "Then why did you dance with him?"

"He asked me." At least that was true.

Despite rejecting Alaric's offer, she seized a glass of champagne from a tray carried by a passing footman. She gulped some wine, hoping it would help her through the next few minutes. "He wants to play down the gossip about a feud with my family after that mess with Juliet. As Juliet's on the Continent and Viola's in Hampshire, I'm the only Frain available."

There. That almost sounded convincing. And not a bad excuse, given she'd come up with it on the spot.

"I see." Kate's noncommittal response didn't sound as if she saw at all.

Portia's self-satisfaction faded, especially when Leighton joined the conversation. "I saw His Grace in the park yesterday with a dog any self-respecting poacher would turn his nose up at owning."

Oh, dear. Portia bit back the urge to defend Jupiter, who she liked more every time she saw him. He mightn't be pretty, but he made up for that with character. "Did you? How nice that Granville has found a pet."

She struggled to sound like none of this mattered. Even in her own ears, she didn't succeed.

The Shelburns watched her as if awaiting a

confession. Plague take them, they weren't going to get one.

"I imagine the duke's felt rather friendless since last year's scandal," Kate said, still in that careful tone.

"The funny thing is I immediately thought of the dogs you foisted on us. Not an ounce of pedigree in any of them," Leighton said.

"I thought you liked your dogs," Portia said with some heat to divert them from Granville's new canine companion. Her annoyed tone would explain the color surging into her cheeks.

"We do," Kate said. "They're part of the family."

"That's good, then." Portia decided to lead with her chin. "If the duke has adopted a stray, I applaud him."

"So you had nothing to do with the acquisition?" Leighton asked.

"On my morning ride, I've seen the duke and his dog. I didn't think to question his choice of pet. Clearly it's a major issue that a man should walk his dog in Hyde Park. I'm surprised it's not in the *Morning Post*."

"There's no need for sarcasm," Kate said.

"Isn't there?" Portia said in a thorny tone. "Even if I gave His Grace a dog, it's not a hanging offense."

"No, but it's...out of character. For you. And for him. I'd have said, at best, you barely tolerated each other."

Portia hoped her belligerent tone would discourage speculation. She also hoped that only Kate and Leighton had made the link between stray dogs, Portia Frain, and the Duke of Granville. "What are you trying to say, Kate? Are you suggesting a romantic intrigue with Granville? The man my sister jilted? The most proper fellow in Mayfair?"

Kate didn't back down. But then, Kate had run

successful textile mills in the Midlands since she was a girl. "You're a beautiful woman. I'll wager Granville isn't blind to that fact."

Portia snorted. "That's very kind of you, but I'm too harum-scarum to be the Duchess of Granville, thank you very much. Granville chose Juliet, for heaven's sake, because she was the most well-behaved lady in England. I'm not in the running for a proposal."

To her overwhelming sorrow, none of that was a lie. She'd always known that no wedding ring waited at the end of their affair.

"Perhaps after two broken engagements, he's decided well-behaved ladies aren't for him," Leighton said. "If you'd like a man's point of view—"

"Which I don't," she said stiffly.

Leighton ignored her. "...the duke looked more than a little interested when he danced with you."

Portia realized with a sinking heart that if she wanted to deflect interest in her relationship with Alaric, she'd chosen precisely the wrong tactic. Her vehement responses only fed her friends' questions.

"He was just being polite. Remember, he's the most proper gentleman in London." She went on to say what she knew to be the unadulterated truth. "Anyway, even if he is looking for another woman to marry, he's not going to consider a Frain. When Juliet abandoned him to go off and marry Evesham, he went through the gossip mills and he'd hate that."

"If you say so," Kate said grudgingly.

Portia so wished that this topic had never arisen. She answered in a more conciliatory tone. "You and Leighton are still like April and May, despite a couple of years together. You see romance wherever you look."

Kate didn't smile. "We just want you to be happy, Portia. When I saw you two together, there was something...right about it."

That made Portia feel like a worm. And a liar. Because while marriage to Alaric most definitely wasn't on the table, an affair was. Kate and Leighton might approve of her resolution to seize what happiness she could. After all, Leighton had once been a famous rake.

But even if she confided her plans – and she couldn't confess all in the middle of a crowded ballroom – she couldn't bear the thought of anyone talking her out of her decision.

Portia glanced up. To her relief, Alexander Comerford crossed the room to her rescue. "You're both unhinged. Granville would laugh himself silly if he could hear you. If he had an ounce of humour, that is. Which we all know he hasn't."

Before Leighton or Kate could argue, Alexander extended his hand. "I believe this our dance, Lady Portia."

The broad smile that she fixed to her face made Alexander look startled. They were friends, but there had never been a hint of romance between them. She wanted Kate and Leighton speculating about her and Alexander and not her and Alaric. "How utterly wonderful. I can't wait."

CHAPTER TWELVE

*H*er heart in her throat, Portia crossed the small square in front of Mary's house and darted into the side alley where Rankin always waited while she visited her former governess. Today there was no familiar closed carriage, drawn by horses from the Frain stable. Instead, there was a black curricle with the hood up and a pair of bays far more impressive than anything her father owned.

The ton didn't frequent unfashionable Marylebone, so it was unlikely that anyone she knew would see her. Nonetheless, she lowered a veil from the brim of her bonnet.

"Did you have any trouble?" Alaric asked softly, leaning forward past the rim of the hood. One gloved hand held the reins, and the other stretched out to take her small valise. He, like her, was dressed in plain traveling clothes and he'd pulled his hat down over his face. He set her bag behind the seat before helping her up.

"No. Everything went like a dream." By now, she should be used to the zap of heat when they touched. Yet even through two layers of leather, the effect remained as disconcerting as ever. "It doesn't seem right for fate to cooperate with our plans."

He laughed softly. "The devil must be on our side."

She climbed up to sit beside him. Under the canopy, the light was dim. It was afternoon and this early in spring, the day already started to draw in. On the narrow seat, her hip squeezed against his. More heat radiated from where their bodies met.

"Papa has gone down to Hampshire to see Viola and Toby and Benedict. Rankin dropped me at Mary's and will collect me there on Friday afternoon. She didn't even blink when I told her I was heading into Essex to rescue a dog."

Under the brim of his hat, green eyes searched her face. "You sound as if you want to be called out on your plans."

Self-mockery turned down her lips. "I've been so afraid something would stop me leaving. I keep waiting for the gun to go off. I'm a nervous wreck."

"You can change your mind, you know." He kept hold of her hand. "Go home and sleep the sleep of the innocent tonight."

As she studied his face, her fear receded. "Do you want to abandon our plans?"

"God, no!" Even through her veil, she saw how appalled he looked. He sounded it, too. "But the decision remains yours."

Reassured by his vehemence, she settled into her seat. "Then let's go."

"I want to kiss you." The fervent admission launched her heart on a string of exuberant cartwheels. "But we're not safe yet."

"I wish you could, too," she said with a touch of wistfulness.

The searing glance he shot her dowsed the last of her doubts.

He released her and seized the reins in both

hands with a purpose that should have terrified her. After all, the purpose was her seduction. But his determination was uplifting. There was something to be said for falling in love with a supremely competent man.

She and Alaric remained silent, as he guided the light carriage out of the alley and into the traffic. Portia huddled back against the seat, although the veil hid her face and the vehicle's hood protected her from casual curiosity.

Alaric's skillful driving and the compact vehicle meant that even through crowded streets, they made good progress. Soon they were bowling along the highway toward Windsor, where they'd turn south for Surrey.

He urged the magnificent horses to a gallop. "There's a rug under the seat if you're cold."

"Thank you, but I'm fine." She sucked in what felt like her first full breath in hours, and her hands shook as she lifted the veil off her face. Immediately the scenery snapped into focus. The hedgerows on either side were white with blackthorn flowers and bare fields stretched to the horizon. It was that time of year where spring and winter vied for supremacy. The day was gray with squalls of rain, so the hood offered shelter against the weather as well as prying eyes. "How long is the journey from here?"

"Two hours if all goes well."

Two hours didn't seem long. Nerves raised their head again, despite the bolt of anticipation slamming through her. At last, they'd be alone with no risk of discovery. They'd never enjoyed that luxury. The prospect was both daunting and exhilarating.

"Are you hungry? There's a basket in the back, if you want to stop. We'll have a hot meal once we get to Surrey. I've arranged for the staff to leave the lodge stocked, and they've got orders not to come near the place until Friday afternoon."

"No, I'm not hungry." At least for food. Over the last few days, they'd met in the park for brief conversations, and last night, they'd been partners in a quadrille at Lady Chastain's ball. Each meeting left behind a storm of futile longing.

They hadn't risked waltzing again, after she told him about Kate and Leighton's curiosity. Since that uncomfortable conversation, she'd avoided the Shelburns. Luckily, the crush at the events they all attended allowed her to do that without being too obvious. Or at least she hoped so. She couldn't face another interrogation and having to tell more lies. Especially when she suspected that neither Kate nor Leighton believed a word she said.

Portia curled her fingers around Alaric's arm, feeling the slide and release of his muscles as he controlled the horses with impressive ease. She hadn't wanted to distract him when he negotiated London traffic.

He'd stuck to the city's less fashionable areas, where they were unlikely to encounter people that they knew. The fine horseflesh might draw a second glance, but in the capital's workaday sectors, people were too busy to stop and speculate on who drove the natty little carriage.

"Do you...bring women to the lodge often?"

He tensed under her grasp. "Portia..."

She bit her lip. "I know it's none of my business, but..."

His jaw firmed, although he didn't shift his gaze from the road ahead. "You're the only woman I've brought to my house in Lorimer Square. And you'll be the only woman who's visited my hunting lodge."

His voice rang with sincerity. She couldn't doubt that he spoke the truth.

Gladness eased the tension inside her. She couldn't help smiling. "It shouldn't matter—"

"But it does."

"I'd hate to be a forgettable affair in a long line of forgettable affairs."

His snort poured scorn on that shaky statement. "No fear. There's been nobody like you, and there will be nobody like you. Ever."

Because Alaric Dempster wasn't given to extravagant statements, his words left her reeling. Silence descended for a minute or two, as she summoned the courage to ask the next question. "Can we...can we stop now?"

The glance he cast her was concerned. "Are you feeling ill?"

"No."

The bays slowed to a halt. "You haven't changed your mind?"

Portia realized that Alaric, too, had suffered bouts of uncertainty. It made her feel better to know that she wasn't alone in that. She liked that he didn't take her for granted. "No, of course not."

"What is it, then?"

Her grip on his arm tightened, and she shifted to face him. The patrician features were clouded with worry.

"There's nobody around. It feels like a good time to kiss me."

Astonished joy filled his expression. And a good dose of relief. He'd definitely been worried that she meant to withdraw from their arrangement. "I don't deserve you."

He loosely knotted the reins over the bar at the front of the carriage and slid his arms around her. She sank into immediate heat and a security which was absurd. But every time he touched her, she couldn't help thinking that everything was going to be wonderful.

His lips explored hers with a thoroughness that set her blood rushing and stirred up that now familiar weight in the pit of her stomach. It was both alarming and thrilling to think that soon he'd fill that emptiness inside her, the ache that had started the first time he'd kissed her.

By the time they drew apart, both were panting. His smart gray hat had fallen to the floor of the carriage.

"Oh, my," she sighed, opening dazed eyes. She shaped her gloved hand to that chiseled jaw. "This last week has been endless."

"Hasn't it just?" His lips quirked in self-deprecation. "Every time I saw you, I was tempted to steal you away and to hell with the consequences."

An elated smile lifted her lips, as her heart expanded against her ribs. "Now you have stolen me away."

His answering smile was free of all restraint, as it so rarely was. "Lucky me."

The evening drew in as the curricle turned between a set of gates and followed a winding avenue of lime trees. Portia tightened her hold on Alaric's arm, as the house came into view past a mellow brick wall and another gate.

"It's lovely," she said.

The lodge was four floors high, with a pavilion on the roof. Pairs of tall casement windows formed symmetrical lines along the cream stone façade. A graceful double staircase rose to a door beneath a carved pediment. Forest encroached on the garden, emphasizing the fairy-tale atmosphere.

Alaric drew the tired horses up on the gravel turning circle. "One of my ancestors built it for his mistress in the reign of Charles II. The story is that he wanted to keep her out of the king's clutches."

"Did he succeed?"

"By all reports, he did. He married her, once he was free to do so. It caused an almighty scandal."

So this had always been a house for lovers. It still was. Alaric didn't love her, but Portia loved him enough to make up for that. "How romantic."

Alaric's smile held no shadows. "It was rather. She was a parliamentarian's daughter who gave up everything to follow her heart. She ended up a countess." He looped the reins over the bar at the front of the carriage and descended from his seat. "Let me help you down."

She held out her hand, experiencing the familiar jolt of awareness when his fingers curled around hers. "Do you come here much?"

"Not often." His sly look set a host of butterflies fluttering inside her. "But that may change."

A huff of amusement escaped. "Now you have a mistress of your own?"

Wry humor twisted his lips, as she stepped down from the carriage. "Now I have need of a bower that offers privacy I lack in London."

After sitting so long, her knees were stiff and she stumbled. Alaric easily caught her and drew her into his side. When his arm circled her, she nestled closer. The air grew colder, and he was so big and warm.

"You must be cold. Shall I take you inside? I'll settle the horses then follow you in."

She tipped her face to gaze at him. She couldn't help smiling, which didn't say much about her grip on morality. Here she was, ready to be ravished by a man who wasn't her husband, and she'd never been so happy in her life.

"Let me come with you. Many hands make light work, after all." She didn't want to be parted from him, not even for the half hour that he needed to care for his horses.

She and Alaric had a mere three nights together. He already spoke as if they'd come back here. Knowing that he planned to continue their affair after this rendezvous was reassuring. But she knew the world well enough to recognize that another opportunity to meet mightn't arise in a hurry.

"What are you thinking about?" he asked, then laughed. "As every lover since Adam has asked the woman he wants."

"'Gather ye rosebuds while ye may.'"

He placed a quick kiss on her lips. "I approve."

Before she could respond, he released her and took the horses' heads to lead them around the side of the house to a neat stable block. "I could have kept the staff on, but I thought you'd prefer us to be alone. However it means that we have to fend for ourselves and feed the horses."

"I like looking after animals, as you know."

"I do know," he said dryly.

"You could have brought Jupiter." She set out after Alaric. The cobbles beneath her half boots were wet, and the air had a delicious freshness. Or perhaps that was only because the whole world fizzed like champagne. "I'd be more than happy to tend to him."

Alaric's look expressed mock disapproval. "I'll have you know I'm more than capable of handling him on my own. I've become a dab hand at washing him. Which is a good thing. Every time I take him out, he finds something disgusting to roll in."

"That's what dogs do."

"No wonder my grandparents never let me have a

puppy. They hated disorder."

He never spoke of his upbringing with bitterness, but she couldn't help thinking that it sounded like a horribly cold way to rear a little boy. "I thought you hated it, too. You were always so proper."

"It turns out I don't mind at all." When he held his hand out, she took it.

"I'm so glad he's decided he'll put up with Matty."

"Getting the lad to feed him was genius."

Given that the duke had once treated her as if she couldn't cross the street without falling over, she basked in the compliment. "Thank heaven it worked."

Portia slipped forward to lift the latch that kept the stable doors closed. She stood back to let Alaric bring the horses and curricle under cover.

"Let me light a lamp or two," he said from somewhere forward of her in the gloom. With the cloudy day and the early sunset, it was as dark as a coal mine inside, despite a line of windows high up near the roof.

She heard Alaric move about and the scrape of a flint. Golden light bloomed around them.

They stood in a big bare space, designed to hold several carriages. Against the far wall, hay was piled in bales and loose mounds. Behind her, a short corridor led to a closed door. On either side of the corridor, half a dozen stalls waited empty.

Alaric lit more lamps. She removed her gloves and started unharnessing the horses.

"They're beauties." And perfectly trained, standing docile as she unbuckled the leathers.

"I bought them last week at Tattersall's." He stood on the other side, working on the second horse. It whickered in welcome and butted him with its splendid head. "I didn't want anyone recognizing the blacks that I usually drive."

"You bought two expensive horses for discretion's sake?" she asked in a reedy voice.

"Of course." His tone was light, as if what he'd done was a mere trifle, hardly worth mentioning.

"But they must have cost—"

He broke in before she could speculate on how many hundreds of guineas he'd laid out on the bays. Papa wasn't in the Corinthian line, but she'd danced enough with Ivor Bilson to know what bloodstock of this caliber cost.

"Worth every penny. I promised that I'd keep your good name safe."

Portia shouldn't find his efforts moving, but she did. Before she'd set out this morning, she'd had a serious word with herself about quelling any sentimental impulses. This was a short-term affair, and she intended to enjoy herself. She wasn't going to waste these few precious days on hopeless yearning.

But when Alaric did things like this, it was almost impossible to remember that this affair didn't include love as part of its definition. At least for Alaric.

She swallowed the poignant emotion blocking her throat. "I didn't expect you to beggar yourself for the sake of a few nights with me."

"There's a couple of pence left in the Dempster coffers. I promise I'll do better than bread and water tonight."

She didn't laugh, although she could tell that he didn't want to dwell on his extraordinary extravagance. Her voice shook with emotion. "That's the nicest thing anyone's ever done for me. Thank you."

"Then life has shortchanged you," he said. "I intend to treat you like the treasure you are."

Before her boggling mind could summon some

response, he went back to murmuring praise to the horse. She heard him pat the horse's neck. "It's all right, Poll."

When she spoke, she'd gained a little control over her tumultuous reactions. Her voice emerged with a dry edge. "Poll? Isn't he a gelding?"

"Apollo and Dionysus. But that's too much of a mouthful for a sensible man."

"Dionysus?" She took a guess. "Di?"

"Right first go."

They each took a horse and led them into the stalls. "They're all set up with food and water."

Alaric was checking Poll's feet on the other side of the chest-high partition. "Yes, a housekeeper and a gamekeeper, a married couple, live here when I'm not using the house. On the rare occasions when I host a hunting party, I send staff from London. I wrote to the Johnsons last week, requesting them to prepare everything. They're visiting their daughter in Godalming right now."

Portia brought Di up to the filled manger. She rubbed him down, as he drank noisily from the bucket. She'd been in a state since she'd arrived at the lodge, but the familiar rhythm of caring for a horse calmed her.

She patted Di's shoulder and went to stand in the aisle. "Your new horses have lovely manners."

"Yes, you did me a favor when I bought them." He came out of the stall and shut the gate behind him. His coat draped over his arm, and he was in his shirtsleeves.

For a long moment, Portia studied him. Lord above, he was a treat for the eye.

He regarded her with a quizzical expression. "What?"

Color flooded her cheeks, which was mad when so far she hadn't done anything to raise a blush. "You're so handsome. You quite dazzle me."

He blushed, too, which she found charming. "What a load of nonsense."

She loved it when he revealed this unexpected boyish side. She saw it when he was with Jupiter and now with his horses. And with her. It wasn't something that he allowed free rein in society. If he had, perhaps it wouldn't have taken her so long to realize how likable he was. "It needs to be said."

"Then thank you," he said with more of that charming self-effacement. "Shall I show you the house?"

She squared her shoulders and summoned all her courage. "Not yet."

He guessed at least part of her intention. "You want a kiss?"

She wanted more than that. But a kiss made a good start. "Yes, please."

CHAPTER THIRTEEN

Granville loved how open Portia was about her desire. Being a duke put one at the top of the aristocratic order. But nothing in his life compared to how powerful he felt, knowing that this one remarkable woman couldn't keep her hands off him. It made him feel ten feet tall.

The first time he'd kissed her, she'd wrapped him in sunshine. The week since had kept that glow alive. Away from Portia, the world was cold and sharp and unwelcoming. By Jericho, he intended to stay as close to her as he could.

Which meant responding to her every overture.

He let his heavy coat slip from his hand and drew her into his arms.

All day, he'd kept a short rein on his passions. Now they were alone, and three days of joyous exploration lay ahead. He could hardly wait.

When she yielded, all willing femininity, he abandoned restraint without a second's hesitation and took her lips with desperate hunger. On a soft growl of encouragement, she opened her mouth to his sensual invasion.

Heat flooded him, turned his veins to rivers of

fire. He couldn't doubt how much she wanted him. It was clear in the way that she pressed close and in the flicker of her tongue around his. It was in her muffled little sounds of pleasure, incoherent pleas to keep going. To give her more.

Her rich scent, floral soap and aroused woman, tinged with horse sweat, filled his senses. Became the air he breathed. Blazing darkness crammed his head, so that everything outside the circle of Portia's arms receded to nothing. It all disappeared, except Portia and the aching heaviness of his balls. He was immediately hard for her.

At last, he allowed himself to discover her body as he'd longed to do. Still kissing her, he ran his hands down her back to the sumptuous rump. He curled his fingers into that delectable softness and gloried in her whimper of approval as she wriggled closer. She'd know now just how much he wanted her.

Granville buried his hands in the silky tumble of hair, making a nonsense of what remained of her chignon. Raking his hands through the luxuriant locks, he brought her closer for more of those intoxicating kisses.

She changed the angle of the kiss, so it turned even more ferocious. Her shaking hands hooked around his shoulders, claiming him as irrevocably as he claimed her.

He'd feared that she'd be hesitant and afraid. But Portia wasn't a woman who lived in fear, praise the angels. He'd always admired her courage and her wholehearted approach to a challenge.

He admired her even more when she joined this unleashed exploration of desire. Her hands slid up and down his arms with feverish intent. With only a thin shirt separating his skin from hers, her touch shuddered through him like an earthquake.

Those seeking hands ran across his back then

lower to catch his hips. His dick swelled at the prospect of her touch, but he reminded himself that this was a virgin. However eager she was, he doubted that she'd stroke his breeding organs before her first tumble.

Tomorrow perhaps?

She pulled back an inch, and her question was a humid brush of breath across his sensitized lips. "You're laughing?"

"I'm happy."

"So am I."

She'd always had more life than anyone else he knew. Right now, she lit up like a Catherine wheel. In the soft lamplight, her golden beauty was incandescent.

With sudden determination, she seized his shirt. Stumbling backward, she drew him down the aisle between the stalls.

He supposed that she headed for the house so they could finish this in a bed. He hoped so. Hell, he'd carry her upstairs right now, if he could convince himself that she was ready.

They were back in the carriage house. Eyes dark and heavy-lidded with passion didn't shift from his face. Somewhere in his reeling mind, he wondered if she tried to send him a message. But he was too drunk on Portia and kisses and rampant desire to have an icicle's chance in hell of deciphering her expression.

Apart from that she wanted him, too. The clutching hands and ragged breath told him that. Even without the searing kisses.

She pushed him hard up against the side of the curricle. He landed so heavily that the vehicle rocked behind him.

Granville reached for her to keep his balance. He reached for her because she was the most glorious being in the world and he never wanted to let her go.

Portia surged to meet him halfway, so they crashed together in wild appetite. He wrapped his arms about her, using teeth and lips and tongue to arouse her. A lopsided waltz ensued that soon had them standing on a thick carpet of hay.

She wrenched away, breathing in tattered gusts. "Stop being a gentleman, Alaric," she gritted out.

Before he could decode that, she shifted further into the hay store. Perforce, he backed up, too. She placed her palms flat on his chest and pushed.

"Hell's bells!" Caught unprepared, he tumbled backward onto the hay, taking Portia with him in a tangle of arms and legs. With an oof, she landed right on top of him.

"Are you all right?" he forced out, as all that alluring softness plastered to his yearning body made him see stars. Stars edged with fire. Her squirming tested his control. Good grief, at this rate, he'd burst out of his breeches. They already felt tight enough to throttle his tackle.

"I'm fine. Better than fine." She struggled up on her elbows to look down at him. This corner of the stables was darker than the stalls, but there was enough light for him to read the strain in her features. Strain and need and purpose. "I want you now."

Everything went still. His heart. His breath. Fortunately Portia. He wasn't sure that he could endure much more of her body rubbing against his.

She stared down at him with a silent entreaty that cut him like a knife. Her lips were red and swollen. When she sank white teeth into that cushiony lower lip, he bit back a groan.

Granville swallowed to ease his parched throat. "Do you...do you want to go to the house?"

"No, I want to stay here." She regarded him with

a frustration that the dim lighting didn't conceal. He was frustrated, too. He'd been mad for her for a mere week, but desire didn't count time like a clock. Desire counted every hour that he wasn't touching her as a year.

Now that she was no longer crushed tight to his throbbing prick, he should feel less frantic. But she was still too close, and the hay made for a good mattress. The change in position didn't relieve his lust. Her scent eddied around him, drawing him nearer and nearer to the point of no return.

"If we stay here, I'll have you. Your first time should be in a bed."

"We can go to bed later." Emotion cracked her voice. When she cupped his jaw in her hand, the touch crashed through him like thunder. "Please don't make me wait anymore."

"Portia..." The idea of deflowering a delicately bred lady in a stable shocked him to the toenails.

He started to roll away as she turned and grabbed his arm, overbalancing him. For a sizzling moment, he splayed over her, squashing her into the hay. He drowned in the wonder that was Portia.

Just as she moved in his direction, he shifted to create some room between them. When he reached down blindly to find his balance, his hand closed on her breast.

She gasped and raised a hand to hold him there. He told himself to let her go, but his hand flexed over that lovely round bosom. Despite layers of clothing, he felt the jut of her nipple. When he increased the pressure, she exhaled in surprised response.

"Yes," she sighed, arching into his touch.

He was lost. By God, he was only human. He caught her in his arms for a famished kiss, then pushed her into the hay beneath her.

CHAPTER FOURTEEN

*R*elief flooded Portia. She sensed the precise moment that Alaric yielded. The resistance drained from his body, and his hand shaped her breast with delightful purpose.

She made an incoherent sound of pleasure, as sensation arrowed down to concentrate in that yearning space between her legs. She'd wanted him to touch her breasts forever. Thinking about his hands on her body had kept her awake or twisting in feverish dreams.

Her nipples tightened with such wicked longing that they hurt. When he plucked at a pearled peak through her clothes, she whimpered.

"You're a devil." The heat in his voice made the words sound more like praise than criticism. "I can't resist you."

She channeled her fingers through his thick, fair hair. "I'm *your* devil."

A faint smile lightened his features. "You are, at that."

His lips on hers always transported her into another world, so it took a few seconds to realize that he tackled the buttons down the front of her pelisse. It took her even longer to note that he performed the action with a smoothness that betrayed his familiarity with getting ladies out of their clothes.

She drew back from the kiss. "Goodness me, you do that well."

With a huff of laughter, he shifted to the side to support himself on one elbow. "I have done this before, I'll have you know."

"There's never been any gossip about your affairs." Her pelisse was open as far as her waist.

"That should reassure you that I can be discreet." He dipped his head and kissed the slope of her breasts above the gown. "I approve of the ensemble."

A thrill rippled through her, then another as his teeth scraped across her skin. "Do that again."

He laughed against her skin and squeezed her breast at the same time as his lips explored her décolletage.

She glanced down. "It seemed sensible to wear something that I could undo myself." How did she manage to put two words together when he stirred up such marvelous feelings?

He raised his head and studied her with a focus that was arousing. "Good for you."

As he undid her gown down to its high waist, his hands were sure. With a shiver of anticipation, she imagined what those hands would soon do to her.

Gently, he brushed the edges of the dress aside to reveal what lay beneath. The top of her stays and her white shift. The corset pushed her breasts high against the linen. Her beaded nipples were raspberry pink through the frail covering.

When he didn't speak, a twinge of uncertainty had her biting her lip. His features were stern. Once that had fooled her into thinking that he had no feelings. She knew better now, but the taut silence made her nervous. "Please say something."

"Portia..." The word trailed away to nothing.

"Yes?" Her voice wavered.

When she'd pulled him into the hay, she'd brimmed with confidence. Now that he undressed her, she was less self-assured. Especially as it became clear that Alaric was adept at the sensual game, while she remained a rank beginner.

At last he looked up. The glitter in his eyes incinerated her insecurities. "You're so beautiful."

Joy blossomed inside her. She stretched up to kiss him in an excess of desire and gratitude. As he met her with unabashed enthusiasm, she curled her hand around his neck. He deepened the kiss and stroked the skin above her shift. Every cell in her body came alive to his caresses. He teased her, edging closer to her shift without delving beneath.

At last he slipped his fingers under the linen and cupped her naked breast.

Portia wriggled in wordless encouragement, as the ache in her nipples sharpened. Then released a muffled cry when he pinched one peak between thumb and forefinger. She dissolved into liquid heat, and her body softened as it prepared for his possession.

The sensation of his fingers on her bare breast sent her up in flames. In an instinctive plea for more, her hips jerked toward his hardness.

He loosened the drawstring, allowing her breasts to spill out. The awe on his face made her feel as beautiful as Venus. And proud of that beauty.

She spread her shaking hand over his chest, feeling his heart thunder beneath her palm. Heat radiated from him, alluring as a fire blazing in a hearth.

Alaric pressed his mouth to hers and pushed her skirts higher. The needy hollows of her body grew slick with excitement, as his hand traced her thigh under her loose drawers. In an agony of suspense, she waited for him to touch her there, in the secret place that ached for him. So many powerful urges assailed her, she wondered why she didn't explode.

Earthy female arousal tinged the air, along with dust and hay and horses. And something musky that she guessed was male arousal. It smelled like Alaric, but it also smelled like masculine need.

When he took his hand away, she wanted to howl in disappointment. She ripped her lips from his to demand, beg, that he keep going, but he spoke first.

"Spread your legs for me, Portia." His gruffness reflected his urgency.

She obeyed with alacrity. She was hot and wet and empty, and she needed him to fill the yearning space. He found the slit in her drawers and insinuated his hand inside. When he cupped her mound, she shuddered in surprise. And pleasure.

Over the pulse in her ears, she barely heard his choked sound of approval. Her hips rose toward that teasing hand, and her fingers circled his arm.

When he lingered at a particularly sensitive place, pulses of searing desire blasted her. The crumpled froth of skirts and petticoats around her hips stopped her from seeing what he did. That just made the experience more evocative. Every sense woke to this seduction.

"Do...it." Talking was almost impossible.

Alaric frowned, although his hand continued its unsettling explorations. "I don't want to hurt you."

She quivered under his touch and spread her legs wider. "It hurts to want you like this."

Still touching her between the legs, he kissed her again, lips voracious. She sucked his tongue into her mouth and pressed up in a plea to take this further.

Portia felt pressure between her legs. With a shock, she realized that his finger was inside her. She gasped against his mouth. The sensation was strange, a little uncomfortable. Almost pleasurable, especially when she tightened around the invasion.

Alaric raised his head to watch her as he slid his finger in and out. Deeper pressure told her that he now used two fingers. Her body clung to him, as he established a steady rhythm that beat in her blood.

It wasn't enough. She wanted him to give her everything. She attained such a pitch of craving that she didn't care if it hurt. "I want you now."

"You're so tight," he said unevenly.

"I'm ready." With daring born of desperation, she tore at the buttons on his breeches.

His rod strained the gray buckram. It looked huge. Impossibly huge. How on earth would that fit inside her? The prospect should terrify her. But even that wasn't enough to discourage her.

"I'm trying to do the right thing." He sounded as if it hurt to talk.

To her frustration, he stopped touching her and caught her seeking hand. She stared up into his eyes, seeing the war that he fought with himself. That rampant flesh between his legs and the hunger she read in his expression revealed that he was as mad to have her as she was to be had. But the Galahad jaw was set like stone, and the telltale muscle flickered in his cheek.

Portia took a moment to appreciate Alaric's consideration. She couldn't love a selfish man. But she wanted the key to the mystery that had tormented her since their first kiss. She couldn't deny herself any longer. She couldn't deny him.

"The right thing is for you to make love to me." Desire roughened her voice.

"Portia..."

"Please." Tears stung her eyes, and her voice cracked with need. She twisted her hand out of his grasp and flattened it against the bulge in his breeches. His member surged against her palm, and he shuddered. Without thinking, she fitted her hand around him.

Alaric released a long, guttural groan and his hips jerked forward to further the contact. "I can't resist you."

"Don't resist me." Triumph filled her. When she angled up to kiss him, his lips tasted of surrender. "We both want this."

She waited for him to protest in his knight-in-shining-armor way, but she'd vanquished his qualms at last. His kiss turned fierce, exciting her to the point of madness.

Through the daze of pleasure, she felt his hand moving between them. Then he slid over her, settling between her parted legs. He propped himself on his elbows and stared into her face, as if it offered a compass bearing toward home in a storm. She raised her chin and managed a smile. A tad shaky, but a smile nonetheless.

"I want you, Alaric." Sincerity deepened her voice to a husky contralto. "I want you so much."

It was true. Despite trepidation. Despite a lifetime of chastity.

"And I want you, Portia." His face was flushed, and his eyes were black with desire. "Bend your knees and tilt toward me."

Excitement speared her. Without hesitation, she obeyed his orders.

Something hot and smooth nudged her. A stretching sensation had her inhaling sharply. This felt different from his fingers.

He reached down with one hand, using his other arm to keep his weight off her. She guessed that he guided himself in. "Don't hold your breath or I'll hurt you," he said jerkily.

With an audible puff, she released her pent-up

breath. She closed her eyes and hooked her hands over his shoulders.

When he surged forward, she cried out. White-hot pain sliced her. Her hands formed talons in his shirt, as she fought the urge to weep. He sank onto her and buried his face in the curve of her neck and shoulder.

Even as she fought to overcome the agony, her body shifted and changed. Pain ebbed, replaced by a feeling of fullness. The intimacy beggared her torrid imaginings. This was so much more substantial, as if life grounded her in a connection as invincible as the planets' orbit or the rising of the sun.

Her deathly grip eased to a caress. With every second, she became more accustomed to having him inside her. The pain faded to a memory. The present was closeness and heat, and air laden with the scent of sexual desire.

Alaric had a talent for making the rest of the world disappear. It happened when they danced. It happened when they kissed. Pinned beneath him, spread-eagled across a pile of hay redolent of sweet summer, she lay safe in a radiant bubble.

He was heavy, and he occupied every inch of her. She'd never been as close to anyone. She loved him so much, she overflowed with adoration. Her hands shifted from his shoulders to snag in the soft curls at his nape. She settled into the hay. A soft gasp escaped, as the new position changed how he felt inside her.

He tilted up on his elbows, looking concerned, looking like he cared. Portia reminded herself not to succumb to romantic dreams, even if an unwise woman might mistake the glow in his eyes for love.

"Are you all right?"

She summoned another smile. "Yes, I'm wonderful."

Portia loved being connected to Alaric. She loved the raw physicality of this experience.

He smiled back. "You are indeed." Before she could bask in the compliment, he frowned again. "I'm sorry I hurt you."

"I don't mind." She touched his cheek, feeling whiskers under her fingers. "I'm so glad we got to do this."

He adopted a knowing air. "We're not done yet. Not by a long chalk."

Her eyes rounded with astonishment. "But you've…"

Pushed inside me. Taken my virginity. Claimed me as yours.

"There's more."

More? The mind boggled. She frowned. "Will it hurt?"

"I hope not. Shall we see?"

She stretched out and curled her toes in exquisite anticipation. The movement awoke a flutter deep inside her. Akin to when he touched her between her legs with such combustible effect.

What he'd done so far fitted with Juliet's description of the marital act. While the actual deed was richer and more complicated, at least she understood the path that she was on. Now she wasn't nearly so sure.

"Yes, please." She lifted her knees again and curled her arms around his back. She loved that she could touch him as much as she wanted.

Upon a faint laugh, Alaric kissed her. Despite his light tone, his kiss was long and intense. Portia surrendered with wholehearted passion. She couldn't confess her love. Not in words, at least. But when they kissed like this, her heart declared how precious he was.

The ardent kiss distracted her, so when he moved,

he caught her unawares.

Instinctively, she went taut to keep him where he was. A muttered protest escaped her, and she bumped her hips up.

As he lifted his head, his groan was heartfelt. "Do that again."

"Do what?"

"Squeeze me tight."

This time, she did it on purpose. Rapture washed over his features. "Yes," he purred.

He shifted again. Still away.

Her nails dug into his nape. "Don't go."

"This is part of the more."

"Oh," she said, then "oh" again in a different tone altogether as he pulled back. She felt every inch of the withdrawal. She dug her fingers into his back, where his muscles clenched and released through his shirt.

Without quite leaving her body, he thrust forward. There was no pain, only the intoxicating sensation of her body adjusting to him. Portia sighed with enjoyment when he went deeper. The next time, she knew what to expect. She'd seen animals mate. How stupid she was not to understand that humans were animals, too.

Alaric established a rhythm as relentless as waves rushing up a beach. Flickers of pleasure ignited to become torment. Every nerve in her body awoke to what he did. She moaned and bowed up to take more. Heat and hunger surged higher and higher.

She strained for something that remained just out of reach. Her next moan verged on a sob. "Alaric..."

"Come for me," he crooned.

She didn't know what he meant. She bit her lip hard as the beckoning became red-hot demand. Still, he kept up that steady movement, taking her further with each plunge until she felt likely to shred into a thousand pieces.

His breath was ragged, and his skin turned into a furnace as she writhed beneath him. Under her hands, his back was hard like granite. Warm, living granite.

He shifted his weight onto one arm and slipped his hand between her legs to seek that hidden place that gave her such a frisson. Tension coalesced into a blast of light and heat.

Suddenly Portia soared free through the storm. The experience transcended anything that she'd ever known. Ecstasy crashed through her like lightning. The world turned gold and bright. She cried out and pressed closer to Alaric as molten fire coursed through her.

His rhythm faltered and turned choppy. His breath emerged in audible gasps. With a guttural groan, he wrenched out of her arms and slumped face down in the hay.

The abrupt end pierced her pleasure like a slap. She opened shocked eyes to watch him. He jerked in what looked like pain and groaned again.

"Alaric, are you all right?" The words scraped over a throat sore after her cries of pleasure.

He lay unmoving, face buried in his folded arms. It was difficult to brush aside the mists of pleasure, but she was worried. Forcing a body as loose as wet string to move, she rose on her elbows and turned her head to study him.

It seemed to take him a year to answer, but finally he turned onto his back with a heavy sigh. He still breathed with great gusts, as if he starved for air. His eyes remained shut.

She couldn't help glancing down to his gaping breeches, but the loose shirt preserved his modesty. "What is it?" she asked, disquiet knotting her stomach.

"I promised I'd save you from a baby," he muttered. He looked as far from the elegant Duke of Granville as it was possible to be. His face was drawn, and his hair was disheveled. His golden whiskers caught the lamplight.

"Yes," she said. Then after a pause, "Thank you."

His lips twitched and to her relief, he looked more familiar. "You're welcome."

Another silence fell. Portia hadn't expected to feel awkward after that breathtaking intimacy. But she wasn't sure how to handle this taciturn man who had been such a superb lover.

At last, Alaric glanced over and took her arm. "How are you?"

"I'm fine," she said in a flat voice.

"Good."

She didn't understand the look that he directed at her. But then, she didn't understand most of what had happened since he'd so unceremoniously broken away.

With growing surprise, she realized that he felt awkward, too. That made her feel less inadequate. She was terrified that his strange reaction was rooted in dissatisfaction. Just because she'd stormed the gates of heaven didn't mean that he'd experienced a similar epiphany.

Her shaking hand tugged up her shift. In the heat of passion, she'd reveled in his pleasure in her body. But lying here while her lover turned away, she couldn't help but feel a bit cheap.

Too little, too late, she couldn't avoid acknowledging.

"Can you bear to kiss me, do you think?" he asked in a diffident voice.

That sounded more promising. "Do you want me to?"

The dark gold brows lowered in displeasure. She

was – almost – sure he was displeased with himself and not with her. His words confirmed that suspicion. "I'm sorry, my darling. I'm acting like a blasted idiot. You were such a wonder in my arms, I nearly stayed too long."

Calling her a wonder mollified hurt feelings. The "my darling" was even better. He'd never used the endearment before. He didn't have to tell her that he wasn't given to insincere pronouncements. While calling her his darling didn't mean that he loved her, it indicated an affection that she'd started to doubt.

Even better, he sounded like himself now. Like the kind man she knew.

"I was worried that I'd done something wrong," she admitted in a shaky voice. Crazy to feel like weeping, after the most sublime experience of her life.

But she discovered that giving her body to a man pierced her deepest emotions and left her vulnerable in ways she'd never been vulnerable before.

Through hazy vision, Portia saw his face scrunch into a grimace of self-disgust. His grip on her arm changed to a caress. "You did everything right. You did so much right, you damn near broke my heart. Mere mortals aren't made to dwell in paradise."

Her megrims receded, as she understood that Alaric had undergone a similar emotional experience. She blinked away the last of her silly tears and blindly turned toward him. Strong arms enclosed her. His lips met hers, and she yielded to the magic of his kiss. When he lifted his head, she was nestled into his side and her hand rested above his pounding heart.

"I've never made love in a stable before," he said, his voice still choked.

"Me either," she said, then sneezed violently.

CHAPTER FIFTEEN

Granville held Portia's hand and drew her up the stairs to the lodge's door. It was full night now. While the sky remained cloudy, the rain had stopped. He inserted the massive iron key that he'd retrieved from its hiding place in the stables into the old-fashioned lock.

As he pushed the heavy, wooden door open, Portia remained quiet. She'd been quiet since that blazing encounter in the stables. He wished to heaven that he knew what she was thinking. She said that she was fine, but he wasn't so sure. Not being sure drove him to distraction.

She carried a lamp in her free hand. Her other hand curled around his. She didn't seem averse to touching him, and their kisses had been as ardent and sweet as ever. But he'd always appreciated the ease between them, especially as most people were too aware of his rank to treat him like a fellow human.

Now she wasn't easy. Not at all. She seemed willing to stay and touch him, but beyond that, he had no idea what went on in her head.

The lamp revealed a dark entry with a corridor

leading off it. The house was small and simple, at least in ducal terms. A narrow foyer across the front, with a modest drawing room and dining room off the corridor. Kitchens and storerooms in the basement. A pair of bedroom suites on the next floor. Smaller rooms for visitors above that. Servants' quarters in the attics beneath the roof, with its pretty terrace and views over surrounding woods and hills.

Plenty of room to entertain a mistress, if the mistress was in a mood for entertainment. "Shall we go down to the kitchens and see what the Johnsons have left us for dinner?" He hated his false heartiness, but her quietness made him edgier than a cat in a dogs' home.

"Do you know the way?" she asked, as if he'd said that he was about to paint himself purple.

"I usually cater for myself when I'm here. It's one of the few places where I don't need to keep up the Duke of Granville's dignity."

She shook her head, more in puzzlement than denial, he thought. "I really did have you wrong."

He wanted to ask whether she understood him better now, but to his shame, he was afraid of her answer. Damn it, he'd imagined that becoming her lover would bolster their closeness, but she'd never felt more like a stranger.

She hadn't felt like a stranger when he was deep inside her, relishing the joy that she took in his possession. Then he'd been convinced that he united with the other half of his soul.

The physical pleasure had surpassed anything in his experience, but it was the emotional union that had astounded him. Tupping Portia Frain turned out to be a gift of the spirit as well as the flesh. He couldn't wait to do it all again.

Once he'd fathomed what troubled her. The thought of her unhappy tied his gut into tangles. The thought that she could be unhappy because of something he'd done or said made him feel like he'd eaten bad fish.

He released her hand to let her precede him inside. "So dinner?"

She placed the lamp on a demilune table beneath a gold-framed mirror. For a moment, he caught her beauty twofold. The real Portia and her shadowy image in the glass. "I'd like a wash if that's possible."

What a dunderhead he was. She'd traveled from London. She'd rubbed down a horse. She'd scrambled his brains with that tumble in the hay. "I'll take you upstairs and show you your room. Then I'll fetch some hot water."

She glanced at him. "My room? Aren't we sharing?"

That sounded promising. "If you'd like to."

He picked up a candle from the table and lit it from the lantern. Perhaps if he could see better, he'd have a clearer idea of her mood.

"Yes."

He waited for more. Nothing came.

Granville headed for the staircase that rose to the upper floors, but stopped when she spoke. "Why don't I come down to the kitchens with you?"

"You don't have to."

"I know."

Bristlingly conscious of Portia following in his wake, he lit a couple of lamps near the base of the stairs. He continued toward the back of the house where a narrow stairwell led down to the kitchens.

"Watch out. It's steep." Catching her hand again, he went ahead with the candle held high.

The fire in the range was banked, but it provided heat and shadowy light. Portia leaned back against the scrubbed pine table and glanced around with interest.

It was his first chance since they'd been in the hay to have a good look at her. He took full advantage of the moment.

She looked thoroughly debauched – and more beautiful than ever. When he already thought her the most beautiful woman he'd ever seen.

Her hair tumbled around her in golden waves. Her face was flushed. The dim light lent her blue eyes sensual mystery.

"What is it?" she asked.

He made no attempt to hide the fondness in his smile. "You brought a few souvenirs back from the stables."

He plucked a couple of strands of hay from her hair and dropped them to the floor. He'd never had sex in a stable before. It turned out that he'd been missing out.

Her dress was in complete disarray. The pelisse hung loose and open, and one lone button closed her bodice over the crumpled shift. Her magnificent bosom threatened to spill free.

A powerful memory jolted him. Dear God, those breasts were glorious. Full and white and firm. Lavish and round in his hands. Crowned with the sweetest pink nipples.

His arousal was unexpected. Unexpected, not because he didn't always want her. He did. But he'd only just lost himself in an orgasm that had drained him to the lees.

Granville didn't live at the mercy of his baser impulses, however thoroughly he'd enjoyed his previous liaisons. But Portia Frain awoke his animal urges. All he could think about right now was having her.

Which was out of the question, bugger it.

He'd just taken her virginity. He couldn't start heaving about on top of her again so soon. Clumsily, he set his candle on the plain wrought iron mantelpiece and told himself to settle down.

But when he turned back toward Portia, she regarded him with such blatant longing that he couldn't stop himself from crossing the flagstones and seizing her in his arms. She tumbled into his embrace as if she, too, couldn't bear any space between them. From the instant their lips met, the kiss was urgent.

He caught her rump with eager hands and hoisted her onto the table. Lifting her skirts as he advanced, he pushed forward. With a naturalness that set his heart racing, she parted her legs and hooked them around his thighs.

At this angle, kissing her was uncomfortable and superb at the same time. She hung off his shoulders as her lips tormented his. He lashed his arms around her back to prolong the contact.

Catching the lower lip in his teeth, he bit down gently. She let out a muffled cry and licked his top lip. Still using his teeth to tease her, he eased her back onto the tabletop. He propped himself above her and broke the kiss. Her lips were red, and pink marks on her cheeks and chest showed where his whiskers had chafed her.

Dismay added an awkward note to his desire. He was about to apologize and step back to help her to sit up, when she reached to undo the single button fastening her dress.

Gulping for air, he sought her gaze. Her blue eyes were languid and shaded by thick dark gold lashes.

"Portia?" He couldn't tell if the word was protest or plea.

The lush mouth, glistening after his kiss, curled into a smile that possessed all the sensual knowledge in the world. Granville tried to tell himself that she'd been a virgin until an hour ago. That her innocence deserved respect and care.

But that smile invited him to join her in ecstasy. That smile told him that she wanted more of him. That smile belonged to a temptress who knew exactly what she needed.

Her wicked hand brushed the green edges of her dress aside to reveal her shift. He couldn't help noticing her nipples peaking against the linen. His fingers curled against the worn wooden surface of the table, and his balls tightened into agony.

With one hand, she released the tie at the neck of her shift. His gaze fastened on her breasts. Then very slowly, so slowly that he feared he might explode before she finished, her fingers drifted down to dip into the valley between her breasts, lowering her shift to reveal more and more skin.

Granville swallowed to moisten a mouth as dry as the Sahara.

Her smile widened into catlike satisfaction, before that fiendish hand pushed down the sagging shift to reveal perfect breasts.

"Touch yourself," he said in a voice like gravel, every drop of blood in his body rushing to his erect prick.

Her hand went still, and she regarded him with faint puzzlement. Then with an action that pummeled all the breath from his body, she took one nipple and rolled it into a point.

By all that was holy, she'd kill him before she finished. With a guttural groan, he shifted his weight onto one arm as he reached down to rub his cock.

"Like this?" she asked in a throaty voice.

Portia began to tease her other nipple. Her erratic breathing set her creamy flesh rising and falling in a riveting display.

"Yes, like that." The sight of her slender hand fondling those beaded crests was the most arousing thing that he'd ever seen. His hips rocked against his hand, as he struggled not to lose control.

Frantically, he ripped at the buttons on his breeches. One clicked on the stone floor as it flew off. He gave a great exhalation of relief and closed his hand around the thick shaft.

Still it wasn't enough. It would only be enough when he was thrusting between those pale thighs.

He swooped to kiss her with a passion that verged on frenzy. She arched up to kiss him back and tightened her legs around his buttocks to bring him closer.

Shaking as if he had a fever, he wrenched back to delve beneath her skirts. A couple of ruthless tugs tore her damp, stained drawers. She gave a muffled squeak, as shreds of white material drifted downward.

Granville paused long enough to survey the feathery dark gold hair protecting her sex. Last time, he hadn't lingered to enjoy the view.

He was too stirred up to delay. When he shucked his breeches down to his knees, his dick bobbed free in hungry readiness.

Seizing her hips in eager hands, he pulled her toward him. He plunged deep into her body. Heat. Pressure. Welcome. The sweetest welcome in the whole wide world.

She shuddered under his thrust, her hands closing on the naked skin of his hips. Her fingers dug into his flesh, as she convulsed around him. Her swift reaction astonished him. She was the most responsive lover he'd ever known. He loved that his merest touch set her on fire.

He closed his eyes and fought to contain his impulse to spill. As her orgasm went on and on, control became more arduous. His hands formed fists on the wood, as her intimate muscles clenched.

The pleasure was so intense, it was almost violent. The urge to take this extraordinary joining to its natural end rose. Only the last threads of honor reminded him that he'd promised to save her from conceiving.

Damn it to hell, it was agony to pull out.

He gritted his teeth and wrested free, while she quaked against the table. Shaking, he shoved her skirts and petticoats up to uncover her stomach, twitching with contractions.

While hot seed spurted onto her skin, he held his tumescent dick in one hand. Catching her hand, he curved it around him as the mighty release faded. She fumbled for a breathtaking moment before she got the idea. When she squeezed, the pleasure took the edge off the grim practicality of his actions.

Unfocused dark blue eyes surveyed him. She looked dazed and satisfied and exhausted. And lovely enough to steal his heart.

When Granville released the hand that he'd jammed around his dick, she didn't let him go. Her touch flowed through him like balm on a war wound.

Gently he disengaged her fingers, trying to ignore the shadow of complaint on her face. He straightened to tear his shirt over his head and tug up his breeches.

He wiped the sticky mess from her stomach, then flung the ruined garment to the floor. She stroked him once more, then let her arm drift to her side. He loved that she wasn't coy. She made no attempt to hide her carnal satisfaction in their couplings.

Granville drew her up for a kiss that he hoped conveyed what a miracle she was. He wanted to tell her that she was marvelous. He wanted to praise and explain and soothe. But his ability to muster a coherent sentence forsook him.

Portia, too, it seemed. She hadn't spoken since

their bodies united.

He'd find words later. This time, he had no doubts that she was happy.

When he lifted her off the table, she was floppy with weariness and satiation. She sagged against him, as if all her bones had disintegrated in that titanic wave of pleasure. He caught her lush arse, and she curled her legs around his hips. Her arms circled his neck, and she buried her face in his chest.

A couple of tottery steps before he collapsed into a cushioned armchair beside the fire. It took little effort to arrange her on his lap. Which was lucky, because he wasn't in much better form than she was. Her head rested on his shoulder and her lovely legs splayed loose across his knees.

Granville put his arms around Portia and held her close as ecstasy receded. It was a long time later before he said, "Next time, I'm taking you to bed."

It was cold and rainy outside. Here beside the banked fire in the lodge's kitchens, Portia was beautifully warm. The man she loved held her safe in his arms.

She stirred from sleep to squint at the plain slate clock on the mantel. Nearly an hour had passed since that thrilling encounter on the table. She must have dropped off straightaway. Hardly surprising after she'd been so on edge all week, afraid of what might happen once she and the duke were alone. Even more afraid that something would stop her going away with him.

Not to mention the overwhelming emotional reaction to losing her virginity and discovering what pleasure awaited in a lover's arms. This lover anyway.

She glanced up at Alaric, the movement setting off a volley of unfamiliar pangs and twinges in her body. He slept, too.

His musky scent teased her nostrils. Sandalwood and Alaric, the perfume of paradise. With a little bit of horse included. Her lips twitched, as she pictured his self-deprecating smile if she shared that thought with him.

Heavens, she must be crushing him. She should move, although it was the last thing that she wanted to do.

Gingerly she eased herself up from where she curled in his lap. Not gingerly enough. Hazy green eyes opened, and he gave her a smile of such heart-stopping sweetness that she wanted to cry. For most of their acquaintance, those eyes had been remote and watchful. Joy filled her, now that he'd removed the barriers between them.

His arms tightened. "Where the devil do you think you're going, madam?"

"I'm squashing you." Sleep weighted her voice.

His lips quirked. "It's a lovely way to die."

Love crammed her heart, as she aimed a playful punch at his arm. "Ungallant, sir."

Laughing, he folded her back against him. "Your pardon, my lady."

He caught her chin and brushed his lips across hers. Not a kiss of passion but one of such tenderness, her heart tilted.

Portia glanced down and noticed that her breasts were bare. She tugged her shift into place but didn't bother buttoning her dress.

She rested her head on his shoulder. If she could summon the energy, she'd be scared out of her wits at the revelation that she wanted to cuddle up to Alaric until the crack of doom. She'd arrived determined to remain levelheaded. Yet already on their first night, she fell victim to impossible daydreams.

She'd slipped into another doze when he spoke. "Tell me why you seduced me in the stables."

He sounded interested, not resentful, she was relieved to hear. The hand that she pressed over his heart moved in a caress. It was bliss to touch his naked skin. "Stables have been rather lucky for us, don't you think?"

His chest expanded on a soft laugh. "Undoubtedly."

She placed a kiss on his pectoral.

"Why are you giggling?" he asked idly, his hand playing with her tangle of hair.

"The hair on your chest tickles my nose." She loved the evidence of how his masculine body differed from hers. Places he was hard and she was soft.

With gentle insistence, he tugged on her hair to raise her face to his. This time, his lips lingered. "Better?"

Portia wrinkled her nose. "It's certainly nice." She laid her hand flat on his cheek. "You've got hair here, too."

"I should have shaved. I would have."

If she'd waited. She owed him an explanation. But how to put it into words? She stared at his chest, as she thought how to phrase this. "You're such a gentleman, Alaric."

He gave a self-derisive grunt. "After today, I'm not sure that's true."

She smiled at his rueful tone. "No, you're still a gentleman."

"Isn't that a good thing?"

He sounded confused and a little hurt, which was what she'd feared before launching into this awkward confession. "Of course it is. I love that I trust you to protect me. I love that your word is sacrosanct. I love that you treat me with such respect."

I love you.

She couldn't say that. Not now. Perhaps never. A rift split her heart. A rift that would only widen over time.

"Why do I feel there's a 'but' coming?"

Because there was. "I've been as jumpy as a flea all week."

"It's natural to be nervous."

"It is. But I felt like I'd swallowed a volcano."

His laugh was short and sharp. "That sounds frightfully unpleasant."

"Not altogether. It was exciting, too. But when we arrived, I realized that you meant to ease me into your bed. Dinner. Conversation. Everything elegant and measured."

"It seemed the civilized choice. I've never been a woman's first lover. I didn't want to frighten you."

She sent Alaric a direct look. "I wasn't afraid. I was desperate. This last week of seeing you in snatches left me feeling like I starved to death inches away from the world's most lavish banquet."

"Portia..." Heat flared in his eyes. This kiss held a promise of passion. "I felt like that, too."

Reassured, she continued with more confidence. "I didn't want you treating me like spun glass. I didn't want you undressing me piece by piece. I didn't want you waiting and waiting and waiting. I didn't want to wait either, getting fidgety about what was coming."

Humor turned his lips down. With his rumpled golden hair and wry amusement, he looked so charming, she wanted to melt. "Instead you shoved me into a haystack?"

After this evening, she'd imagined that she'd lost the ability to blush. It turned out that she was wrong. "Did you mind terribly?"

His smile deepened. "It was the most glorious thing that's ever happened to me." He paused. "With perhaps the exception of having you on the kitchen table. By now, it should be clear that I can't resist you."

She stretched up to kiss him, taking her time. "I can't resist you either, which makes us a good match." Oh, no, did that imply marriage? She rushed on. "I look forward to joining you in a bed."

"So do I. I want to undress you at my leisure, if you can bear the delay. I can't believe we're still in our clothes."

"Almost." She raked her nails through the soft fur on his chest. His skin twitched beneath her fingers.

He caught her hand and brought it to his lips. "Let me be a gentleman now and allow you to wash and have something to eat." A wicked light flared in his eyes, turned them richest emerald. "After all, you'll need your strength."

Anticipation made her shiver. "Oh?"

His smile turned wicked, too. "Later."

"I'm so glad I found that haystack." Over her raised wineglass, Portia cast Alaric a teasing glance. "I wouldn't have been able to eat a thing otherwise. Which would be a pity, when Mrs. Johnson cooked us that delicious dinner."

He responded with an amused grunt and surveyed the ruins of their meal spread across the mahogany table. The dining room was small enough to feel cozy, even with only two occupants. Heavy green velvet curtains kept out the night air. A fire in the hearth added its flickering light to the candles. "I'd hate you to miss that chicken and leek pie."

"And the cheese savories and deviled eggs," she said after a sip of wine.

"My sacrifice paid dividends." His solemn tone made her choke on her wine.

The meal had been surprisingly lighthearted. Conversation had flowed. Alaric was at ease here in a way that she'd never seen before. Or perhaps like her, he found that satisfying their sexual appetites allayed their tension.

"I salute your heroism, Your Grace." She suited action to words.

Setting down her glass, she studied her companion. He wore another beautifully tailored coat. The unadorned black emphasized his magnificent form.

After they left the capacious armchair in the kitchen, he'd brought their bags in. She'd had a wash and changed into a clean gown, and Alaric had put on a fresh shirt. The shirt that he'd worn earlier had ended up in the fire.

Now he relaxed in his chair, eyes slumbrous. With casual grace, he dangled his half-empty wineglass from one hand. He had beautiful hands, long-fingered and elegant. The light glinted off the heavy gold signet ring and turned the wine to gleaming ruby. Portia couldn't help remembering those hands on her skin, trailing heat wherever they touched. The images stirred a lazy ripple of arousal.

Portia wanted Alaric so much, she was nearly sick with it.

With a decisive gesture, he set his glass down. "What would you like to do now? I've got some books in the drawing room, or we could play cards. There's a piano, too, if you fancy some music."

"I'm not very accomplished on the piano."

"Do you sing?"

"Like a crow with a sore throat."

That made him laugh. She loved his appreciation for her odd sense of humor. She loved the way that every time he laughed, he become less the formidable Duke of Granville and more charming, endearing Alaric Dempster. "God help us."

"The comparison is unfair to the crow." She put down her glass and shot him a direct look. "Do you really want to stay down here, doing the pretty as if we're polite strangers? Or are you being a gentleman again?"

His answering look was equally frank. "I don't want you thinking that the only thing I value about you is that beguiling body."

Gratification flooded her. "You haven't seen much of the beguiling body yet. Aren't you curious?"

His strangled response combined a groan and another laugh. "What do you think?"

Portia sucked in a shaky breath. Her breasts swelled against her bodice, as if they strained toward his touch. "I think we've got three days to enjoy each other. We can play cards in London."

Without raising an eyebrow, his gaze dropped to her bosom, revealed to advantage under a scooped décolletage that she usually covered with a scarf for modesty's sake. Not tonight. Modesty remained behind in London. She loved how he ogled her cleavage.

Heat spread from her brimming heart to her extremities. She shifted on the chair to ease the erotic weight. For pity's sake, she was in a bad way. He just had to look at her, and she melted with female need.

Smile lines deepened beside his eyes as he watched her squirm, although his lips retained a serious line. She had no doubt that he knew how he affected her. "Are you saying it's time we both retired upstairs?"

"You promised me a bed, I believe."

He rose and proffered his hand. "Then, my darling, let's go."

Portia didn't move straightaway. She couldn't. It was that blasted "my darling." It always turned her silly.

Scolding herself for being a sappy lackwit, she stood and took his hand. "Excellent plan, Your Grace."

CHAPTER SIXTEEN

Granville put away the last of the plates from their dinner and turned to watch Portia wipe down the table where he'd enjoyed the most explosive sexual encounter of his life. While he'd loved what they'd done in the hay, his awareness of her inexperience had helped him maintain some vestige of control. Astonishing to think that soon afterward, he'd swive Portia in brazen abandon across a table.

She was the most exciting woman he'd ever known. Even here in the kitchen performing the most everyday of tasks, something about the sway of her hips and the deft movements of her hands het him up like a randy adolescent.

He was in a ferment for her. He'd hungered for that exquisite body. Now that he'd had her twice, he should feel less on edge. But the craving to tup her again left him strung as tight as a violin.

"We could have cleaned up in the morning," he said with a mildness that in no way reflected his desperation.

She glanced up with a smile, as she untied the apron that she'd found in the larder and laid it over the back of a wooden chair. "I know."

"But you like things done right."

For all his ravening impatience, there was something deeply pleasing about watching this woman he wanted beyond all others pottering about like a middle-class housewife tending to the man in her life.

"Juliet made sure her sisters were proficient in the domestic arts. She said we couldn't run a household if we didn't know how to do everything ourselves."

"That sounds like Juliet."

His attempt at a neutral tone must have failed, because Portia cast him a troubled glance. "I suppose you hate her. With good cause. But she's my sister, and I love her."

"As you should." He might have no experience of the love between siblings, but he'd noted that the three Frain sisters formed a close-knit unit.

"I won't mention her again." He hated to see her mouth turn down with a hint of sadness. "But she was like a mother to me, and she sacrificed so much to bring us up. Papa was useless."

Her father was completely stagestruck. Unless the topic was Shakespeare, he had no interest in it. Granville blamed Lord Portdown's inadequate parenting for the recent scandals that had engulfed the Frain family.

"You mustn't feel bad talking about Juliet." He examined his feelings. "You know, I don't hate her."

"You're being a gentleman again."

His gesture was apologetic. "I can't help myself."

"No, you can't." Her smile indicated that she wasn't displeased.

However she teased, something told him that she liked him as he was. And for who he was. Not because he held a great title and had riches to burn. "I mean it. I don't hate her."

Her flattened lips dismissed his statement. "She treated you shabbily. I love her, and even I think that."

"But you see, that's it. She didn't love me. She loved Evesham. I despise the bastard, but I'm sure he loves her back. Better all round that they marry each other, than someone else, don't you agree?"

Portia still didn't look like she believed him. "That's very generous."

"Not at all." He'd never eaten his heart out over Juliet, although she'd given his pride a good wallop when she eloped with his worst enemy. "Anyway..."

"Anyway?"

"If I'd married Juliet, you and I would never have come together." He spoke from absolute conviction. "I'd give up an awful lot, if the end result was having you to myself like this."

She stood stock-still and regarded him with an expression that he couldn't altogether read.

"Say something," he said, half-joking.

She shook her head, as if aligning thoughts in complete disarray. "I'm..."

Another silence.

"Pleased? Relieved?"

The soft light in her blue eyes made something unfamiliar inside him unfurl like a flower opening to the sun. The sensation verged on painful.

She raised her hand to her lips, as if holding back a confession. That newborn corner of his soul reached toward her, but when she spoke, it was in answer to his remark. "Pleased."

For a charged moment, they stared at each other. Granville couldn't help but feel that a separate conversation took place out of earshot. He'd hand over half his fortune if he could eavesdrop.

"That's...that's good," he said gruffly.

She blinked as if fighting tears, which made no

sense. Her smile hinted at a tremble, too.

He couldn't bear the thought of her crying. It made him want to rampage around, breaking the expensive china. Given how carefully she'd washed up, she wouldn't appreciate that at all.

Then brave, forthright Portia returned. She squared her shoulders and held out her hand. "Did you say you'd take me to bed?"

Her voice sounded normal, with a rich undercurrent of sultry invitation. Relief tinged Granville's exhalation, although for the life of him, he couldn't say what had scared him just now.

Portia wanted sex. Sex he could give her. He forced that strange, vulnerable part of him back into the darkness, where he hoped it would fade away and die. He strode past the table and lashed his arms around her, kissing her until she turned into a bundle of molten pleasure. If truth be told, his knees felt a little unsteady, too.

"Have you finished down here?" he murmured, nipping her earlobe.

She gave a start. "I have."

"Good." He released her and went around the room, extinguishing every lamp but one. After stopping to kiss her again, he took her hand. He collected the last lamp from the bench and mounted the stairs.

Granville pushed open the door to his suite and placed the lamp on a chest. Before Portia's arrival, he'd always slept alone in this house. It felt significant that she was the first woman to share the big bed with the carved oak headboard.

Portia gave a muffled giggle. "I feel like a heroine in a gothic novel, lured to her doom by the seductive villain."

She giggled again when with a fiendish laugh, he pushed her against the door. "There's no escape, my pretty."

Placing her hands on his waist, she spoke in an exaggerated tremolo. He approved of a heroine with a heaving bosom. "What shall I do?"

He nibbled a path along her elegant neck. "Yield to my satanic demands, my dear."

She whimpered with pleasure, and her hand slid down to fondle his buttocks, bringing him closer. He stiffened in an instant and groaned, as his lips explored the shoulder bared beneath her stylish blue gown. Her breath changed, and she squirmed against him.

"You're not supposed to encourage your evil seducer." His voice was rough and unsteady. He enjoyed the game, but he had trouble thinking past the ache in his balls. "They'll banish you from the league of Minerva Press heroines, if you keep doing that."

"I'll have to take up a career as the evil villain's mistress." Her words emerged in fits and starts. The game turned serious for Portia, too.

He flattened his palms on the door and pushed back to break the contact. "The evil villain is on board with that."

Her theatrical pout made him laugh. "So why is my ruthless seducer playing coy?"

"Because this time he wants to savor the experience." His voice lowered into longing. "I've dreamed of seeing you naked more often than you can know."

"Why do you say things like that?"

"Because they're true?"

"How on earth can I say no?"

"I hope you won't."

She observed him through her lashes. The effect was intoxicatingly seductive. "You know, I'd rather like to see a naked man myself."

"A naked man or *this* naked man?"

"Do I have another option?"

He laughed and swung her toward the center of the room. "No, you do not, my lovely."

"In that case, I'll settle for what I've got."

She rose on her toes and kissed him quickly. Before he got too interested, she stepped back. "What should I do?"

Granville told himself to simmer down. To think, he'd once considered himself a civilized man. He'd certainly believed that he was immune from ever becoming a slave to physical impulse. Portia Frain transformed him into someone at the mercy of animal appetites, someone he had difficulty recognizing.

"Take down your hair." The words emerged as a command. This close to the edge, soft entreaties were beyond him.

She pouted again. Somewhere since he'd stumbled across her in Wapping and now, she'd learned a coquette's tricks. Damn it, those tricks worked far too well. "I've got to do all the work?"

A self-derisive laugh. "Better I keep my hands to myself for the moment."

The answer didn't placate her. "From whose point of view?"

"Portia..." he growled with a mixture of reproof and pleading.

She sighed and lifted graceful arms to the loose confection of gold curls. The posture arched her back and raised her opulent bosom until she threatened to overflow her dress. Her eyes made promises that she was his for the asking.

Her gaze clung to his as very slowly, she drew out a pin. One long tress unraveled downward.

Air was suddenly in short supply. Something about the leisured play of her hands in that shining mass of hair and the sulky look on her face turned Granville's blood to steam.

She must guess how aroused he was, because the next pin came out even more slowly. She held it in her hand before dropping it to the carpet.

His hands closed so tight that they ached. How could she do this when he wasn't touching her? How could she do this when he'd already lost himself twice this evening?

For pity's sake, she was touching her hair. Only her hair.

How the devil was he ready to explode, just looking at her bedamned hair?

Another three pins. Another three serpentine locks draping those magnificent curves. Another shuddering inhalation from Granville.

Most of her hair remained up, displaying her slender neck. To his surprise – and discomfort – she stopped playing with her coiffure and her hands descended to filmy blue skirts.

"What are you doing?" Could that strangled voice be his?

Her glance was searing enough to melt iron. Portia knew exactly what she did to him, and she relished every moment. "Undressing."

Granville closed his eyes in frustration. Only briefly, because he didn't want to miss a moment of the spectacular show. "God help me."

Her lips twitched. She didn't look sulky anymore. She looked exultant. If at first his experience had given him an advantage, now they were equals in this sensual world.

Inch by inch, she lifted her skirts. Tormenting him, and glorying in his agony.

His attention dropped from that goddess's face to neat ankles above narrow feet in blue satin slippers. Shapely legs encased in white silk stockings. Higher still to pretty sky-blue garters. She sent him another of those goading glances that threatened to turn him to smoking ash. His breath rasped out, as if he was in danger of suffocation.

Whatever she saw must please her, because skirts and petticoats rose to uncover loose drawers. White, so delicate that they were near-transparent, edged with lace. The drawers split at the crotch to reveal feathery pubic hair.

His groan echoed around the room. Her smile intensified, as she caught her skirts in one hand and settled the other over her mound. "Goodness me, how…damp I am," she purred.

Every inch of his body caught fire. She'd kill him before she was done.

"Portia…" He pressed his palm to the throbbing weight of his erection. It didn't help. "You're enjoying this."

His accusation gratified her, he could see. "Indeed I am."

Her fingers shifted to the string on her drawers. One deft tug and it came loose. The garment sagged to reveal the sinuous curve of her hips. A couple of fiendish wiggles, and her drawers dropped to her feet. Without looking down, she stepped out of them. Instead, she watched Granville with an avid attention almost as arousing as the sight of her disrobing.

"Turn around," he croaked, crushing his hand to his rampant stand.

He wasn't sure that she'd obey. She'd seized control of the encounter. But praise all the angels – or Satan himself, because there was nothing angelic about this seduction – she presented her back. Bunched skirts covered her to behind her knees.

"Lift your dress." His voice sounded like it scraped over broken glass.

Again, she obeyed, although she didn't hurry. By the time he glimpsed the lush flesh of her bare buttocks, he feared that he was losing his mind.

He forgot good intentions. Hell, he came close to forgetting his bloody name.

"Lean over the base of the bed," he growled.

Portia cast him a questioning glance over her shoulder, but something in his face must have convinced her that this was no time for discussion.

Granville wasn't surprised that he looked determined. He was on the brink of going up like a gunpowder store struck by an enemy shell. If his face conveyed even half his hunger, he must look like he wanted to devour her in one bite.

She was still a few steps from the baseboard when he ripped at the fastenings on his breeches. Her skirts had tumbled down, concealing that superb arse. It didn't matter. The sight remained etched in his mind. "Bend over."

She took up her position. "Are you going to…" she faltered out in a breathless voice.

It could be excitement. Or it could be her stance, stooped over the bed.

"God, yes," he rasped, like a dying man given water.

"How…"

His hands seized her waist. He prayed that she wouldn't tell him to stop. If she did, he'd have to, but by God, retreating now would rip him to shreds. "Yes?"

The delay extended forever. In his mind at least. "How exciting."

A gust of relief escaped. "I don't deserve you, Portia."

Granville stepped closer, burying his dick in her skirts. It twitched in longing. So close to where it wanted to be, inside Portia.

"What should I do?"

"Brace yourself," he muttered, shoving silk and linen out of the way. The scent of her arousal was sharp in his nostrils. Even if she hadn't told him that she loved what he did, his senses would know. "Why do women wear so many blasted clothes?"

"To torture our lovers?"

Despite his urgency, a grunt of laughter emerged. "It jolly well works. Spread your legs for me."

Again she cooperated without protest. His heart slammed against his ribs, when he saw her glistening pink vulva. He wanted to taste her there. Take his time. Send her to paradise again and again.

Later.

With an unsteady touch, he stroked her, relishing the slickness and heat. The sight of his hand toying with those rosy folds made him bite back a groan. She moaned as his finger found her clitoris. With another of those heart-stopping wiggles, she pushed back.

He caught her hips and took in the perfect view. Portia's feminine roundness, and the long, graceful back, and the untidy golden hair. The intriguing valley between her legs.

Her hands curled into claws on the embroidered silk coverlet. "Don't...wait," she panted, angling her arse higher.

As if she had to beg. He was utterly at her command.

On that thought, he plunged forward. Heat. Sumptuous constriction. *Home...*

Portia's soft cry didn't sound like distress. Even more encouraging, she bumped back to take more.

On a profane prayer of gratitude, Granville closed his eyes and began to move.

CHAPTER SEVENTEEN

*P*ortia's body stretched in a most satisfying way as Alaric pushed into her. She hardly noticed the slight burn on flesh unused to a man's possession before today. The faint sting was worth it in return for the bliss. What had seemed so unnatural a few hours ago now felt like the most perfect act in the world.

The sensation was marvelous, and in this rather shocking position, different from their earlier lovemaking. He settled so deep, she was sure that he must touch her womb. She released a shuddering breath, as she accommodated his size. She adored this moment when their bodies united and she basked in intimacy before the rise to transcendent release.

Although she loved that, too.

The bed's carved baseboard dug into her stomach, and it seemed odd not seeing Alaric's face. On the other hand, the act contained a delicious suspense.

She squirmed to encourage him to continue. And to see how that felt at this bizarre new angle. It turned out to be wondrous. A whimper of exhilaration escaped her.

Alaric leaned forward, pressing her into the mattress. He kissed her ear, the side of her face, her nape.

She twisted her head until her lips made clumsy contact with his. The kiss was succulent and untamed and frustrating, because their current position made a full exploration impossible.

After an interval as exasperating as it was arousing, he retreated. She gave an involuntary gasp. Every time he shifted, he stimulated a different place inside her.

Alaric began a long rhythmic glide, forward, back, then forward again. Every time he reached his limit, she felt as if he claimed her forever.

Portia clenched her hands in the coverlet beneath her, as the now familiar spiral toward rapture began. An incoherent sigh of surrender emerged.

He moved faster, although still with that purposeful, rocking action. Her excitement built toward release. Her muscles tightened around him, as the peak approached, irresistible as a flood tide.

When he made a guttural sound of approval, she contracted around him. He slid a hand down to squeeze her breast. Her arousal notched higher. Then higher again, when that seeking hand slipped under her bodice to tease her nipple. She gave a strangled moan.

By now, her entire body was a quivering mass of yearning. Her blood beat in time with his strokes, and her vision went foggy. Further and further she flew as she hurtled toward ultimate pleasure. The experience edged toward torture, as she teetered on the brink of losing herself.

All that gathering tension erupted into a blinding flash of sublime pleasure. With a harsh cry, she spasmed around him.

For a fraught moment, Alaric went still. Then he withdrew and bent over her, arms holding her tight. His hardness rubbed the small of her back before she felt the hot, sticky rush of his seed.

Gasping, still caught in that extraordinary whirlwind, Portia sagged under him. Fighting the urge to cry, she shifted to find a more comfortable position.

He'd launched her into a new and shining universe that touched all of her, heart and soul as well as body. How on earth could she remember that this was just a passing affair, when he took her to such heights? It wasn't fair. The beauty of what happened when their bodies united was so pure, it broke her heart.

What a fool she was. She'd believed that she understood what she agreed to when she came away with Alaric. It was too late to regret that she hadn't known enough to fear the way sharing her body would change her.

When he shifted, pleasure still rippled through her. She trembled under the brush of what she guessed must be his handkerchief, as he wiped his sperm off her bare skin.

Gently he brushed her hair aside and kissed her cheek. The action's tenderness deepened her emotional reaction to what she wished had been mere physical satisfaction. Nobody had ever cherished her like this. Her heart brimmed with joy, but it was joy pierced with longing for what she could never have.

Why must he treat her as something precious? She loved it, but it made accepting the bitter truth of her situation even harder. She couldn't reveal how she grieved that he didn't love her. He'd loathe causing unhappiness. He might even decide to end their affair.

That thought galvanized her into action. She pushed against the bed to straighten and released an involuntary groan.

"What is it?" Alaric was at her side immediately, supporting her elbow. "God forgive me, I didn't hurt you, did I?"

His frantic concern for her well-being only sharpened her worries. She must hide her unrequited love. Desolation might await once he finished with her, but that didn't mean she intended to forsake him until she had to.

"No, of course not." She battled to sound composed, but the catch in her voice betrayed her.

His hand tightened on her arm. "But you're in pain?"

Now he'd buttoned his breeches, he almost looked like nothing had happened between them. Except for the color along those slashing cheekbones and the fullness of his mouth.

Her laugh was wry. "I'm not in pain. But I've discovered muscles today that I didn't know I had."

He didn't look reassured. "You must have been uncomfortable while I took my pleasure."

She summoned a smile and trailed a finger down his cheek. He'd shaved before dinner, but now she felt the prickle of whiskers. "And I found my pleasure during... What should I call what we do?"

Juliet had spoken of conjugal union, but not only was that far too clinical for these fiery encounters, there was nothing conjugal about what she did with Alaric. And not likely to be either.

"You want to talk about vocabulary?" he asked in disbelief. He shifted to link his hands loosely about her waist. "After that?"

She rose on her toes and kissed him, appreciating that she could do it properly this time. When he kissed her back, she sensed that what they'd just done had given him more than physical satisfaction, too. His kiss and the shocked "after that?" told her everything that she needed to know.

Portia's disquiet had receded by the time she drew away. Her smile felt more natural, as she slid one hand behind his neck and gazed up at him. "How else will I know what to ask for?"

His laugh still held a trace of incredulity, even as his brows lowered in thought. "There are plenty of unacceptable terms."

"Good."

This time, he kissed her. "You're a rebel against your class, Portia Frain." Once if he'd said such a thing, she'd assume that it was criticism. Now she heard admiration in the musical baritone. "I should avoid you. You'll overturn the status quo before you're done. Then what will a dispossessed duke do with himself?"

He made her sound brave and daring, instead of a hopeless misfit in the society that she'd been born into. "This particular duke is welcome to work in my kennels." Sincerity crept in, despite her teasing. "I'm so impressed with how you've handled Jupiter. It's a waste that you've never owned a dog. You have such a deft touch with him."

And with women. A shiver rippled through her, as she recalled Alaric filling her to the hilt from behind.

His lips quirked with the ironic humor that always made her heart contract with longing. "That's all right, then. At least I won't starve."

"Should the revolution break out, I'll keep you in bread and cheese, Your Grace."

"Fresh bread?"

She stifled a giggle, enjoying his nonsense. "Don't push it."

He laughed. This time, his kiss was more intense. She was breathless by the time he raised his head.

He stared down at her as if he'd never seen anything so wonderful in his life.

Portia reminded herself not to trust that expression. This was only their first night together, and already she was melting into a lovelorn puddle. If she wasn't careful, before they were done, he'd guess that she loved him and that her offer of a trouble-free affair was only so much hot air.

He bumped his hips forward. "I like to push things."

Heat bubbled through her, although she wasn't sure that she was up to another bout. She wanted him. She always wanted him. But so far, they'd come together in a variety of unorthodox places. The hay. The table. Bent over on a bed. She'd loved everything that he'd done, but the unaccustomed activity left her aching.

"I know you do." Her eyes narrowed on that striking face. "Stop avoiding the question. If I want you, what should I say?"

"Just that."

"What?"

"I want you."

"Really?"

He shrugged. "Works every time."

"What else can I say? Just in case I prefer some variety."

The fond tolerance in his sigh made her fall a little bit more in love with him. "You just want to hear all the dirty words, don't you?"

She tugged the curls at his nape. "I am after all a rebel."

The green eyes gleamed with approval. "Very well."

When he didn't continue, she gave his hair a sharper pull. "Alaric."

"There's swiving and tumbling and tupping and

bedding and rutting. Coitus."

"Yes?"

"Any of those will do."

She frowned. "They don't sound very dirty. You can do better, I'm sure."

"Copulate. Fornicate. Have intercourse. Know in the biblical sense. Lie with. Seduce."

"More." Even with her sparse experience, most of those seemed too banal.

His lips twitched. "Portia, you're a lady. A man minds his tongue in the presence of a lady."

"Not always. I like what your tongue does."

He looked startled before chuckling with such surpassing salaciousness that her secret places clenched in involuntary response. "You don't know the half of what my tongue can do, my sweet little lamb."

She laughed at the description, even as curiosity sparked. What did he mean? "That sounds like you're going to lick me all over."

Sly humor lit his eyes to dark emerald. "We'll just have to wait and see, won't we?"

She responded with a growl. "Stop treating me like a fool, Alaric. And tell me what I need to say if I want you to...swive me."

"That will work."

"But there's more?"

He gave another long-suffering sigh. "I suppose so."

"If I wasn't a lady, but an amorous milkmaid, what would I say?"

"Roger me?"

"That sounds awful." Her nose wrinkled in displeasure. "I've never met a Roger I liked."

"You'd like it if I rogered you."

A huff of shocked laughter. "No doubt."

"The thing you could say..."

"Yes?" She found this discussion titillating. She feared that she was no longer the lady Alaric called her.

"Fuck me."

The word was short, sharp, vivid. And she was sure utterly forbidden in polite company. How delicious. An exultant smile curved her lips, as she gathered the nerve to speak. "Fuck me, Alaric."

CHAPTER EIGHTEEN

God God, he was turning into the worst kind of satyr.

Granville drew a deep breath and battled to remember that up to a few hours ago, Portia had been a virgin. Since then he, heaven forgive him, had tupped her three times. In a bedamned evening. He was in perpetual heat for this woman. Where the hell did he find the energy?

Watching Portia's pink, cushiony lips framing filthy words made him hard again. What the devil was she doing to him? She possessed a powerful magic. She just had to look sideways for him to think about having her.

Now here she was saying "fuck" with such innocent relish and turning him molten with desire. He told himself to calm down. Then he remembered something else that she'd said while he pronounced words he'd never spoken to a gently born woman in his life. The idea entering his mind was so explosive, he swelled against his breeches.

"Alaric?" she asked in a suspicious tone. "You look rather wild."

Wild? He was a rampaging beast, ravenous for

the sweetest flesh he knew. She had no idea what awaited.

"I believe I interrupted you," he purred, scenes of depravity careering through his mind.

"When I said fuck me?"

He gritted his teeth. She really needed to stop saying that or he'd fuck her indeed. "No. Before."

"Before?"

"Before I had you from behind."

A smile of astonishing lewdness curled her lips. "That's the way animals mate."

Arousal thundered through him, but he'd noticed her discomfort and felt like a brute. So no matter how overheated he became, she needed time to recover. Even if restraint was likely to incinerate him to embers. "Did you mind?"

That provocative expression intensified. "It was the most exciting thing that's ever happened to me. And I say that as a woman who has had the most exciting day of her life."

He grimaced. "I'm trying to do the right thing, my darling. You're not helping. I promised we'd make it into a bed."

Her gaze softened at the endearment. "We almost made it last time."

He wanted to stop talking about last time. Otherwise she'd end up under him again.

"You were taking down your hair." Granville couldn't believe that he was yet to see her naked. And hadn't she expressed an interest in seeing his body, too?

She ran her fingers through the untidy mane. "You've since taken care of that."

"Now it's time to take off your dress."

"You first."

Startled, he stepped back. "What?"

Portia's jaw set in a determined line. It was a

touching reminder of the woman he'd rescued in the East End. "You've seen considerably more of me than I've seen of you. It doesn't seem fair."

He laughed with unfettered pleasure. "I love how direct you are."

"Does that mean you agree?"

His hand already reached for his neckcloth, which a glance in the cheval mirror in the corner told him was in a woeful state after that unforgettable rogering. "I warn you, I'm nowhere near as beautiful as you are."

"Let me be the judge of that." Folded arms plumped her breasts in a most intriguing way. Granville swallowed, reminding himself that he possessed some self-discipline.

He tugged the neckcloth free and dropped it to the carpet. He tried not to glance toward her discarded drawers. If he dwelled too long on the fact that she was bare beneath her gown, he'd be on her.

His shirt fell open, uncovering his body halfway down his chest. She'd seen him without his shirt before, so the greedy lick of her eyes on the vee of skin surprised him. By Jericho, it felt like she touched him with hot fingers, even if a couple of feet separated them.

"Now the coat." Her husky tone betrayed sensual curiosity.

"You're very imperious," he said idly.

Another of those devastating, self-assured smiles. They were new today. Every time, they shot an arrow of fire straight to his balls. "You like it."

Damn it, he did. He was putty in her hands. Well, putty, if the definition of putty included something as rock-hard as his dick.

Granville liked that she felt confident enough to give him orders. He liked that she kissed him when the urge struck. He liked that she found his never-ending desire for her as piquant as he did.

The coat went. He threw it down beside his neckcloth. Hobbs would have a fit. Now Granville stood in front of Portia in shirtsleeves and the gray silk waistcoat with its exquisite embroidery.

"That's pretty." Portia pointed at him. "Take it off."

He shot her a direct look. "Your turn."

How he wanted her to remove her dress. He wanted it with the kind of urgency that kept a man awake all night. But when she crossed to sit on a chair near the fire, he recognized that she set out to torment him first.

She lifted her skirts. All the saliva evaporated from his mouth, as he wondered if she meant to display herself. But after a gleaming glance under her eyelashes, she positioned herself to show only her knees and two nicely curved calves in white stockings.

With deft hands, she untied the ribbons around her ankles that kept her slippers in place. She raised her skirts higher to reveal the pretty garters that held up her stockings. A few quick tugs to loosen them, before she dropped each garter to the carpet. Then using her skirts to preserve her modesty, she perched her heel on the edge of the seat. Slowly she unrolled one stocking and laid it on the floor near her garters.

Breathing became more difficult as Portia revealed each inch of bare skin.

A faint smile hovered around her lips, while she repeated the action for her other leg. Even slower. She knew exactly what she was doing, the beautiful witch. When she set her bare feet on the floor and rose, he wanted to beg her to keep going.

"The waistcoat," she said. "I've done my bit."

"For now," he gritted out, as his fingers fumbled

with the silk-covered buttons down the front. It took an eon to undo them, but finally he shrugged out of the garment and consigned it to the floor.

Only shirt, breeches and boots remained. Portia's eyes dropped to the bulge in his breeches, and her smile deepened. "You seem to be in extremis, Your Grace."

He grimaced. "This is what you do to me."

"Aren't I clever?"

"Portia…"

She remained unmoved. "Shirt next."

"What about your dress?" He sounded like he starved, and she dangled a juicy steak just out of reach.

"In time. I'm slightly ahead when it comes to undressing, you may recall."

How the hell could she sound so calm? While he balanced on the edge of a precipice.

"Very well," he rasped, struggling out of his shirt. The blasted rag suddenly had ten sleeves.

Finally he stood bare-chested. He was gratified to note that she didn't look so sure of herself anymore. Her gaze ate him up, and hectic color marked her cheeks.

"Goodness me, you're a magnificent sight," she said in a reedy voice. "You should give up wearing clothes altogether."

He snorted with amusement, even as he reveled in her praise. "And break my tailor's heart? Not to mention my valet."

"More noblesse oblige, I see," she said with a hint of dryness.

She stepped forward and placed both hands on his pectorals. He shuddered under the contact. Her erratic breath betrayed rising excitement, spoiling the illusion of control. He caught her hips in loose hands, resisting the urge to seize her and bundle her over to the bed.

The reward for restraint was the chance to drink in the wonder on her face, as she explored his chest. Raking her fingers through the light covering of dark blond hair. Running her hands up and down his arms in a breathtaking mix of caress and curiosity. Toying with his nipples.

Granville bared his teeth. "You should stop."

He could tell that she begrudged looking away from his chest. "Don't you like it? I hoped you might. I like it when you do this to me."

How he loved hearing that she enjoyed his touch. Self-deprecation turned his mouth down. "Of course I like it. Too much. I'm on the brink here."

She traced the line of his collarbones before lifting her hands. "Can I help with your boots?"

He realized with a shock – and a pang of self-disgust – that he was yet to have her without taking off his boots. A reminder of why for the moment, he needed to keep his head. "Thank you."

She caught his hand and led him across to the chair. He collapsed onto the seat and watched her fall to her knees before him.

God help him, he was doomed. His good intentions became more threadbare by the second. He wouldn't be human if seeing her now didn't stir thoughts of her taking him in her mouth.

When he'd planned this meeting at his isolated hunting box, he'd assumed that Portia would be unsure and hesitant. They'd already done more than he'd imagined in his wildest dreams.

She'd been thrillingly willing. Perhaps over the next few days, he might coax her to accept his dick into her mouth. The thought made his already stiff cock swell.

Granville pushed the incendiary prospect out of his mind. He already had enough difficulty clinging to self-control.

He stretched one leg toward her and watched as she gripped the heel and toe and gave the boot a good tug to remove it. That generous bosom jiggled. Which didn't help his self-control either.

More enticing heaving of breasts with the second boot's removal, then she took off his light stockings. She remained where she was, staring at his feet with an attention that he was sure they didn't deserve. "Portia, is everything all right?"

Wonder edged her smile. "Even your feet are beautiful."

Granville glanced down at his toes. He couldn't see it.

"You're just lost in a fog of pleasure." He was, too.

She rose on her knees to kiss him. He expected passion, but her lips were tender. With Portia, sweetness was as mighty as passion. It had the ability to stab straight through to his heart. By the time she was on her feet, he lay back in a complete daze.

A daze that vanished in an instant when she turned her back and swept her hair out of the way. "Can you undo my dress, please?"

At last. At last. Hallelujah, at last!

With unsteady hands, he unlaced the blue gown until the dress fell away to reveal the pale skin of her back. "Your stays, too?"

"Yes, please."

He placed a nipping kiss on one shoulder. "I'm done."

Her shiver was visible. "Ooh, that was nice."

She turned to him, eyes heavy with desire. Her hands clutched the drooping bodice to her breasts.

"Will you show me?" he asked gently. "Please?"

After a brief hesitation, she lifted her hands away and gave one of those alluring wiggles. For a suspenseful second, the dress clung to the perfect slope of her breasts, before slithering to the ground to reveal her remaining undergarments.

As if the loss of her gown marked a turning point, Portia quickly discarded her corset and untied her petticoats. Only the cotton, knee-length shift remained.

Granville noted the lavish curves made mysterious under sheer white material. The breasts that had haunted his fantasies. The intriguing dip of her navel. The shadowy delta between her thighs.

He stepped forward and swung her up into his arms. With a startled laugh, she hooked her hand around his neck. "What are you doing?"

"You'll see." He carried her across to the bed and placed her crosswise on the mattress, letting her bare legs dangle to the floor.

"But…"

When she tried to wriggle away, he caught her leg. "Trust me, Portia."

An uncertain blue gaze focused on him. Whatever she saw there must have reassured her because she lay flat again and stared at the ceiling. "I do."

That shouldn't sound like a declaration of love, but somehow it did. His heart overflowing with joy and gratitude, Granville fell to his knees and caught her thighs.

"Let me show you what my tongue can do, my lady," he murmured, carefully pulling her knees apart. Anticipation was headier than wine.

He delayed a moment to remind himself to take his time and do this properly. He also lingered to take in the beautiful sight of her cleft, satiny with readiness.

When he didn't begin, she tensed under his touch. "You're looking at me, aren't you?"

Her voice was higher than usual. She must guess his plans.

"You're gorgeous everywhere." Granville smiled with wolfish eagerness, so perhaps it was a good thing that she looked anywhere but at him right now.

He saw her swallow. "That's...lovely to hear. But I feel rather—"

"Self-conscious?"

"That's one word for it."

His smile widened. "The woman who seduced me in a haystack won't let a little embarrassment stop her."

"If you say so."

"I most certainly do." He filled his lungs with the scent of Portia's need and placed his lips on her clitoris.

"Alaric!" she cried, bucking in surprise. Then cried out again when he flicked his tongue against the sensitive bud.

So many new experiences had assailed Portia on this extraordinary day that she felt inured to surprises.

Until Alaric put his mouth in a spot that she'd never imagined a man would want to kiss. She'd never imagined that she'd want a man's lips down there either. If the thought had occurred to her. Which of course it wouldn't.

That fiendishly clever tongue traced her cleft and teased the place that gave her such pleasure. On a choked cry, she buried shaking hands in his soft hair. He made a muffled sound of encouragement and drew on her. As lightning bolts of response juddered through her, she widened her legs.

Familiarity didn't lessen the glorious magic. If anything, the rise to release became faster and easier. After three days of this, she'd go up in smoke at the mere sight of Alaric.

When he deepened the pressure, the throb of her blood turned urgent. She lifted her hips to catch every second of the remarkable and shocking things he did.

Another shudder shook Portia, as he pushed his tongue inside her. In a paroxysm of pleasure, she writhed against the bed. She was so close. So tantalizingly close...

He penetrated her with one long finger. She jerked in helpless reaction and tipped over into a fiery universe. Through the inferno, she waited for him to unite their bodies. He'd been ready for most of the night.

Instead, his fingers moved in a ruthless invasion that lifted the crest of her response. She'd just started to come down from the outer edges of the cosmos when her muscles spasmed again.

"Alaric?" she asked in bewilderment, as her insides turned liquid. With another cry, she tumbled into another titanic climax.

"That's perfect." His growl rumbled through her. "Go with it."

As if she had a choice when a tide of euphoria swept her into the middle of a turbulent ocean.

He leaned in and used his tongue as well as his fingers. She felt battered by rainbows, dazzled by flares of light, transformed to flowing rivers of silk. This time, when she broke, she crumbled into shards of flaming starlight. A broken cry emerged from a throat tight with emotions – and words that she could never speak aloud.

He persisted, his touch turning gentle. The last wave of pleasure was as sweet and soft as a shower of rain on a hot summer's day.

Gasping, she lay upon the mattress, legs as loose as muslin draped on either side of him. While she subsided into a pool of exhausted satiation, her hand slid from his hair to lie open at her side. Closing her eyes, she struggled to fill lungs as empty as a tinker's pocket.

She'd lived through an earthquake. Several earthquakes. Aftershocks quivered through her in luscious little surges.

She heard him shift and stand. "Portia, say something."

She didn't open her eyes.

"Portia?"

She swallowed, hoping her voice worked. "You can't expect me to talk after that."

"You liked it then?"

A faint smile tugged at her lips. "Stop fishing for compliments."

He gave a soft laugh. The bed dipped as he curled up next to her and took her into his arms. She went unresisting. Heavens, right now, she doubted that she'd summon an ounce of resistance if a bear sprang out of the wardrobe to eat her.

He kissed her on the forehead. Even through the weariness, his tenderness made her smile.

When she stirred, Alaric stretched out beside her, leaning on one elbow. He watched her with a light in his green eyes that made her susceptible heart ache with futile longing. This, what they did together, was wonderful. It would be more wonderful still if he loved her.

Mentally, she kicked herself. What was the point of howling after the moon? In fact, if she did, it would mar her present happiness. Which would be a tragedy indeed.

She *was* happy. Her body felt sleek and replete and heavy with animal satisfaction. Her hand traced a wandering path up his bare chest. She loved touching him. He was warm and hard and altogether a treat to discover. Her hand snaked behind his neck.

One thing that she'd never questioned about Alaric Dempster, even when dismissing him as too dreary for words, was his cleverness. He got the hint straightaway.

His kiss made her toes curl into the coverlet.

When he lifted away, his eyes were dark with arousal. That slumberous look kindled simmering heat in the pit of her stomach.

He caught her chin. "What's wrong?"

Portia released a breath laden with both puzzlement and self-disgust. "How can I be interested in…you know again?"

His lips twitched, as his hand dropped to toy with the ribbon that closed the top of her shift. "All those dirty words I taught you and 'you know' is the best you can do?"

She didn't smile. "Is there something wrong with me?"

It was his turn to frown. "No, you're utterly perfect."

"I wouldn't say that." Although it was nice to hear.

"I would." He tugged at the ribbon with more purpose until her shift gaped.

She glanced down to see her breasts on flagrant show. "Is it normal to want to keep doing…"

"You know?"

She tugged at his hair. "You're not taking me seriously."

His smile widened. "Yes, I am. You're worried that I think you're a brazen hussy, because you can't keep your hands off me."

Oh, dear, she wasn't wrong about him being clever. That wasn't what she was saying, but she knew enough to understand that the world despised women with unquenchable sexual appetites. She braced to ask the question. "Do you think that?"

Alaric gave a short laugh. "Portia, you're hardly an example of unbridled debauchery. For pity's sake, you were an innocent until you fell into my nefarious hands."

She bit her lip and regarded him uncertainly. "We've...swived three times. As well as whatever you call it when you kissed me between the legs."

"Lick-twat."

She winced. "It's much nicer than it sounds."

"I'm glad you think so." He cupped one breast. His touch was casual, but the air became more charged by the second. He focused on her breast with a concentration that turned the weight of arousal between her legs liquid.

She spoke in a rush, with embarrassment and also because her heart accelerated with excitement. "Now here I am, wanting to do it all over again."

Something about the curve of Alaric's lips expressed his contentment with that state of affairs. Or perhaps he looked so pleased because he toyed with her breast. "I want to do it all again, too. And I was there for everything else we've done today."

"But you're a man."

His hand stilled and at last he looked at her. Lazy sensuality shone in his eyes. "I've never fucked a woman three times in a matter of hours. Going on a fourth time. You're utterly irresistible to me."

Portia stared into his eyes, reading a conviction that assuaged her fears. "That's good," she faltered, shaping her hand around his nape in a caress.

"It is." He closed his eyes briefly in visible enjoyment of her touch. She couldn't interpret it as anything else. "It's even better that I seem to be utterly irresistible to you."

"You are," she admitted.

"Heaven knows why."

"You're..." She struggled to find an adequate word

to describe him. Thrilling? Lovable? Potent? Unforgettable? "...superb."

He kissed her again, taking her nipple between his thumb and index finger. As he tugged at the point, she whimpered in helpless surrender.

"I think you're superb, too, you know." The way he fondled her breast had her shifting against the bed.

"Mutual enchantment?"

"The best sort of enchantment."

This time, she pulled him down for a kiss. Still kissing, he hauled her up to sit on the edge of the mattress. He nibbled a devastating trail down her neck. He paused at the curve of her shoulder. The sensation of his breath on her skin stoked her arousal.

"Shall we take off your shift? It's time."

His musky scent tinged the air that she breathed. "Very well."

Alaric's smile was one of the sweet ones that always made Portia feel like her world was made of bonbons and champagne and daffodils. "Thank you."

She shifted out of his arms to stand before him on trembling legs. His Adam's apple moved as he swallowed.

"You take my breath away." His voice cracked with emotion.

She gazed back, her unruly heart cramping with painful longing. "You make me feel..."

"Yes?"

"Like a goddess," she whispered.

He didn't smile. "Good."

He rose and kissed her again. Her head whirled by the time he released her and caught her shift in his hands. "Lift your arms for me," he murmured.

Without hesitation, she obeyed. Alaric pulled her

shift over her head and tossed it away. For the first time in her life, Portia stood naked before a man. Her heart lodging in her throat, she avoided his eyes. It was an effort not to shield herself with her hands.

A tiny voice in her mind said that self-consciousness was absurd after all they'd done. But Portia felt more virginal than she had before losing her virginity in that glorious tussle in the hay.

"Say...say something," she stammered, blushing hotter than the sun.

When the silence continued, she forced herself to look at him. What she saw punched the breath from her lungs until lights flickered behind her eyes.

She hadn't been sure how he'd react to her nakedness. With lust? Possessiveness? Pleasure?

In truth, all three were present in his expression. But mostly, she saw wonderment.

His gaze devoured her, and his hands opened and closed at his sides as if he hardly dared to touch her. If she hadn't already loved him, she'd have fallen in love with him at that moment. Forever.

"I'm not worthy." Awe edged his voice. "You *are* a goddess."

She'd become used to his wry humor. But his hushed statement held no trace of irony. He sounded completely overcome.

Her shyness receded, and she drew herself up to stand proudly. It was a silent presentation of all that she was and all that she had to this man she adored. This time, when she sought his gaze, she didn't falter.

Portia wasn't ashamed of her desire. Because she realized with growing elation that he wanted her to match him in passion.

With a single stride, he crossed the space between them and hauled her into his arms. His mouth was hot and demanding. The kiss told her that he burned for her. She responded with unconstrained fervor.

Alaric toppled back onto the bed, taking her with him in a fury of touching and kissing. When he rose above her, she placed a shaking hand on his shoulder and smiled into his vivid features. "Nothing more happens until you take off your breeches, Your Grace."

He already reached for the buttons.

CHAPTER NINETEEN

*M*rs. Bilson's ball had been a highlight of the season since her daughter, Lily's debut in 1816. Lily's engagement to Alexander Comerford had been announced a week ago, so this year's event celebrated the betrothal. Portia couldn't miss it without her absence being questioned.

Before she'd spent three days in the country with her lover, that had seemed simple. It didn't seem simple tonight as she arrived at the Bilsons' house with Kate and Leighton. She hadn't wanted to return to London. She hadn't wanted to part from Alaric.

The Portia who came back to Town was a different person from the Portia who had left. It was a shock to arrive home to discover that everybody treated her as they'd always done. That easy acceptance irked her, even if it was safe.

Since Juliet's marriage, she'd stayed with Papa because he needed someone to run his household. But now he was back in London, he was busy with his theatrical interests. He was home so rarely that a good housekeeper could manage the house without him noticing much difference.

Perhaps it was time for Portia to set up her own

establishment. An establishment that she could fill with stray dogs and nobody to tell her nay. An establishment that offered a little privacy.

She couldn't avoid housing a chaperone, but she could choose one who wouldn't examine her comings and goings too closely. Mary would be ideal. Aunt Mabel would be happy to relinquish her current responsibilities and return to her dower house in Derbyshire. London was too noisy and crowded for her these days.

As Portia stepped out of the Shelburns' carriage, she had a sense that a new life beckoned. A new life where she could live on her own terms at last.

Tonight, she'd see Alaric. And tomorrow morning. They couldn't kiss or touch, but she'd bask in his presence, however briefly. It wasn't enough, but it would have to be until they arranged another tryst. Maybe the next time that she left London for Surrey, she'd depart from a house of her own.

"You're looking very jolly all of a sudden," Kate said with a hint of sourness, when she turned to check on why Portia lagged behind.

Startled, Portia gaped at her friend. "I'm happy for Lily."

She was. Alexander and Lily would go along together very well.

"I'm sure," Kate retorted, taking Leighton's arm and stepping toward the front door.

"Aren't you?"

"Of course I am, but you've been as dismal as a wet Sunday since we collected you."

"I haven't." She dipped her head to avoid the light of the torches blazing on the house's front steps.

"Definitely quieter than usual," Leighton said, tucking his wife's arm in his crooked elbow.

"I'm a little tired," Portia said. Both true and a massive understatement. Alaric's voracious sexual appetite had kept her awake for most of the last few days. During the week before that, nerves and longing had robbed her of sleep.

"You're looking a bit peaky," Kate said thoughtfully.

"How kind," Portia responded. "When I tried so hard to be at my best."

That was also true. She thought her new dress in teal-green satin became her. She'd spent more time than usual titivating, and Betty had put her hair up in a tumbling mass of curls. Portia wasn't too proud to admit that she wanted Alaric to admire her. In fact, she wanted him to take one look and burn to cart her off to bed.

They couldn't do anything about that in Mayfair. But if she had to hunger for him, by heaven, she wanted him hungering for her in return.

Leighton cast his wife an unimpressed glance before he smiled at Portia. "You look lovely."

"Thank you." Portia took his other arm, as they entered the tall, white house and swept up the elaborate staircase.

Luckily, the ballroom was so crammed with the bluest blood in the land – Lily and Alexander were a popular couple and they belonged to influential families – that once inside, Portia could avoid Kate without being too overt. Her friend had sharp eyes, and she was already suspicious of Portia and Alaric.

Portia was thankful that her sisters weren't in London. They'd know immediately that something significant had happened. The moment they saw her with Alaric, they'd guess who to blame.

A quick survey of the room as the dancing started allowed her to locate him partnering Lady Colville. Kate and Leighton danced together, and Portia accepted Ivor Bilson's invitation. He was so excited about his sister's engagement, he only mentioned fishing twice.

The ball went along as most balls did. Usually, Portia enjoyed the social whirl, but tonight her mind was focused on Alaric and how soon they could be together again. The first waltz took forever to arrive. When he crossed the room to claim her as his partner, she was with the Tierneys.

"Lady Portia, I believe this is our dance," he said, after acknowledging the others.

He looked like the man who had proposed to Juliet. Composed. Restrained. Elegant. He sounded like that man, too. Cool. Uninvolved. A stranger to passion.

But after three tumultuous days in his arms, Portia knew better. Her body still hummed with the pleasure that they'd shared.

Which made it difficult to appear unmoved as she dipped into a curtsy. "Your Grace."

He took her hand and bowed over it. It was even harder to hide her immediate physical reaction to his touch. A wave of sensual memories assailed her, turning her knees to water.

The orchestra played the waltz's opening. Her hand tightened around his, and she dared to meet his eyes. He appeared wary, not like her insatiable lover at all. But the hand at her waist was possessive, and she was close enough to hear his shuddering exhalation at the contact.

The dance floor was crowded and offered no real privacy. But something jagged and restless inside Portia settled, now they were together.

"I thought my time would never come." Despite its quietness, his tone conveyed a fierce longing that had her stomach performing a dizzying swoop. "What do you mean by dancing with all these other buffleheads instead of me?"

Her hand moved in a surreptitious caress on his

shoulder. Those aristocratic nostrils flared as if he drew in her scent.

"Those buffleheads are your friends," she protested on a splutter of laughter. Mostly because she was so happy to be in his arms again. She'd been in emotional tatters since she left him.

She didn't want to think about what that meant for her future. Because amidst all the joy and passion and intrigue, one thing remained clear. This was an affair, not a lifetime commitment. At some unspecified time, Granville would choose a wife, a perfect duchess, the kind of woman Portia could never be. And Portia would be left bereft and brokenhearted.

The familiar twitch of his lips. "Not anymore."

"Heaven help your political career." Like him, she kept her voice to a murmur.

"To buggery with my political career. I want you to myself."

For a blazing moment, she stared into his eyes. She realized that while he might joke about his frustrations, he was deadly serious. His urgency made her heart race with forbidden excitement.

Her hand tightened on his shoulder. "When can we go away again?"

"That's up to you."

"It will look strange if it's too soon," she said with a pang of regret. Right now, she was ready to consign society and its notions of propriety to Hades.

"Then meet me in the square after the ball."

"Alaric..."

He whirled her in a reckless turn, but she was already off-kilter with desire. "I have to kiss you."

"Not here," she managed to force out, struggling to look as though she despised the Duke of Granville.

"Damn it, I know." He sounded like he suffered.

"Don't look at me like that," she whispered.

"People will talk."

His grip on her waist firmed, even as he tried to adopt the blank expression that he always wore dancing with her. He wasn't very successful. She suspected that she made a similar dog's breakfast of hiding her turbulent emotions.

"This is...more difficult than I thought it would be."

"Yes." Desolation weighted the word. Because Portia didn't just mean avoiding the gossips' notice. She meant needing to behave as if she didn't love this man more with every breath.

Before she'd gone to Alaric's bed, the charade had been onerous enough. Now after he'd buried himself deep inside her, it was nigh impossible to treat him like a mere acquaintance.

Even worse, for as long as she lived, she must act as if the duke meant nothing to her. They moved in the same social circles. Unless she emigrated to France or America or far Cathay, they were fated to encounter each other every season. The idea of the torture ahead left her feeling like she stood poised at the mouth of hell.

"Can I take you out onto the terrace?" His voice was stiff with the effort of concealing his feelings.

"People will notice."

"I'm devilish sick of *people*." He spat out the last word like a curse. Right now, Portia could only agree.

She chanced a quick glance into his eyes, then wished she hadn't. He looked like he wanted to eat her up with a spoon. The humbling truth was that she was more than willing to be devoured.

But not here.

She looked away and licked dry lips. His growl expressed intolerable frustration. "Don't do that."

"What?"

"Lick your lips. It always makes me mad to kiss

you."

And other things, she knew. In their three days in Surrey, he'd introduced her to so many debauched acts. Carnal memories sent blood rushing to her cheeks.

"Portia, stop it," he hissed.

He knew what she was thinking. Of course he did.

"I can't help it." Her voice vibrated with a frustration that matched his.

"Say you'll meet me tonight, if only to save my sanity."

With a feeling of grim inevitability, she heard the waltz move into the coda. Her time with Alaric had been so short. Now it reached its end. They hadn't even been alone. If they'd been alone, they'd be kissing.

"I'm sure that's an exaggeration." She strove to inject some mundanity into this fraught conversation.

His lips flattened. "It doesn't feel like one."

"If I stay until the end of the ball, I'll have to go home or Papa will lock me out."

"You could stay at my house."

Temptation tugged at her. A night with Alaric would be bliss. Last night, she'd slept alone. Except that she hadn't slept. Even after a few days sharing his bed, Portia had been unable to settle without him by her side.

She maintained enough grip on common sense to see the pitfalls of his suggestion. "Your servants would know. Heavens, my servants would know. The story would soon be all over London."

He was pale and determined, and the grip of his hands conveyed craving. "Then leave now," he said tersely.

Could she? It was easy enough to claim a headache. The Shelburns had already noted her edgy mood.

"Portia, for the love of heaven, say you will."

How could she resist? "Yes."

The tension seeped from his features, and he swung her in a triumphant circle. "Thank you."

"An hour?" she asked breathlessly.

"Yes."

The music ended with a clash of cymbals and a harp glissando. She hated seeing him step away, even with the promise of a tryst ahead. "Shall I take you to the Shelburns?"

"Yes, please."

He caught her arm and made his way through the crowd. Portia struggled to maintain a neutral expression. She felt a battery of curious eyes upon her. Or perhaps that was her guilty conscience speaking.

Leighton and Kate waited near the refreshment table. They turned to watch Portia and Alaric approach.

"My lord and lady, Lady Portia is feeling unwell. Perhaps she should go home."

Alaric's voice was smooth, not at all like it was when he'd confessed his hunger. It expressed precisely the amount of concern a man should feel for the sister of his former fiancée.

"I'm sorry to hear that," Kate said. "It's very close in here. Would a breath of air help?"

Portia sagged against Alaric in what she hoped was a convincing display of weakness. "I think...I think I'd rather just leave. Will you please make my apologies to Mrs. Bilson?"

"Of course," Leighton said.

"Shall I request your carriage, Lady Portia?" Alaric asked.

Kate came up beside Portia and took her arm. "She came with us, so please ask for our coach."

Alaric released Portia and bowed. "I hope you soon feel more the thing, my lady. I'll call tomorrow afternoon to check on your welfare."

"That's very kind," Portia stammered, performing a shaky curtsy. It might be kind, but it wasn't a good idea. He'd never called on her before. After their dance tonight, it would cause talk. Everything that they did risked unwelcome notice. She hated it. "I'm sure it's nothing serious."

"Nonetheless I'd like to reassure myself." Alaric bowed to the Shelburns. "My lady. My lord."

Portia struggled not to watch him stride away through the crowd. "I'm sorry to be a nuisance," she said to Kate.

Kate put her arm around her and helped her toward the double doors leading to the stairs. People assembled for the next dance, so nobody paid attention to two ladies making for the exit. "You'll be yourself in no time. Send me a note in the morning and tell me how you are."

Alaric waited downstairs. "The coach should be here soon. One of Mrs. Bilson's maids will accompany you, Lady Portia."

"Thank you, Your Grace," Portia said. "You're very thoughtful."

He was. She'd learned to appreciate his attention to detail when he'd spent three glorious days making love to her. He bowed again and left them alone in the foyer, apart from two silent footmen at the door.

"Shall I come home with you?" Kate asked. "You're looking rather flushed."

Without doubt, she was. She was in a flurry of anticipation at the prospect of seeing Alaric. "No need to spoil your evening. It's just across the square. The maid is chaperone enough for such a short trip."

"Very well."

To Portia's relief, Kate only spoke about trivialities before the carriage rolled up. How pretty and happy Lily looked. The extravagant ruby ring that Alexander had given his fiancée. Lady Colville's daring gown. The massed lilies adorning the room, a compliment to the daughter of the house.

Portia had feared that Kate might subject her to another inquisition about the Duke of Granville. Only when she settled into the carriage, a shy Irish maid sitting opposite, did it occur to her that Kate's silence on the subject of Alaric made a stronger statement than a barrage of questions.

CHAPTER TWENTY

The Duke of Granville's early departure from the ball would rouse little curiosity. A man of his rank often called on several different events over any given night to lend his consequence to more than one hostess.

But if the duke followed Portia too quickly, some sharp-eyed observer might note the coincidence. Despite his blood rushing at the thought of seeing Portia alone, he lingered to chat to a few political cronies, he partnered an incandescently happy Lily Bilson in a contredanse, and he made sure to appear in no particular hurry when he strolled out of the Bilsons' house half an hour after Portia's exit.

Behind him, the ball continued, a triumph for Mrs. Bilson and a memorable celebration for the engaged couple. Ahead was a rendezvous with the woman who occupied his every thought. He knew that he'd got the better end of the deal.

It wouldn't do for anyone to see the dignified Duke of Granville running through the streets of Mayfair. Once he was outside, and only with difficulty, he restrained himself to a swift, purposeful walk, even as his heart thundered like a whole battalion of drummers.

When he reached Dempster House, he even realized that he had the perfect excuse for staying out as long as he liked.

"Your...Your Grace," Matty said in shock, as Granville loomed out of the lamplit gloom. Jupiter let out a joyful yip and strained at the leash clutched in the lad's hand.

"Good evening, Matty." Two streetlamps stood near the front door, so it was easy to read the expressions on both the boy's and the dog's faces.

The boy performed a shaky bow. He wasn't quite as overawed in his employer's presence as he used to be, but he wasn't yet at ease. "Sir."

Granville gestured to Jupiter. "Sit."

Jupiter sat, his attention riveted on Granville. He'd been in alt ever since Granville's return to London this afternoon. He put up with Matty because he had to, but his heart was set on his master. Despite that master not taking any nonsense. Granville remained surprised at how fast he and his unconventional pet had established a perfect understanding.

"I'll walk him tonight. I feel like a stroll." Granville extended a gloved hand. "You get off to bed."

"Thank you, Your Grace." Matty passed the lead across. "It's a fine evening."

It was more than fine when it offered Granville a chance to meet Portia away from prying eyes. His smile was probably inappropriately bright when he responded. "It is, at that. Good night, Matty."

The boy cast him a startled glance before bowing again and making his way up to the front door.

"Shall we go and find our Portia?" Granville asked Jupiter, who was on his feet and wagging his tail.

Another surprise for Granville was how quickly he'd taken to conversing with the hound. It wasn't much use regretting the lack, but he wished his stiff-rumped grandfather had let him have a dog when he was a boy. He'd been a lonely child, and even these short days with Jupiter had proven what good company a dog was.

With Jupiter trotting at his side, he crossed the empty street to the garden in the center of the square. As he slipped through the black iron gate, he heard the chimes for eleven o'clock. Most society events wouldn't finish until around two, so with a bit of luck, he'd enjoy a couple of hours with Portia.

She wasn't waiting in the copse, which he supposed was a good thing, even if every second without her seemed wasted. Lorimer Square was among the safest places in London, but an unescorted woman shouldn't be out on her own in the dark.

Although knowing Portia, Granville wouldn't be surprised if she carried her pistol. She stood on her own two feet, and he admired her all the more for it.

He removed his gloves and unclipped Jupiter's lead so the dog could snuffle around in the bushes. Leaning back against a tree trunk, he strove to rein in his impatience. He took a deep breath and told himself to enjoy the anticipation. It was difficult, but he should look at it as the sauce that added extra spice to his need.

Until he'd met Portia, his life had – most of the time – been packed with undeserved pleasures, if not precisely exciting. Meeting Portia had catapulted him out of a black-and-white etching and into all the drama of a Caravaggio oil painting. His days had color and flavor and impetus in a way that they never had before.

He hoped to hell that she never changed her mind about wanting him. The idea of reverting to that dull, gray man sent a chill down his spine.

In the quiet night, he heard the gate on the other side of the garden click and the scuff of her boots on the path. He straightened and every cell in his body tingled with exhilaration.

He was so attuned to her, he caught her hand without seeing it. She wasn't wearing gloves either, although she had at the ball. The warm slide of skin on skin smacked the breath from his lungs.

"You came," he murmured.

"Of course I did." Her fingers laced through his with gratifying eagerness. "It's been so long since you kissed me."

With a muffled laugh, he drew her closer, close enough to catch her floral perfume. When they'd danced together, that scent had tempted him to do things that had no place in a ballroom. Now they were alone in the dark, and he didn't have to act the gentleman. "Let's fix that."

His lips descended for a kiss clumsy with need, evoking poignant memories of the first time that he'd kissed her in his stables. Could that only be a week ago? He'd been through a lifetime since then.

With a broken moan, she plastered herself to his body. He stroked her derriere. Even through her skirts, he felt the luxuriant curves. She'd worn silk at the ball, but she'd changed into something in a heavier material that presented more of a barrier.

By God, he wanted her naked. He wanted her in his bed. He wanted her with him for the rest of the night. He wanted to wake up with her and spend the day at her side.

He just wanted.

Portia wanted, too. She never made any secret of that. Good intentions fled the moment that she stepped into his arms. She was so warm and ardent. So perfect and passionate. How could he go on without her?

He swung her around until her back collided with the tree. She gave a faint gasp against his lips, then snarled her hands in his hair to drag him nearer. He hitched up her skirt and caught her under the buttocks, hauling her up until her quim was level with his aching prick.

"Oh, yes," she sighed, crooking her legs around him. She hooked her hands over his shoulders. He staggered as he took her weight, then braced her against the tree.

"I didn't…I didn't mean us to fuck," he grated out, pressing his cheek to hers and breathing air that smelled like Portia.

"Don't stop," she whispered and scraped her teeth along his jaw in an unmistakable invitation. "Please don't stop. I've missed you so much."

He'd missed her, too. Mad as that was, after less than a day apart. Only now that she was here did his world seem right. "Hold on to me."

She grasped his shoulders, as he shifted one hand from her glorious arse and ripped at his pantaloons. He was panting as if he climbed a mountain. During those heady days in Surrey, they'd come together like this several times. She knew what to do. Resting her thighs on his hips, she arched forward.

He released his cock and holding it, leaned in to find the slit in her drawers. His nostrils flared to take in more of her rich scent. The whole world turned into Portia.

She tilted her hips and took the tip of his dick inside her. The sensation became even more compelling when she clenched around the sensitive head. She was already hot and wet, and he fought the urge to lose himself before she climaxed.

"Stop teasing me," she rasped into his ear, then bit the lobe.

"Very well," he grated out and thrust hard. A blast

of heat threatened to blow the top of his head off. When she nipped his ear more sharply, his balls contracted in pleasurable agony.

He began to move in heavy plunges that sheathed him to the hilt. The world exploded into a storm of bliss. Her rhythmic little moans spurred him on.

Her moans emerged more quickly as she approached her release. Her battle to muffle her cries stoked his arousal. He loved her ardent surrender. He lifted her higher to change the angle. With a muted cry, she succumbed to rapture.

His balls tightened, his blood turned to flame. With a mighty groan, he filled her with his seed. For a measureless interval of delight, he pumped into her, giving her everything he had, everything he was.

Struggling for air, he collapsed against her. His bones had turned to syrup. Thank God for the tree. He wasn't sure his legs would support him, let alone her as well. She quivered with the aftereffects, and her breath emerged in sobs.

For a long time, Granville remained where he was. He struggled to breathe. He struggled to think. Hell, he struggled to stay standing after that titanic release. He basked in having her in his arms. Just where he wanted her.

Through his exhaustion, he felt her bring her legs down. He slipped free, but didn't shift away. Now that he wasn't carrying her, he twined his arms around her. He loved fucking her. But he also loved these luminous moments, once the crisis had passed. He fumbled between them to fasten his pantaloons.

After a long while, she pressed her lips to his neck above his high collar. Yet again, they'd set the heavens alight, yet remained fully dressed. He turned his head and caught her mouth for a kiss that expressed his joy in her.

She kissed him back, embracing him so he sank

into those voluptuous curves. He surrendered to a dark paradise where he and Portia stayed together like this forever.

Portia drew away first. "Alaric?"

"Mmm?" He wasn't sure that he was capable of conversation. In such a perfect moment, reality was an unwelcome intruder.

"That was spectacular."

"Yes," he said on a long exhalation. "Yes, it was."

She stroked his cheek with a tenderness that he felt to his toes. "Spectacular. But you didn't pull out."

All Granville's glorious peace, the peace that was Portia's greatest gift to him, evaporated. He jerked upright and stepped back, heart clanging like a badly-tuned bell.

Stupid. Stupid. Stupid.

"Hell, Portia, I'm so sorry."

He reached for her, but she couldn't see him in the stygian gloom. She didn't take his hand. She didn't speak.

For fuck's sake, don't let her hate him. She'd hated him once. How would he survive if she went back to despising him?

Her silence had him rushing into speech in a way that the august Duke of Granville never did. "It's no excuse to say I want you so damned much that I can't put two thoughts together. I promised to look after you and I failed."

Still she didn't speak. By God, he wished that he could see her face. She had such expressive features. They always betrayed her thoughts, right back to her disapproval of her beloved sister marrying the man who she dismissed as the driest of dry sticks.

His heart lodged in his aching throat, while his stomach dived to his boots. He went on in a frantic gabble. "I beg you to forgive me. I beg you to give me another chance."

She wore a dark dress and it was black as the lowest pit of hell in the copse, but he sensed that she shifted. He braced for anger, but her voice was even. "I know you didn't do it on purpose."

He sucked in a relieved breath, his first full breath since he'd realized the vast extent of his sin against her. "You don't hate me?"

A faint huff expressed her scorn for that question. "As if I could."

Granville didn't speak. He was clever enough to know that more was coming. What would he do if she said that she'd never risk tupping him again? Until he seduced Portia, he'd merely existed. Only with her had he truly lived.

Her voice remained calm but stern. "I know this isn't what you want, Alaric. But if it turns out I'm carrying a baby, you'll have to marry me."

Shock had him speaking before he considered strategy. When strategy had guided him ever since he'd first kissed her. "I'll marry you tomorrow, if you like. I've had a special license in the top drawer of my desk since the day after we rescued Jupiter. If you say you'll become my wife, I'll be the happiest man in England."

CHAPTER TWENTY-ONE

The ground shifted beneath Portia's feet. Nothing that Alaric said made sense. Not in any world she lived in. Her hands fisted in her creased skirts. "But you don't want to marry me."

His sigh was audible. She wished to heaven that they weren't having this conversation in the middle of a lightless grove of trees. She'd dearly love to see his face and his stance, to get some idea of his feelings. She had a dreadful suspicion that he was tensed up like a hunted animal. That beautiful baritone sounded cold and grim, despite him saying he wished to marry her.

"I decided to marry you when you pulled out your pistol and threatened to shoot that ruffian."

While she should be happy to hear this, it didn't fit with what she knew to be true. "But...but you didn't like me then."

"It seems I did."

"You've never mentioned marriage."

"The moment you agreed to come away with me, marriage was inevitable. Credit me with a little honor. You're a gentlewoman. You were a virgin. If I debauched you, I owed you a wedding ring."

She hadn't been as daring and free as she'd thought. That was disappointing, although she shouldn't be surprised. From the start, she'd recognized Alaric's ironclad ethics. Usually she admired them, but right now, she couldn't help feeling that he'd been less than candid. He might be a gentleman, but it was clear that he'd manipulated her.

"Why didn't you say something?"

"Because you told me in no uncertain terms that you didn't want a husband."

"So you'd bed me until we got caught and had to marry?" Bitterness edged her tone. "A third Frain sister rushed to the altar in a hail of scandal?"

"No. On my soul, no. It would be easy enough to spark a scandal, if I was unprincipled enough to engineer one. You know how I've tried to hide our affair."

To be fair, she did. "Why?"

"I didn't want to force your hand."

That was something, she supposed, still feeling at a disadvantage. "You were giving me time to decide to marry you?"

His answer held a hint of apology. "I hoped you might warm to the idea."

"Thanks to your fatal charm?" She didn't soften the irony in her question.

"You like me. Or at least you did." Alaric stopped, as if waiting for her to agree, but she remained silent. He went on in a more subdued tone. "And we're tremendous in bed together. That has to count for something."

Tremendous in bed. And against trees and walls and doors. And on tables and chairs and carpets. "It means I want you," she said flatly.

"And I want you."

That was no comfort. Desire didn't solve the problems between them. "I'd make a dreadful duchess."

"You're perfect for me."

He sounded so sure, she almost believed him. "What about my animals? I'd turn your life upside down. You'd hate that."

Alaric sighed again. "Portia, you can empty the Royal Menagerie and move the exhibits into my back garden, if that's what it takes to accept my proposal. Dogs and cats and lions and tigers and...hell, dragons are welcome, as long as you say yes."

She wanted to say yes. She wanted to believe him. But she couldn't. Not yet, anyway. "That's all very well to say, but you require a respectable, biddable woman who never sets a foot wrong. My feet are wrong all the time. So is the rest of me."

She thought he might laugh at that, but clearly he was at such an extremity that his sense of humor abandoned him. "You're right for me. The question is whether you think I'm right for you."

"None of this is like you, Alaric." He wouldn't see her bewildered gesture. "You're the most gentlemanly gentleman in the ton. If you wanted to marry me, why not court me in the accepted manner or ask Papa for my hand? He'd love me to marry a duke, especially without a scandal forcing the groom's hand."

"Portia, darling..."

The anguished "darling" went some way to smoothing her ruffled feathers. "Yes?"

"I'd already conducted two conventional courtships. Both came to disaster. This time, I'd found a woman I really wanted. A public wooing always led to the wrong outcome. A different strategy was called for."

"At least I couldn't run off with Evesham, now

that he's married to Juliet," she said drily.

This time, a faint huff of laughter rewarded her. "That's something, I suppose."

"I may not have a baby, you know. Wouldn't you rather wait and find out?"

"No. I want you with me." His voice shook with the power of his emotions. "I want to claim you as my wife in the full light of day. I want you by my side without having to lie and deceive and pretend that I don't think you're the most marvelous creature in the world."

Her eyes widened in shock. "That's...that's strong stuff."

"My feelings are strong. I know we haven't been together for long. I'm willing to delay, if that's what you want. But if it was up to me, I'd marry you this very moment. It's not enough to see you for a few minutes in the park and act like our meeting isn't the center of my entire day. It's not enough to dance with you once at a ball now and again. It's not enough to have you in my bed for a few days, then do without you until the next time you can sneak away." He sucked in a broken breath. When he resumed, desperation turned his voice hoarse. "And everything I saw of you tonight tells me it's not enough for you either."

He was right. It wasn't enough. It would never be enough. But would it be enough for her to marry him, when so far he hadn't come near to mentioning love? Was half a cake better than no cake at all?

Portia had a vile inkling that if she said no to his proposal, she wouldn't even have half a cake. As a result, she'd starve to death.

She twined her shaking hands together at her waist and told herself that she couldn't confess her love. At least until she knew whether she carried Alaric's child. If they had to marry, it was better that he never knew of her aching, hopeless devotion. She'd loathe living with a man who tiptoed around her feelings.

"Is it enough, Portia?" he asked when she didn't reply.

"No, it's not." Misery laced her voice. "But I don't want to destroy your life."

"The only way you could destroy my life is to leave me."

He was saying – almost – all the right things. He wanted her in his life. He wanted *her*. "If we marry, everyone will say that you only took me on because you couldn't have Juliet. The ton will forever call me your second-best bride."

"I don't give a flying fuck what the ton says. My happiness is more important than a bit of malicious gossip." His violent response told her that he veered close to the edge. Alaric didn't in general use coarse language. "You don't think I'm pining for Juliet, do you?"

"No, I don't," she said, and for the first time, she really believed him. This distraught, ardent man had no interest in her older sister. Alaric and Juliet might be a perfect match in so many ways, while Portia was the last person that he should marry. But she now accepted that Alaric pursued one woman and that woman was Portia Frain.

"I'm glad," he said with a relieved sigh. "I wondered if that would always be an obstacle between us."

The time for protecting herself had passed. Whatever damage her confession did, she couldn't hide the truth any longer. She squared her shoulders. "Alaric, I'm honored by your offer—"

She heard his breath catch. "For the love of God, Portia, don't refuse me. I beg you."

Drawing on all her inner resources, she licked dry

lips. "I believe marriage should be a meeting of equals."

"So do I," he said quickly.

She sliced the air with one hand to silence him. He must have sensed the gesture, even if he couldn't see it, because he stopped speaking.

"A marriage where one person is in love and the other isn't will make us both wretched." Her words hurtled into the space between them like a boulder crashing down a mountainside.

The silence this time lasted a long time. Long enough for Portia's heart to shrivel. His lack of response was all the answer that she needed.

"You're right, damn it." His voice was expressionless as it never was. "I'd hoped..."

What? That she'd get over her inconvenient love? That wasn't going to happen. She was a stalwart soul. Once she committed herself, she didn't waver.

It was humiliating to realize that Alaric had guessed her feelings. And it further complicated what was already an odiously complicated situation. Regret grated in her voice. "I won't change, Alaric. I'm sorry."

"There's no chance you could ever love me?" he asked in that same toneless voice.

"There's no chance I..." She broke off, as she realized that he hadn't said what she'd expected. "Wait. What are you saying? You love me?"

"You know I do. That's why you're refusing me." He sounded like all the light had been sucked out of the world. She *hated* the way he sounded.

Since their frantic, ecstatic union against the beech tree, nothing had made sense. This capped it all. Portia drew a fragmented breath and reviewed what he'd said. If she got this wrong, her whole life would be empty.

"I'm...I'm not refusing you," she said on a breath

of sound. A joyous smile curved her lips, doubly wonderful when she'd feared that everything she wanted was out of reach for eternity. "I said I...I don't want to marry you when I'm so in love with you that I could die. Not when you aren't even a little bit in love with me."

He caught her arms in a desperate grip. "But I've been in love with you since that first day."

This radiant happiness would illuminate the rest of her life. "That's only fair, because I've been in love with you since the first day, too."

"My darling girl." He hauled her close as the choked words escaped. "I thought I didn't have a prayer."

This kiss was unlike any they'd shared before, miraculous as those had been. Love met love without any concealment. By the time Alaric raised his head, she was warm from her toes to her crown and leaning against the tree in a satisfied daze.

"I love you, Portia," he said, as if making a solemn vow.

"And I love you, Alaric. So much."

This kiss was longer and set the seal on their commitment. She twined her arms around his neck and gave herself up to the man she loved.

When they came up for air, Alaric rested his chin on her head. "You'll marry me?"

She muffled a cracked laugh against his heart. It seemed bizarre to cry when she was so happy, but tears stung her eyes and coagulated in a tight ball in her throat. "I'll be the world's worst duchess."

"I don't care. I'll be the world's happiest man."

"And I'll be the world's happiest woman." She laughed. "I *am* the world's happiest woman. It broke my heart when I was sure you didn't love me while I loved you so madly."

His arms tightened. "Love me madly forever,

sweetheart."

"I will. Forever."

More kisses until Portia felt like she flew up to the stars.

The sound of a carriage rattling into the square brought her back to earth with a bump.

"I should let you go." Reluctance weighted Alaric's statement.

"Soon we can be together all the time." An invitation to bliss.

The carriage stopped on the other side of the square. Doors opened and closed and there was a brief conversation before the carriage rolled away, leaving the square empty once more.

"Portia, my exquisite Portia, will you marry me?"

"Yes, with all my heart."

"Will you marry me tomorrow? Well, today really. It's after midnight."

Dizzy with the swift change from despair to jubilation, Portia drew back, wishing she could see Alaric. "I'd love that. Can we manage it?"

"I don't see why not. I'll talk to the rector of St. James's on Piccadilly. He'll be delighted to perform the ceremony."

"Oh, Alaric." She rose on her toes and kissed him quickly. "I can hardly believe this is happening."

He brought her back for a more thorough kiss. "Believe it, my darling."

"Soon I'll be your wife."

"I'm so happy." He paused. "What about your father? Should I ask his permission to marry you?"

Portia frowned into the darkness. "If we involve Papa, this will turn into an extravaganza. Especially as this time, he isn't marrying a daughter off to quash a scandal. I don't want an extravaganza."

"Nor do I." Even without seeing Alaric, she knew that he shuddered. "My wedding plans have come under enough scrutiny."

"If Papa gets involved, we won't be able to marry for weeks. Months even."

"I don't want that either."

"We could present it to him as a fait accompli."

"Would that hurt his feelings?"

Portia smiled, her heart spilling over with gratitude and elation. "You know, that's one of the many reasons I love you."

"Because I can't make a decision?"

She laughed and placed a hand on his cheek. "No, because even when you have every right to be selfish, you care about other people."

"He's about to become my father-in-law."

Portia gave an exaggerated gasp of horror. "I should have mentioned that when I listed all the reasons not to marry me." Even without his monomania for Shakespeare, her father was a handful.

Alaric's embrace firmed. "It's too late to wriggle out of taking me. I've got your promise."

"I'm sure Papa would like to be involved, but he was really terrible to Juliet. I'm in no mood to indulge his vanity if it means putting off our wedding, especially—"

"Especially when you could be carrying my child."

A glow that had nothing to do with passion and everything to do with love expanded inside her. "I'd love that."

"So would I." More kissing. Portia's brains were addled by the time they stopped. Their closeness filled her with contentment. She and Alaric were together and would stay that way.

"Tomorrow?" he asked.

"Yes, tomorrow."

"Shall I send a note to the stables?"

"I've got a better idea. I'll ask the Shelburns to be

our witnesses. Kate already suspects something's going on. It will cheer her no end to discover she's right. If I leave for the church from Leighton House, I can dress there without anyone wondering what I'm up to. I'll send her a note first thing."

Another flurry of kisses. Breathless, Alaric raised his head. "Damn it, I want to see you. I never imagined getting engaged in the dark."

She laughed. "It's romantic." She caught his hands. "Alaric, are we really going to do this extraordinary thing? Everyone will say we're the most mismatched couple in England."

"We'll be too happy to care about gossip."

"How wonderful."

"But you should go inside. We've tempted fate long enough."

"Kiss me first."

It wasn't a speedy farewell, and Portia was trembling by the time she stepped back. "I love you, Alaric." Having held the words inside for so long, she exulted in repeating them over and over.

"I love you, my treasured Portia."

"And tomorrow we're getting married. I can hardly believe it."

"You'll believe it when you're standing in front of the parson saying 'I do.'"

What a perfect thought. One more quick kiss.

"Let me call Jupiter, then check nobody's around," he said.

She collapsed against the convenient tree, as she struggled to comprehend that such joy existed and that it belonged to her.

CHAPTER TWENTY-TWO

With Jupiter back on his leash, Granville stepped from the garden onto the street outside Dempster House. Nobody seemed to be around, although that would soon change. He'd checked his pocket watch as soon as he had light to see. It wasn't far off two.

He was about to whistle to let Portia know it was safe to come out of the trees when a growl from Jupiter warned him that he was no longer alone.

"What is it, boy?" he murmured.

He heard footsteps before he saw the hulking figure approaching. "What have we here? The noble thief himself, eh? And my dog."

Despite a single meeting several weeks ago, Granville recognized the coarse voice straightaway. Jupiter kept growling, a low rumble of hostility, and he shifted closer to Granville's side.

"Jim Jones," Granville snarled. "What in Hades do you want?"

Nothing good, that was for sure. He was disgusted with himself for coming out unarmed. His sword stick was inside, as were his pistols. But then, he'd never imagined the brute having the gall to accost him in the middle of Mayfair.

"I want my dog back."

"You were paid for your dog." Granville raised his voice to make sure that Portia heard and stayed put. The idea of her encountering this bruiser when Granville had no way of defending her turned his blood to ice. He prayed that Jones had just appeared on the scene, and didn't guess that Granville had company other than Jupiter.

"Not enough."

He'd been paid more than a working man earned in a month.

"I'm not giving Jupiter back. He's my dog now." Granville was surprised at how strongly he felt about that.

"Well, my lord high and mighty, that would sound a hell of a lot more convincing if we weren't standing out here in the dark, with nobody around to help you, and me with a pistol in my pocket."

The bastard was right. Granville was a big, muscular man who regularly sparred at Gentleman Jackson's salon, but Jones had a gun, even if one discounted that the sod was built like a mountain. In a hand-to-hand fight, Granville had no hope of prevailing. And he had Portia to worry about as well, damn it.

But be buggered if he meant to hand over Jupiter. Especially as Jones would put him straight into a dogfight. Granville wouldn't tolerate the idea of his beloved pet being ripped to pieces, purely to make money for a bunch of yahoos.

But what the devil was he going to do?

He fell back on ducal authority. "If you dare to threaten me, I'll have the law on you faster than you can say good morning. The judiciary take a dim view of criminals accosting their betters."

They were just across the road from Dempster

House and its streetlamps. Granville wished to Jericho that he couldn't see Jones's expression. The warning left the man remarkably unmoved. "That's as may be, Your Grace."

Jones knew exactly who Granville was. Of course he must. He wasn't in Lorimer Square by chance. Granville's image regularly appeared in the illustrated papers. It wouldn't be hard to track him down if someone took the trouble. Jones had taken the trouble. "Your best choice is to sink back into the mire you sprang from."

"Fine words from a man with nothing but his own superiority to save him."

"Just a friendly piece of advice. You can't hope to escape punishment if you assault me and steal my dog."

Jupiter kept up his growling, but he trembled against Granville's leg. Granville tightened his hold on the leash. Jupiter was a breath away from springing at Jones, and he was terrified that the man would shoot.

Giving your heart away was hellish. Right now, the idea of anything happening to either Portia or Jupiter flooded his mouth with sour bile.

"I don't see why not. Now much as I enjoy hobnobbing with my *betters*..." The contempt dripping from the word conveyed his view of Granville's rank. "...it's past my bedtime. Hand over the dog and nobody gets hurt."

"I'm not giving you my dog."

Jones dug in the pocket of his voluminous leather coat and produced a horse pistol. However frail the hope, Granville had wondered if the man lied about being armed. "I'll happily kill you, Your Grace. I can disappear into the shadows faster than a rat shoots up a drainpipe."

"If you shoot that thing, the square will fill before

you can snap your fingers." Granville kept his voice steady.

Right now, while he was undoubtedly afraid for himself, he feared Portia's reckless courage most of all. She wouldn't stand by if things turned ugly. He credited her good sense in staying hidden until now, but he couldn't rely on that discretion continuing.

If Portia intervened, they'd have a full-scale disaster on their hands. Jones was smart enough to know that given a choice between Jupiter's life or Portia's, Granville would have to sacrifice the dog. When he didn't want to lose either of them, damn it.

"Yes, well, you won't care. You'll be dead." When he stepped closer, Jupiter snarled and strained against the leash.

Granville struggled to hold him back. "Don't be a fool, man."

"That dog is going to earn me a fortune. I'm not giving him up."

"He deserves better than you."

"Maybe so. But that don't make no difference." Jones held out his hand. "Give him over, chum. Or take the consequences."

The door at the top of the steps at Dempster House slammed open. "I don't think so," Sheriff said, pointing a gun at Jones from where he stood in the doorway. "Put your weapon down."

When Jones jerked around in shock, Granville saw his chance. He released Jupiter, who lunged. Granville lurched forward to grab the gun.

"Fucking 'ell!" Jones staggered back, his finger tightening on the trigger. There was a deafening bang, but luckily Granville had twisted his arm. The bullet discharged skyward.

Sheriff dashed down to the pavement. Jupiter gave a sharp bark and bit the back of Jones's knee. Jones swore and kicked at the same time, as he tried to fight Granville and the dog off.

Granville wrestled the now-useless gun away, while Matty and Phipps ran up from the kitchens to grab Jones. The man struggled, although he must know that he'd lost.

"Matty, get the nightwatchman," Granville panted. He'd been scared, he wasn't too proud to admit. And furious that just as his life turned in the right direction, he came close to losing it.

"Aye, Your Grace." The lad took to his heels. Phipps picked up Jupiter's leash and with difficulty pulled the dog back from Jones.

Around them, lights went on in houses, doors opened, and windows slid up with a volley of crashes. Dear God, Granville hoped that nobody decided to wander through the center of the square. He needed someone to find Portia and get her away before anyone noticed her presence.

As if conjured up by Granville's worry, Hobbs appeared at his elbow. "Shall I see Lady Portia gets home without attracting attention, Your Grace?"

Shocked, Granville surveyed his valet. "How did you..."

The fellow rarely smiled, so the faint lift of his lips counted as much as a triumphant grin from another man. "When England's tidiest nobleman leaves his apartments in chaos and that chaos includes female clothing, I could tell something was up."

"The devil with it, man. We've tried so hard to be discreet." He wasn't sure whether he was grateful or embarrassed or annoyed. Probably a mixture of all three.

"A man has few secrets from his valet," Hobbs said with a hint of smugness.

People flooded into the street. At this hour, they sported evening clothes and day wear and robes flung over night attire. A few older residents wore nightcaps on their heads, like aged Wee Willie Winkies. As the crowd swelled, buzzing with questions, Jones stood defeated between Phipps and Sheriff.

A smile of his own stretched Granville's lips. "You may be the first to wish me happy, Hobbs. Lady Portia and I are to be married today."

Hobbs's smile widened. "I'm delighted, sir. I wish you and her ladyship every joy."

"Thank you."

Now the danger had passed, Granville crouched to give Jupiter some attention. "Good boy. Good boy."

Jupiter's tail wagged, and he jumped up to lick Granville's face. He was as pleased to stay with his new master as his new master was to keep him.

A couple of brawny footmen emerged from Dempster House to take charge of Jones. Granville looked up at Sheriff from where he patted his dog. "How the deuce did you know to come out?"

"I was with Matty when he walked Jupiter the last few nights. We noticed that rogue hanging around where he shouldn't be. But we were much earlier than this and I suspect there were too many people around for him to chance his arm. Tonight, after you stayed out so long, I came up to wait in the hall, in case there was trouble."

With gratitude jamming Granville's throat, his voice emerged as a gruff rumble. "I owe my life to you. The sod was out to kill me. He'd certainly have killed Jupiter. Thank you."

Phipps's smile as he bowed expressed sincere affection and respect. "It's always an honor to serve you, sir."

The nightwatchman staggered into view. When he came closer, Granville caught a strong whiff of spirits. That at least explained how Jones had infiltrated the square. The man performed an unsteady bow, punctuated by a loud hiccup. "Your Grace, what goings-on. What a fuss."

"We'll get this scurvy fellow in front of the courts, sir," Sheriff said, ignoring the drunk. "Phipps and I will take the brute who accosted you in to Bow Street now and lay charges. We've seen enough to make sure that this ruffian causes no more trouble."

Jones had threatened a peer of the realm, a duke no less. He'd be lucky to escape a hanging. At best, transport to the horrors of Botany Bay on the other side of the world awaited.

The ruffian clearly reached the same conclusion and didn't much like it. "No harm was done." His arrogant air was less convincing than it had been when he'd pointed a pistol at Granville.

"No thanks to you," Sheriff said.

"And no thanks to you," Phipps said to the nightwatchman with audible disgust.

A carriage rolled past, followed by another, signal that London's entertainments finally ended for the evening. Soon the square would be bustling with traffic.

Granville didn't want to get involved in a hundred recountings of the night's events to people arriving home and agog to hear the news. He was getting married in a few hours. He'd rather think about that than the last half hour's tribulations.

He picked up Jupiter's lead. "I'll leave everything in your capable hands, Sheriff."

When he glanced across the crowd, he saw Hobbs on the fringes of the gathering. His valet's nod told him that Portia was safely back at home.

His mind already shifting to the joys awaiting in the morning, Granville climbed the steps, Jupiter at his side.

CHAPTER TWENTY-THREE

*P*ortia and her maid, Betty, stood on the pavement outside the tall, white house that Kate and Leighton used in London. Around them, Grosvenor Square was quiet. It was too late for the tradesmen to be out doing deliveries to the grand houses and too early for the ton to be awake and active.

Unless this particular member of the ton was born into the diligent middle classes and still ran the factories that her father left her. Not to mention the presence of a baby in the house. Master Richard Anstey, Viscount Lemaire, was two months old now and the thriving center of his doting parents' lives.

When the footman opened the gleaming black door, Kate rushed up behind him. Richard was in her arms, and she wore a floral dimity gown in a becoming shade of pink. "Frederick, please look after Lady Portia's maid."

"Yes, my lady," the footman said with a bow.

Betty and the valise she carried disappeared into the depths of the house. The girl didn't know the reason behind this visit. Portia had packed her own bag before she'd called Betty this morning. In fact, she'd packed by candlelight somewhere around three. She was too excited to sleep a wink, not to mention on edge after that dreadful scene with Jim Jones and Alaric.

Once they were alone, Kate turned to Portia with unconcealed curiosity. "I received your mysterious note. Do come in and tell me what this is all about. Don't say that you've fallen out with your father. That will make three sisters out of three."

Portia couldn't help laughing at her friend's impatience. "And good morning to you, Kate."

Kate gave a dismissive exhalation. "I have no time for silly civilities. I've been on tenterhooks since I got your message. Come straight through to the morning room."

Portia let her friend whisk her away to a sunny room, where a tea tray awaited. Kate shut the door, closing the three of them inside. She set Richard in a cradle near the open French doors and turned back to Portia. "If you've had a fight with your temperamental papa, you're in a remarkably good humor about it."

She took Kate's hands and spoke the words for the first time, words that she never thought she'd say. "Kate, dear, dear Kate, I'm to be married today."

Kate's jaw dropped with such theatrical astonishment that Portia laughed again. "It's mad, isn't it?"

Kate regarded her as if she'd flown in on Pegasus. "I don't know. That depends who you're marrying."

Portia's hold on her friend's hands tightened. "Why, Granville, of course. You knew there was something going on from the first. Don't pretend you're caught unawares."

Except it turned out that Kate *was* caught unawares. Her brown eyes widened as round as pennies. "Granville? The most boring man in

Britain?"

Portia had the grace to blush. "I was wrong about him. He's the most wonderful person in the world."

"I need to sit down to take all this in." Looking poleaxed, Kate drew Portia across to a couch. "You love him?"

"I do." It was also glorious to make that avowal. To someone other than Alaric. Although it was glorious making avowals to him, too.

Kate looked less bewildered, as she subjected Portia to a thorough inspection. "I can see it."

"He loves me back."

"Why wouldn't he? You're adorable." Kate pressed her hands, but a frown drew her dark eyebrows together. "It's just that he's so correct and so aware of his consequence. While you're all heart and independence and determination."

Portia pulled her hands from Kate's. She knew that most people would react with skepticism when they learned of her wedding. Or at least the people who weren't too busy speculating on how inappropriate it was for Portia to marry her sister's cast-off suitor.

To the devil with them all. Except Kate. She wanted Kate to understand and approve. "He's not like that at all. When you come to know him, you'll love him, too."

"He and Juliet always struck me as the ideal couple. Not you and him. Granville isn't looking to you as a stand-in for the woman he really wants?"

Portia tried not to wince. She'd have to get used to hearing about Juliet and Alaric. To think, one of the things that she'd always valued about Kate was her plain speaking.

"No, he really loves me." Portia doubted her ability to become a suitable duchess, but she didn't doubt Alaric's love. Which was lucky, given Kate's misgivings. She spread her hands in an expansive gesture. "I couldn't be happier. I'm so happy, I feel like I could fly. I've never been so sure of anything as I am that Alaric is the only man for me."

Kate grimaced. "Dear Lord, forgive me. Here I am trampling all over your news. I'm the last person to question a match between apparent opposites. Everyone thought Leighton came down terribly in the world when he married me, after all. If you're content with your choice, then I'm overjoyed for you."

Portia smiled. "Thank you. Thank you for believing in me." She leaned forward to embrace her friend.

The hug helped. It really did. By the time they drew apart, they both wiped away tears.

"You're a smart woman. If you say Alaric Dempster is the man for you, he gets my endorsement." Kate gave a husky giggle. "But you do have to tell me everything. Shall I pour us some tea? I might ring for a fresh pot. That one will be stewed now."

Portia was back to smiling. "I'd love a cup of tea and a good chat, but time's of the essence and I need your help."

Kate went back to looking shocked. "Dear heaven, did you say you were getting married...today? It's already ten o'clock."

Portia laughed. "I did. Alaric is at St. James's right now, arranging the ceremony. I assume he'll send a note, once he's spoken to the rector."

"But...but what about banns and guests and a dress and a reception and—"

"Alaric has a special license. My dress is in Betty's bag." A new gown that she'd bought last week with a view to dazzling Alaric. "I'm hoping you and Leighton might consent to be our witnesses. In fact,

I'm hoping you'll let me get ready here."

"What about your father?"

"The plan is to tell him tonight after we're married."

"Just before you move into Dempster House?" Kate asked drily.

Portia shrugged. "You know what he's like. Alaric and I want today to be about us."

Kate's smile was brilliant with approval. "Then let's make it thus."

Portia beamed at her friend. "I can be married from your house and you'll attend the ceremony?"

"I'd be honored. So will Leighton."

"Thank you." Portia hugged Kate again. "There's nobody I'd rather have with me on the best day of my life."

Kate stood and crossed to pick up Richard, who was gurgling happily in his cradle. He was a restless baby, so Portia was grateful that for the moment, his mood was sunny. "Let's find Leighton and tell him his presence is requested, then you and I will go upstairs and make you look utterly spectacular."

Portia rose as well. "You're going to be my attendant as well as my witness?"

"Just try and stop me."

A footman opened the door when Granville arrived at the Shelburns' mansion. He'd known Leighton Anstey, Lord Shelburn most of his life but had never paid a social visit. They moved in different circles, especially in earlier days when Shelburn had been more famous as a rake and a reprobate than today's blissfully happy family man. Granville had only been inside the house once before, when he attended the recent ball to dance with Portia.

Now he mounted the steps two at a time to collect the bride he loved with all his heart.

The footman brought him into an attractive morning room, where the Shelburns sat with Portia. She surged to her feet and rushed over to take his hands. "Alaric, I thought you'd send a message."

He smiled at her. He'd been smiling all day, he was just so damned euphoric. "I decided to come myself. By heaven, you're gorgeous. I'm the luckiest man alive. That's a lovely dress."

Portia glanced down at the ice-blue satin gown that brought out the color of her beautiful eyes. "This old thing?"

He laughed and only just restrained himself from kissing her. "You make a stunning bride."

Lord Shelburn rose and held out his hand. "Congratulations, Your Grace."

Granville realized that he'd completely forgotten his manners. He should have acknowledged his host and hostess first. But how could he think about anyone but Portia on this day of days?

He tore his attention away from his darling and shook Shelburn's hand. "Thank you. And thank you to you and Lady Shelburn for supporting us in our plans for a quiet wedding."

"I'll be the most envied woman in London, once the news is out." Lady Shelburn stood beside her husband and threaded her hand through his arm. "Everyone will want the details of what you wore and what you said and what you did."

"As long as you say the groom was much prettier than the bride." Portia took Granville's hand again. "Hobbs has excelled himself."

Granville sighed with mock self-pity. "The fellow's been pecking and picking at me all morning."

"You look the ideal bridegroom, Your Grace," Lady Shelburn said.

Granville had on a black coat and biscuit pantaloons. His neckcloth was a perfect fall, and he wore his favorite gray silk waistcoat.

"Thank you." He smiled. "Given both of you will play such an important part in my wedding day, perhaps you should call me Alaric."

Lady Shelburn cast him a warm glance. "Then we must be Kate and Leighton."

"What did the rector say?" Portia asked.

"He's at our disposal for the rest of the day."

"Capital," Leighton said. "In that case, let's have some champagne to celebrate before we go."

As if on cue, the butler arrived with a bottle in an ice bucket, followed by a footman bearing a tray of four glasses.

While the butler poured the wine, Kate sent Granville a teasing glance. "Isn't it bad luck to see the bride on the day of the ceremony?"

Portia gave one of her beguiling giggles. "We just might have met after midnight last night."

Kate arched her eyebrows. "You got over your headache fast."

Portia blushed like a rose. "Love is the best medicine."

"We had things to talk about," Granville said, although he suspected that Kate and Leighton guessed that at the very least, kissing had occurred.

Leighton smiled and raised his glass. "May I propose a toast to the engaged couple, Portia and Alaric, and wish you both every happiness?"

"Thank you." Granville already felt like champagne flowed through his veins.

"Thank you, my dear friends," Portia said after a sip.

Kate took a mouthful of wine and set her glass on

the table. She turned to Leighton. "Come and help me choose some flowers from the garden. Portia hasn't thought of a bouquet."

Leighton caught on immediately and drained his glass before setting it next to Kate's. "We can't have our bride missing out on her flowers."

The moment that the Shelburns disappeared behind the closed door, Portia flung herself into his arms. "Alaric, I'm so glad Jim Jones didn't kill you."

He laughed as he clasped her close. It felt like an eon since he'd held her, even if it was only last night. "So am I."

"Don't joke." She gave a shudder. "I was scared to death."

"I was mainly terrified that you were going to fly out of the grove like a Valkyrie and take him on again."

"You don't know how difficult it was, staying put," she mumbled into his shoulder. "I kept telling myself that if I trusted you enough to marry you, I trusted you to handle Jim Jones."

"What's this?" He pulled back to see her face. "I won't have you crying on our wedding day. It's against the rules. Anyway, everything worked out."

"I couldn't bear thinking I might lose you."

"I couldn't bear thinking I might lose Jupiter."

That elicited a watery chuckle. "I was impressed with how you stood up for your dog."

"So was he." Granville dug in his pocket for a handkerchief and passed it to her. "I won't let Jim Jones cast a pall over the greatest day of my life. Let's look forward to our wedding instead. I love you so much, Portia."

"And I love you," she said, voice thick with emotion. The kiss was sweet and leisurely and held no shadows. It spoke of promises made and a life to be shared.

"I like your friends," he murmured, keeping hold of her hand but moving back. "And I appreciate their tact. I was desperate to kiss you."

"I think they noticed." She rose on her toes to kiss him quickly.

He stared down into her lovely face, so in love that he was drunk with the emotion. "No second thoughts?"

"Heavens, no." She returned his searching stare. "What about you?"

"I've never been so happy." Heartfelt sincerity roughened his voice. "You make me happy, Portia."

Her eyes softened, and she cradled his cheek in a tender hand. This time, the kiss was more thorough. By the time he lifted his head, Portia was flushed and breathless. So was he.

She glanced down at her gown. "Perhaps we should get married before my dress is crushed beyond rescue."

He laughed. "You're a beautiful bride, my darling. I don't deserve you."

Her smile was misty, as she raised his ungloved hand to kiss his knuckles. The act of overt homage made his heart cramp into an aching lump of adoration. "You deserve everything in the world that makes you happy, my dearest."

Gratitude flooded him as he smiled down at her. He was feeling rather misty himself. "That's you, my beloved."

The smile that she bestowed upon him was dazzling. "Make me your wife, Alaric. Let's find Kate and Leighton and go to the church. I want the world to know I'm yours and you're mine."

One more quick kiss before he caught her hand. "Forever, Portia."

"Forever, Alaric," she echoed.

They opened the door to find Leighton and Kate

coming up the corridor toward them with an extravagant array of tulips and cherry blossom and irises. Portia accepted the flowers with thanks, then took Granville's arm.

Together, they stepped forth to claim a glorious future.

EPILOGUE

Lancers, Devon, August 1828

August in Devon was heavenly, especially on a sunny day like this, Portia couldn't help thinking, as she sat in a gazebo with a view of the Duke of Evesham's magnificent gardens. On a wicker table beside her chair rested a glass of barley water and a plate of dry crackers.

The expansive grounds resounded with children's laughter. Children's laughter and barking dogs. Over the years, Portia had found homes for many of her strays with her sisters and their families.

"It's lovely to see they've become friends," Juliet said from the chair next to her. She was as beautiful as ever, with a glow of contentment and achievement that warmed the hearts of everyone who loved her. Juliet had indeed turned out to be a perfect duchess. Partly because she was now more forgiving of human frailty. Her own and everyone else's.

Portia glanced across the manicured lawns to where the dukes of Evesham and Granville were involved in an engrossing discussion. "Yes, something of a miracle," she said drily.

Meetings between the reluctant brothers-in-law had been awkward for the first few years, even after Alaric discovered the true reason behind his first fiancée jilting him. But both Lucas and Alaric loved their wives too much to try and keep the sisters apart. Time and familiarity had gradually smoothed most of the rough edges between them.

Lucas had started hosting a house party every August to celebrate Juliet's birthday. Something about being in the country and in the kind of large family gathering that Alaric never knew as a boy had led to a rapprochement between the two dukes. By now, as Juliet said, one might even call them friends, if of the competitive, sardonic kind.

"They're talking about tomorrow's cricket match." Viola looked up from her book. With motherhood, she'd developed the skill of reading and knowing exactly what was going on at the same time.

"No wonder they look so serious," Juliet said. "I wonder which side will end up with Kate."

Kate and Leighton played hide-and-seek with the younger children over near the maze. Portia's sons, Charles and Gerard, six and four. Juliet's daughter Arabella, six. And Viola's youngest three, Orlando, six, and the twins Lysander and Rosalind, who were only three and the babies among the crowd of cousins. At least until after Christmas when Portia delivered the child that she carried. Most of her pregnancies had been trouble free, but this time round, morning sickness lingered – and hadn't restricted itself to mornings either. Which was why she sat in the cool and didn't join in with the hide-and-seek.

"I vote Alaric gets Kate," she said.

Juliet gave a scoffing huff. "Of course you do. Any side that gets Kate is sure to win." Kate, it turned out, was a gun bowler and the secret weapon for any team lucky enough to recruit her.

"We've got a fair contingent of cousins to throw into the mix this year," Viola said. "Now Richard's ten, he's showing signs of talent with the bat, and Benedict always wants to do what Richard does." Benedict, Viola's oldest, was also ten and hero-worshipped his cousin.

"And William is keen to play, too." At nine, Juliet's son was avid to prove that he could keep up with the big boys.

"Jessica and Sylvie and Sophia are old enough this year, too," Portia said, mentioning Viola's daughter, Kate's daughter, and her own eight-year-old darling, her first child and a girl so much after her own heart.

"At least it will give the older children a break from Shakespeare." Juliet shot a not altogether favorable glance over to a makeshift stage near the drive. With the assistance of Miss Donald, Kate's old governess, Lord Portdown was casting parts for *A Midsummer Night's Dream.*

Portia laughed. "Yes, Papa is in alt to have all his grandchildren – and adopted grandchildren – available for theatricals. Doesn't it take you back, Juliet?"

Juliet's grunt was noncommittal, although these days, she'd mostly given up her feud with her harum-scarum father. Portia couldn't help thinking back to the day that she presented her new husband to her father after their rapturous wedding ceremony. Any fears that her private nuptials might hurt his feelings had vanished on the spot. He'd been so ecstatic that the Duke of Granville had deigned to marry his daughter that the issue of missing the wedding hadn't arisen.

The years since that glorious day had overflowed

with happiness and incident and accomplishment. Despite her fears that she'd make the world's worst duchess, she'd soon found a way to combine her independent nature with her duties. Alaric's unfailing support had helped her weather any passing disapproval from society.

Her role even brought some benefits. The Duchess of Granville had influence to bear on the issue of animal welfare in a way that mere Portia Frain didn't. These days, she managed a team of dog rescuers, giving her a reach that she could only dream of before her marriage. Not that she'd surrendered her old ways entirely. Upon occasion, she and Alaric set out to retrieve a mistreated animal. She always enjoyed their adventures together.

Portia watched Viola's husband Toby emerge from the house and cross to join the ducal deliberations. He'd been such a tearaway as a young man, but family life suited Lord Renfrew. Family life and a levelheaded wife he adored. "You know, they could be talking about your birthday tomorrow, Jules."

Juliet shook her head, with a mocking smile. "No, it's cricket. I know my place in the pecking order."

"As if Lucas wouldn't die for you," Viola said. "He worships the ground you walk on."

"You haven't got anything to be jealous of in that department," Juliet retorted. "We've all been lucky to find such loving husbands."

"And all of them were considered so unpromising at the start," Portia said with a fond laugh. "Kate married the worst lord in London, Viola chose a rogue with a reputation for trouble, and you ran off with the most ramshackle duke in the kingdom."

"Don't forget you ended up with the most boring man in Britain, Porsh," Viola said. "And I quote you."

Portia made a dismissive gesture. "He's the most wonderful man in Britain."

"He has some competition for that title," Juliet protested.

Viola laughed. "Indeed he has."

"You sound like hens laying an egg, with the way you're all cackling your heads off." Alaric came up on Portia unawares, while she was busy teasing her sisters.

"We're trying to work out who has the best husband," Viola said, her affection for her grand brother-in-law warming her voice. Viola, unlike Portia, had always had a soft spot for the Duke of Granville.

"It's obvious that Portia wins," Alaric said with the wry humor that had so surprised her before she got over her prejudice against him.

"I wouldn't say that," Juliet responded. Like her husband, she'd been uncomfortable with Alaric at first, given their checkered history. But these days, the things that they'd always had in common cemented a friendship based in his steadfast love for her sister.

"I feel like I might lay an egg." Portia stretched out a hand to her beloved husband. "Do you think you could take me inside, darling?"

The smile that curled his lips held a tinge of anticipation. He knew what she really wanted. With three children and a dogs' home and his political career to run, opportunities for daytime revels had become rare. Here at Lancers, they had a crowd of adults to keep an eye on their offspring and Portia's pregnancy presented them with the perfect excuse to disappear for a nap. Although she'd be surprised if much actual napping was done.

"With pleasure." He took her hand and helped her up, then snapped his fingers at Jupiter who as usual was at his heels. "Come on, old boy."

Jupiter, deaf and stiff with arthritis, wagged his tail and tottered after Portia and Alaric as they wandered back to the stone mansion.

Alaric tucked her hand into the crook of his elbow. "It's nice you're spending time with your sisters."

"And Kate."

"She's like a sister."

"She is indeed. I know we see them all during the year, but there's something special about coming together at Lancers."

"Yes, there is. These days, I can even stomach that scoundrel Evesham."

Portia nestled into his side, loving how big and warm he was. "You don't fool me. You like him."

His sigh was long-suffering. "I suppose I do. In fact, I like all of them." He paused. "Not nearly as much as I like you. In fact, I don't just like you, I love you. More and more each day."

Portia stumbled and clung to Alaric's arm. "You shouldn't say things like that when I'm trying to see straight. You know, how dewy-eyed I get when you turn sentimental."

He laughed and stopped to kiss her. "I love that I can still make you all girlish and confused, even though we've been married ten years and have three growing children."

Portia glanced back to the gazebo. "Everyone's watching us."

Alaric shrugged. "It's not as if they never kiss in public. Every August, Lancers turns into a damned Cupid's bower."

Portia laughed, then gave a surprised squeak as Alaric swung her up into his arms. "What are you doing?"

"Making sure you get to our chambers safely. I

have plans for you, my beautiful wife, and they don't include a sprained ankle."

She curled her hand behind his neck and tugged on the curls at his nape. "Ooh, you mean to ravish me?"

"I do indeed."

"Excellent," she said with unconcealed smugness.

Another laugh. Another kiss. Before Alaric strode inside to join her in paradise.

ABOUT THE AUTHOR

Australian Anna Campbell has written 51 bestselling historical romances. 11 multi award-winning historical romances for Avon HarperCollins and Grand Central Publishing and 40 as an independently published author. Right now, she's working on a new series called Cinderellas of Mayfair, set amidst the glamour and sensuality of Regency London. Anna has won numerous awards for her stories, including *RT Book Reviews* Reviewers Choice, the Booksellers Best, the Golden Quill (three times), the Heart of Excellence (twice), the Write Touch, the Aspen Gold (twice), and the Australian Romance Readers' favorite historical romance (five times).

Anna loves to hear from her readers. You can find her at:

Website: www.annacampbell.com

facebook.com/AnnaCampbellFans

x.com/AnnaCampbellOz

bookbub.com/authors/anna-campbell

The Worst Lord in London: Scoundrels of Mayfair Book 1

Headlong into the unknown...

Independent, willful Kate Starr has cherished a penchant for handsome Lord Shelburn since she was sixteen years old, but as a mill-owning industrialist, she moves in a different world from the libertine earl. Then one fateful day, Shelburn invites her to accompany him in a scandalous race, and immediate physical attraction swiftly turns into blazing passion.

The hunter caught...

Leighton Anstey, Earl of Shelburn, glories in his reputation as the worst lord in London. His fame as an irresistible seducer is unrivaled, although his amours are notable for their explosive heat, not their longevity. The dashing lord has never met a

woman who can hold his wandering attention, until
he tumbles into a liaison with a mysterious woman
who enthrals him, body and soul.

A brief encounter or a forever love?

Neither Kate nor Shelburn views their torrid affair
as more than a shooting star, flaring red-hot for a
brilliant instant, then destined to fade to nothing.
But does the fiery desire raging between them blind
them to the chance of finding lifelong happiness
together?

The Trouble with Earls:
Scoundrels of Mayfair Book 2

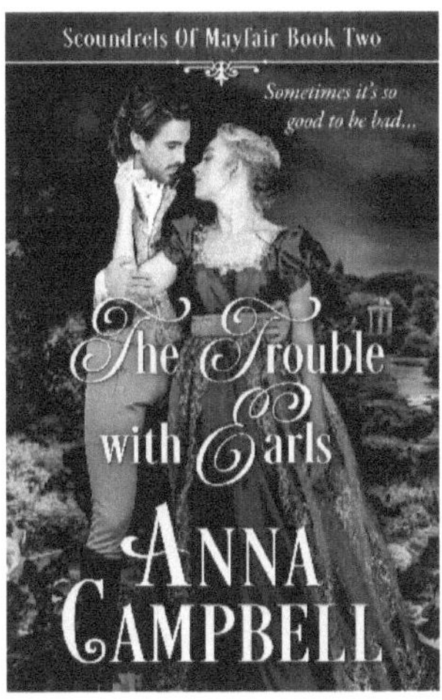

The wild rogue and the wallflower!

Toby Sutton, Earl of Renfrew, is a notorious libertine with no interest in marrying a wellbred young miss and making her his countess. But when he meets lovely Lady Viola Frain, irresistible desire creates an explosive mix with his native recklessness. Within a matter of days, he and Viola are joined in a hurried marriage of convenience, patched together to scotch an almighty scandal.

Marry in haste, repent at leisure?

With two spectacular older sisters, shy Viola Frain is used to being the overlooked member of the family. When handsome Lord Renfrew literally falls at her feet, Viola finally meets a man who thinks she's special. But before the fragile bloom of attraction can flower, she finds herself wed to Renfrew and whisked away to brooding Brazey Castle, where shadows of old tragedy threaten her frail hope of happiness.

The trouble with earls...

Society watches avidly, forecasting disaster for an alliance between two people so mismatched. Can passion unite the rake and the recluse? Or is the truth just as Viola fears? That the trouble with earls is that they're bound to break your heart.

The Last Duke She'd Marry: Scoundrels of Mayfair Book 3

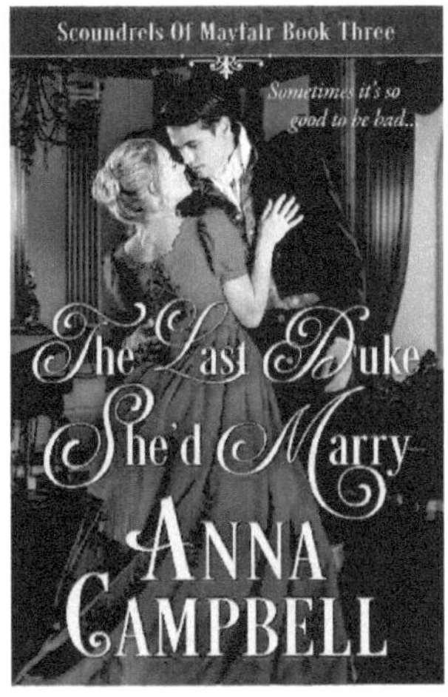

She wants to be a duchess. Just not HIS duchess!

Pure and proper Lady Juliet Frain was born to be a duchess. Everyone says so. Now society awaits the announcement of the elegant beauty's engagement to the dignified and honorable Duke of Granville. However all Juliet's plans go awry when she meets the scandalous but sinfully attractive Duke of Evesham. The wild libertine is the last man Juliet wants to find irresistible, yet somehow she can't keep her hands off him. And suddenly to her chagrin, nobody is calling Juliet either pure or proper!

He's no Romeo…

After ten riotous years on the Continent, Lucas Hebden, Duke of Evesham, has returned to London, trailing a well-earned reputation as a rake and a reprobate. But an unexpected loss in a card game finds him far from London's fleshpots and playing at amateur dramatics in the country. Even worse, he's starting to confuse the poetic passion in *Romeo and Juliet* with the real-life passion that has him pursuing his disapproving but breathtakingly lovely leading lady. It's clear that Lady Juliet Frain has no time for bad boys, and any sensible man would give up – but then nobody ever called Evesham sensible!

When Juliet's suitor Granville arrives to propose, it's the battle of the dukes! Once the curtain falls, which duke will emerge victorious and take the starring role in Juliet's heart?